Queen Lucia

E. F. Benson

Chapter ONE

Though the sun was hot on this July morning Mrs Lucas preferred to cover the half-mile that lay between the station and her house on her own brisk feet, and sent on her maid and her luggage in the fly that her husband had ordered to meet her. After those four hours in the train a short walk would be pleasant, but, though she veiled it from her conscious mind, another motive, sub-consciously engineered, prompted her action. It would, of course, be universally known to all her friends in Riseholme that she was arriving today by the 12.26, and at that hour the village street would be sure to be full of them. They would see the fly with luggage draw up at the door of The Hurst, and nobody except her maid would get out.

That would be an interesting thing for them: it would cause one of those little thrills of pleasant excitement and conjectural exercise which supplied Riseholme with its emotional daily bread. They would all wonder what had happened to her, whether she had been taken ill at the very last moment before leaving town and with her well-known fortitude and consideration for the feelings of others, had sent her maid on to assure her husband that he need not be anxious. That would clearly be Mrs Quantock's suggestion, for Mrs Quantock's mind, devoted as it was now to the study of Christian Science, and the determination to deny the existence of pain, disease and death as regards herself, was always full of the gloomiest views as regards her friends, and on the slightest excuse, pictured that they, poor blind things, were suffering from false claims. Indeed, given that the fly had already arrived at The Hurst, and that its arrival had at this moment been seen by or reported to Daisy Quantock, the chances were vastly in favour of that lady's having already started in to give Mrs Lucas absent treatment. Very likely Georgie Pillson had also seen the anticlimax of the fly's arrival, but he would hazard a much more probable though erroneous solution of her absence. He would certainly guess that she had sent on her maid with her luggage to the station in order to take a seat for her, while she herself, oblivious of the passage of time, was spending her last half hour in contemplation of the Italian masterpieces at the National Gallery, or the Greek bronzes at the British Museum. Certainly she would not be at the Royal Academy, for the culture of Riseholme, led by herself, rejected as valueless all artistic efforts later than the death of Sir Joshua Reynolds, and a great deal of what went before. Her husband with his firm grasp of the obvious, on the other hand, would be disappointingly capable even before her maid confirmed his conjecture, of concluding that she had merely walked from the station.

The motive, then, that made her send her cab on, though subconsciously generated, soon penetrated into her consciousness, and these guesses at what other people would think when they saw it arrive without her, sprang from the dramatic element that formed so large a part of her mentality, and made her always take, as by right divine, the leading part in the histrionic entertainments with which the cultured of Riseholme beguiled or rather strenuously occupied such moments as could be spared from their studies of art and literature, and their social engagements. Indeed she did not usually stop at taking the leading part, but, if possible, doubled another character with it, as well as being stage-manager and adapter, if not designer of scenery. Whatever she did—and really she did an incredible deal—she did it with all the might of her dramatic perception, did it in fact with such earnestness that she had no time to have an eye to the gallery at all, she simply contemplated herself and her own vigorous accomplishment. When she played the piano as she frequently did, (reserving an hour for practice every day), she cared not in the smallest degree for what anybody who passed down the road outside her house might be thinking of the roulades that poured from her open window: she was simply Emmeline Lucas, absorbed in glorious Bach or dainty Scarletti, or noble Beethoven. The latter perhaps was her favorite composer, and many were the evenings when with lights quenched and only the soft effulgence of the moon pouring in through the uncurtained windows, she sat with her profile, cameo-like (or like perhaps to the head on a postage stamp) against the dark oak walls of her music-room, and entranced herself and her

1

listeners, if there were people to dinner, with the exquisite pathos of the first movement of the Moonlight Sonata. Devotedly as she worshipped the Master, whose picture hung above her Steinway Grand, she could never bring herself to believe that the two succeeding movements were on the same sublime level as the first, and besides they "went" very much faster. But she had seriously thought, as she came down in the train today and planned her fresh activities at home of trying to master them, so that she could get through their intricacies with tolerable accuracy. Until then, she would assuredly stop at the end of the first movement in these moonlit seances, and say that the other two were more like morning and afternoon. Then with a sigh she would softly shut the piano lid, and perhaps wiping a little genuine moisture from her eyes, would turn on the electric light and taking up a book from the table, in which a paper-knife marked the extent of her penetration, say:

"Georgie, you must really promise me to read this life of Antonino Caporelli the moment I have finished it. I never understood the rise of the Venetian School before. As I read I can smell the salt tide creeping up over the lagoon, and see the campanile of dear Torcello."

And Georgie would put down the tambour on which he was working his copy of an Italian cope and sigh too.

"You are too wonderful!" he would say. "How do you find time for everything?"

She rejoined with the apophthegm that made the rounds of Riseholme next day.

"My dear, it is just busy people that have time for everything."

It might be thought that even such activities as have here been indicated would be enough to occupy anyone so busily that he would positively not have time for more, but such was far from being the case with Mrs Lucas. Just as the painter Rubens amused himself with being the ambassador to the Court of St. James—a sufficient career in itself for most busy men— so Mrs Lucas amused herself, in the intervals of her pursuit of Art for Art's sake, with being not only an ambassador but a monarch. Riseholme might perhaps according to the crude materialism of maps, be included in the kingdom of Great Britain, but in a more real and inward sense it formed a complete kingdom of its own, and its queen was undoubtedly Mrs Lucas, who ruled it with a secure autocracy pleasant to contemplate at a time when thrones were toppling, and imperial crowns whirling like dead leaves down the autumn winds. The ruler of Riseholme, happier than he of Russia, had no need to fear the finger of Bolshevism writing on the wall, for there was not in the whole of that vat which seethed so pleasantly with culture, one bubble of revolutionary ferment. Here there was neither poverty nor discontent nor muttered menace of any upheaval: Mrs Lucas, busy and serene, worked harder than any of her subjects, and exercised an autocratic control over a nominal democracy.

Something of the consciousness of her sovereignty was in her mind, as she turned the last hot corner of the road and came in sight of the village street that constituted her kingdom. Indeed it belonged to her, as treasure trove belongs to the Crown, for it was she who had been the first to begin the transformation of this remote Elizabethan village into the palace of culture that was now reared on the spot where ten years ago an agricultural population had led bovine and unilluminated lives in their cottages of grey stone or brick and timber. Before that, while her husband was amassing a fortune, comfortable in amount and respectable in origin, at the Bar, she had merely held up a small dim lamp of culture in Onslow Gardens. But both her ambition and his had been to bask and be busy in artistic realms of their own when the materialistic needs were provided for by sound investments, and so when there were the requisite thousands of pounds in secure securities she had easily persuaded him to buy three of these cottages that stood together in a low two-storied block. Then, by judicious removal of partition-walls, she had, with the aid of a sympathetic architect, transmuted them into a most comfortable dwelling, subsequently building on to them a new wing, that ran at right angles at the back, which was, if anything, a shade more inexorably Elizabethan than the stem onto which it was grafted, for here was situated the famous smoking-parlour, with rushes on the floor, and a dresser ranged with pewter tankards, and leaded lattice-windows of glass so antique that it was practically impossible to see out of them. It had a huge open fireplace framed in oak-beams with a seat on each side of the iron-backed hearth within the chimney, and a genuine spit hung over the middle of the fire. Here, though in the rest of the house she had for the sake of convenience allowed the installation of electric light, there was no such concession made, and sconces on the walls held dim iron lamps, so that only those of the most acute vision were able to read. Even then reading was difficult, for the book-stand on the table contained nothing but a few crabbed black-letter volumes dating from not later than the early seventeenth century, and you had to be in a frantically Elizabethan frame of mind to be at ease there. But Mrs Lucas often spent some of her rare leisure moments in the smoking-parlour, playing on the virginal that stood in the window, or kippering herself in the fumes of the wood-fire as with streaming eyes she deciphered an Elzevir Horace rather late for inclusion under the rule, but an undoubted bargain.

The house stood at the end of the village that was nearest the station, and thus, when the panorama of her kingdom opened before her, she had but a few steps further to go. A yew-hedge, bought entire from a neighboring farm, and transplanted with solid lumps of earth and indignant snails around its roots, separated the small oblong of garden from the road, and cast monstrous shadows of the shapes into which it was cut, across the little lawns inside. Here, as was only right and proper, there was not a flower to be found save such as were mentioned in the plays of Shakespeare; indeed it was called Shakespeare's garden, and the bed that ran below the windows of the dining room was Ophelia's border, for it consisted solely of those flowers which that distraught maiden distributed to her friends when she should have been in a lunatic asylum. Mrs Lucas often reflected how lucky it was that such institutions were unknown in Elizabeth's day, or that, if known, Shakespeare artistically ignored their existence. Pansies, naturally, formed the chief decoration—though there were some very flourishing plants of rue. Mrs Lucas always wore a little bunch of them when in flower, to inspire her thoughts, and found them wonderfully efficacious. Round the sundial, which was set in the middle of one of the squares of grass between which a path of broken paving-stone led to the front door, was a circular border, now, in July, sadly vacant, for it harboured only the spring-flowers enumerated by Perdita. But the first day every year when Perdita's border put forth its earliest blossom was a delicious anniversary, and the news of it spread like wild-fire through Mrs Lucas's kingdom, and her subjects were very joyful, and came to salute the violet or daffodil, or whatever it was.

The three cottages dexterously transformed into The Hurst, presented a charmingly irregular and picturesque front. Two were of the grey stone of the district and the middle one, to the door of which led the paved path, of brick and timber; latticed windows with stone mullions gave little light to the room within, and certain new windows had been added; these could be detected by the observant eye for they had a markedly older appearance than the rest. The front-door, similarly, seemed as if it must have been made years before the house, the fact being that the one which Mrs Lucas had found there was too dilapidated to be of the slightest service in keeping out wind or wet or undesired callers. She had therefore caused to be constructed an even older one made from the oak-planks of a dismantled barn, and had it studded with large iron nails of antique pattern made by the village blacksmith. He had arranged some of them to look as if they spelled A.D. 1603. Over the door hung an inn-sign, and into the space where once the sign had swung was now inserted a lantern, in which was ensconced, well hidden from view by its patinated glass sides, an electric light. This was one of the necessary concessions to modern convenience, for no lamp nurtured on oil would pierce those genuinely opaque panes, and illuminate the path to the gate. Better to have an electric light than cause your guests to plunge into Perdita's border. By the side of this fortress-door hung a heavy iron bell-pull, ending in a mermaid. When first Mrs Lucas had that installed, it was a bell-pull in the sense that an extremely athletic man could, if he used both hands and planted his feet firmly, cause it to move, so that a huge bronze bell swung in the servants' passage and eventually gave tongue (if the athlete continued pulling) with vibrations so sonorous that the white-wash from the ceiling fell down in flakes. She had therefore made another concession to the frailty of the present generation and the inconveniences of having whitewash falling into salads and puddings on their way to the dining room, and now at the back of the mermaid's tail was a potent little bone button, coloured black and practically invisible, and thus the bell-pull had been converted into an electric bell-push. In this way visitors could make their advent known without violent exertion, the mermaid lost no visible whit of her Elizabethan virginity, and the spirit of Shakespeare wandering in his garden would not notice any anachronism. He could not in fact, for there was none to notice.

Though Mrs Lucas's parents had bestowed the name of Emmeline on her, it was not to be wondered at that she was always known among the more intimate of her subjects as Lucia, pronounced, of course, in the Italian mode—La Lucia, the wife of Lucas; and it was as "Lucia mia" that her husband hailed her as he met her at the door of The Hurst.

He had been watching for her arrival from the panes of the parlour while he meditated upon one of the little prose poems which formed so delectable a contribution to the culture of Riseholme, for though, as had been hinted, he had in practical life a firm grasp of the obvious, there were windows in his soul which looked out onto vague and ethereal prospects which so far from being obvious were only dimly intelligible. In form these odes were cast in the loose rhythms of Walt Whitman, but their smooth suavity and their contents bore no resemblance whatever to the productions of that barbaric bard, whose works were quite unknown in Riseholme. Already a couple of volumes of these prose-poems had been published, not of course in the hard business-like establishment of London, but at "Ye Sign of ye Daffodil," on the village green, where type was set up by hand, and very little, but that of the best, was printed. The press had only been recently started at Mr Lucas's expense, but it had put forth a reprint of Shakespeare's sonnets already, as well as his own poems. They were printed in blunt type on thick yellowish paper, the edges of which seemed as if they had been cut by the forefinger of an impatient reader, so ragged and irregular were they, and they were bound in vellum, the titles of these two slim flowers of poetry, "Flotsam" and "Jetsam," were printed in black letter type and the covers were further adorned with a sort of embossed seal and with antique looking tapes so that you could tie it all up with two bows when you had finished with Mr Lucas's "Flotsam" for the time being, and turned to untie the "Jetsam."

Today the prose-poem of "Loneliness" had not been getting on very well, and Philip Lucas was glad to hear the click of the garden-gate, which showed that his loneliness was over for the present, and looking up he saw his wife's figure waveringly presented to his eyes through the twisted and knotty glass of the parlour window, which had taken so long to collect, but which now completely replaced the plain, commonplace unrefracting stuff which was there before. He jumped up with an alacrity remarkable in so solid and well-furnished a person, and had thrown open the nail-studded front-door before Lucia had traversed the path of broken paving-stones, for she had lingered for a sad moment at Perdita's empty border.

"Lucia mia!" he exclaimed. "Ben arrivata! So you walked from the station?"

"Si, Peppino, mio caro," she said. "Sta bene?"

He kissed her and relapsed into Shakespeare's tongue, for their Italian, though firm and perfect as far as it went, could not be considered as going far, and was useless for conversational purposes, unless they merely wanted to greet each other, or to know the time. But it was interesting to talk Italian, however little way it went.

"Molto bene," said he, "and it's delightful to have you home again. And how was London?" he asked in the sort of tone in which he might have enquired after the health of a poor relation, who was not likely to recover. She smiled rather sadly.

"Terrifically busy about nothing," she said. "All this fortnight I have scarcely had a moment to myself. Lunches, dinners, parties of all kinds; I could not go to half the gatherings I was bidden to. Dear good South Kensington! Chelsea too!"

"Carissima, when London does manage to catch you, it is no wonder it makes the most of you," he said. "You mustn't blame London for that."

"No, dear, I don't. Everyone was tremendously kind and hospitable; they all did their best. If I blame anyone, I blame myself. But I think this Riseholme life with its finish and its exquisiteness spoils one for other places. London is like a railway-junction: it has no true life of its own. There is no delicacy, no appreciation of fine shades. Individualism has no existence there; everyone gabbles together, gabbles and gobbles: am not I naughty? If there is a concert in a private house—you know my views about music and the impossibility of hearing music at all if you are stuck in the middle of a row of people—even then, the moment it is over you are whisked away to supper, or somebody wants to have a few words. There is always a crowd, there is always food, you cannot be alone, and it is only in loneliness, as Goethe says, that your perceptions put forth their flowers. No one in London has time to listen: they are all thinking about who is there and who isn't there, and what is the next thing. The exquisite present, as you put it in one of your poems, has no existence there: it is always the feverish future."

"Delicious phrase! I should have stolen that gem for my poor poems, if you had discovered it before."

She was too much used to this incense to do more than sniff it in unconsciously, and she went on with her tremendous indictment.

"It isn't that I find fault with London for being so busy," she said with strict impartiality, "for if being busy was a crime, I am sure there are few of us here who would escape hanging. But take my life here, or yours for that matter. Well, mine if you like. Often and often I am alone from breakfast till lunch-time, but in those hours I get through more that is worth doing than London gets through in a day and a night. I have an hour at my music not looking about and wondering who my neighbours are, but learning, studying, drinking in divine melody. Then I have my letters to write, and you know what that means, and I still have time for an hour's reading so that when you come to tell me lunch is ready, you will find that I have been wandering through Venetian churches or sitting in that little dark room at Weimar, or was it Leipsic? How would those same hours have passed in London?"

"Sitting perhaps for half an hour in the Park, with dearest Aggie pointing out to me, with thrills of breathless excitement, a woman who was in the divorce court, or a coroneted bankrupt. Then she would drag me off to some terrible private view full of the same people all staring at and gabbling to each other, or looking at pictures that made poor me gasp and shudder. No, I am thankful to be back at my own sweet Riseholme again. I can work and think here."

She looked round the panelled entrance-hall with a glow of warm content at being at home again that quite eclipsed the mere physical heat produced by her walk from the station. Wherever her eyes fell, those sharp dark eyes that resembled buttons covered with shiny American cloth, they saw nothing that jarred, as so much in London jarred. There were bright brass jugs on the window sill, a bowl of pot-pourri on the black table in the centre, an oak settee by the open fireplace, a couple of Persian rugs on the polished floor. The room had its quaintness, too, such as she had alluded to in her memorable essay read before the Riseholme Literary Society, called "Humour in Furniture," and a brass milkcan served as a receptacle for sticks and umbrellas. Equally quaint was the dish of highly realistic stone fruit that stood beside the pot-pourri and the furry Japanese spider that sprawled in a silk web over the window.

Such was the fearful verisimilitude of this that Lucia's new housemaid had once fled from her duties in the early morning, to seek the assistance of the gardener in killing it. The dish of stone fruit had scored a similar success, for once she had said to Georgie Pillson, "Ah, my gardener has sent in some early apples and pears, won't you take one home with you?" It was not till the weight of the pear (he swiftly selected the largest) betrayed the joke that he had any notion that they were not real ones. But then Georgie had had his revenge, for waiting his opportunity he had inserted a real pear among those stony specimens and again passing through with Lucia, he picked it out, and with lips drawn back had snapped at it with all the force of his jaws. For the moment she had felt quite faint at the thought of his teeth crashing into fragments.... These humorous touches were altered from time to time; the spider for instance might be taken down and replaced by a china canary in a Chippendale cage, and the selection of the entrance hall for those whimsicalities was intentional, for guests found something to smile at, as they took off their cloaks and entered the drawing room with a topic on their lips, something light, something amusing about what they had seen. For the gong similarly was sometimes substituted a set of bells that had once decked the collar of the leading horse in a waggoner's team somewhere in Flanders; in fact when Lucia was at home there was often a new little quaintness for quite a sequence of days, and she had held out hopes to the Literary Society that perhaps some day, when she was not so rushed, she would jot down material for a sequel to her essay, or write another covering a rather larger field on "The Gambits of Conversation Derived from Furniture."

On the table there was a pile of letters waiting for Mrs Lucas, for yesterday's post had not been forwarded her, for fear of its missing her—London postmen were probably very careless and untrustworthy—and she gave a little cry of dismay as she saw the volume of her correspondence.

"But I shall be very naughty," she said "and not look at one of them till after lunch. Take them away, Caro, and promise me to lock them up till then, and not give them me however much I beg. Then I will get into the saddle again, such a dear saddle, too, and tackle them. I shall have a stroll in the garden till the bell rings. What is it that Nietzsche says about the necessity to mediterranizer yourself every now and then? I must Riseholme myself."

Peppino remembered the quotation, which had occurred in a review of some work of that celebrated author, where Lucia had also seen it, and went back, with the force of contrast to aid him, to his prose-poem of "Loneliness," while his wife went through the smoking-parlour into the garden, in order to soak herself once more in the cultured atmosphere.

In this garden behind the house there was no attempt to construct a Shakespearian plot, for, as she so rightly observed, Shakespeare, who loved flowers so well, would wish her to enjoy every conceivable horticultural treasure. But furniture played a prominent part in the place, and there were statues and sundials and stone-seats scattered about with almost too profuse a hand. Mottos also were in great evidence, and while a sundial reminded you that "Tempus fugit," an enticing resting-place somewhat bewilderingly bade you to "Bide a wee." But then again the rustic seat in the pleached alley of laburnums had carved on its back, "Much have I travelled in the realms of gold," so that, meditating on Keats, you could bide a wee with a clear conscience. Indeed so copious was the wealth of familiar and stimulating quotations that one of her subjects had once said that to stroll in Lucia's garden was not only to enjoy her lovely flowers, but to spend a simultaneous half hour with the best authors. There was a dovecote of course, but since the cats always killed the doves, Mrs Lucas had put up round the desecrated home several pigeons of Copenhagen china, which were both imperishable as regards cats, and also carried out the suggestion of humour in furniture. The humour had attained the highest point of felicity when Peppino concealed a mechanical nightingale in a bush, which sang "Jug-jug" in the most realistic manner when you pulled a string. Georgie had not yet seen the Copenhagen pigeons, or being rather short-sighted thought they were real. Then, oh then, Peppino pulled the string, and for quite a long time Georgie listened entranced to their melodious cooings. That served him out for his "trap" about the real pear introduced among the stone specimens. For in spite of the rarefied atmosphere of culture at Riseholme, Riseholme knew how to "desipere in loco," and its strenuous culture was often refreshed by these light refined touches.

Mrs Lucas walked quickly and decisively up and down the paths as she waited for the summons to lunch, for the activity of her mind reacted on her body, making her brisk in movement. On each side of her forehead were hard neat undulations of black hair that concealed the tips of her ears. She had laid aside her London hat, and carried a red cotton Contadina's umbrella, which threw a rosy glow onto the oval of her thin face and its colourless complexion. She bore the weight of her forty years extremely lightly, and but for the droop of skin at the corners of her mouth, she might have passed as a much younger woman. Her face was otherwise unlined and bore no trace of the ravages of emotional living, which both ages and softens. Certainly there was nothing soft about her, and very little of the signs of age, and it would have been reasonable to conjecture that twenty years later she would look but little older than she did today. For such emotions as she was victim of were the sterile and ageless emotions of art; such desires as beset her were not connected with her affections, but her ambitions. Dynasty she had none, for she was childless, and thus her ambitions were limited to the permanence and security of her own throne as queen of Riseholme. She really asked nothing more of life than the continuance of such harvests as she had so plenteously reaped for these last ten years. As long as she directed the life of Riseholme, took the lead in its culture and entertainment, and was the undisputed fountain-head of all its inspirations, and from time to time refreshed her memory as to the utter inferiority of London she wanted nothing more. But to secure that she dedicated all that she had of ease, leisure and income. Being practically indefatigable the loss of ease and leisure troubled her but little and being in extremely comfortable circumstances, she had no need to economise in her hospitalities. She might easily look forward to enjoying an unchanging middle-aged activity, while generations of youth withered round her, and no star, remotely rising, had as yet threatened to dim her unrivalled effulgence. Though essentially autocratic, her subjects were allowed and even encouraged to develop their own minds on their own lines, provided always that those lines met at the junction where she was station-master. With regard to religion finally, it may be briefly said that she believed in God in much the same way as she believed in Australia, for she had no doubt whatever as to the existence of either, and she went to church on Sunday in much the same spirit as she would look at a kangaroo in the Zoological Gardens, for kangaroos come from Australia.

A low wall separated the far end of her garden from the meadow outside; beyond that lay the stream which flowed into the Avon, and it often seemed wonderful to her that the water which wimpled by would (unless a cow happened to drink it) soon be stealing along past the church at Stratford where Shakespeare lay. Peppino had written a very moving little prose-poem about it, for she had royally presented him with the idea, and had suggested a beautiful analogy between the earthly dew that refreshed the grasses, and was drawn up into the fire of the Sun, and Thought the spiritual dew that refreshed the mind and thereafter, rather vaguely, was drawn up into the Full-Orbed Soul of the World.

At that moment Lucia's eye was attracted by an apparition on the road which lay adjacent to the further side of the happy stream which flowed into the Avon. There was no mistaking the identity of the stout figure of Mrs Quantock with its short steps and its gesticulations, but why in the name of wonder should that Christian Scientist be walking with the draped and turbaned figure of a man with a tropical complexion and a black beard? His robe of saffron yellow with a violently green girdle was hitched up for ease in walking, and unless he had chocolate coloured stockings on, Mrs Lucas saw human legs of the same shade. Next moment that debatable point was set at rest for she caught sight of short pink socks in red slippers. Even as she looked Mrs Quantock saw her (for owing to Christian Science she had recaptured the quick vision of youth) and waggled her hand and kissed it, and evidently called her companion's attention, for the next moment he was salaaming to her in some stately Oriental manner. There was nothing to be done for the moment except return these salutations, as she could not yell an aside to Mrs Quantock, screaming out "Who is that Indian"? for if Mrs Quantock heard the Indian would hear too, but as soon as she could, she turned back towards the house again, and when once the lilac bushes were between her and the road she walked with more than her usual speed, in order to learn with the shortest possible delay from Peppino who this fresh subject of hers could be. She knew there were some Indian princes in London; perhaps it was one of them, in which case it would be necessary to read up Benares or Delhi in the Encyclopaedia without loss of time.

Chapter TWO

As she traversed the smoking-parlour the cheerful sounds that had once tinkled from the collar of a Flemish horse chimed through the house, and simultaneously she became aware that there would be macaroni au gratin for lunch, which was very dear and remembering of Peppino. But before setting fork to her piled-up plate, she had to question him, for her mental craving for information was far keener than her appetite for food.

"Caro, who is an Indian," she said, "whom I saw just now with Daisy Quantock? They were the other side of il piccolo Avon."

Peppino had already begun his macaroni and must pause to shovel the outlying strings of it into his mouth. But the haste with which he did so was sufficient guaranty for his eagerness to reply as soon as it was humanly possible to do so.

"Indian, my dear?" he asked with the greatest interest.

"Yes; turban and burnous and calves and slippers," she said rather impatiently, for what was the good of Peppino having remained in Riseholme if he could not give her precise and certain information on local news when she returned. His prose-poems were all very well, but as prince-consort he had other duties of state which must not be neglected for the calls of Art.

This slight asperity on her part seemed to sharpen his wits.

"Really, I don't know for certain, Lucia," he said, "for I have not set my eyes on him. But putting two and two together, I might make a guess."

"Two and two make four," she said with that irony for which she was feared and famous. "Now for your guess. I hope it is equally accurate."

"Well, as I told you in one of my letters," said he, "Mrs Quantock showed signs of being a little off with Christian Science. She had a cold, and though she recited the True Statement of Being just as frequently as before, her cold got no better. But when I saw her on Tuesday last, unless it was Wednesday, no, it couldn't have been Wednesday, so it must have been Tuesday—"

"Whenever it was then," interrupted his wife, brilliantly summing up his indecision.

"Yes; whenever it was, as you say, on that occasion Mrs Quantock was very full of some Indian philosophy which made you quite well at once. What did she call it now? Yoga! Yes, that was it!"

"And then?" asked Lucia.

"Well, it appears you must have a teacher in Yoga or else you may injure yourself. You have to breathe deeply and say 'Om'——"

"Say what?"

"Om. I understand the ejaculation to be Om. And there are very curious physical exercises; you have to hold your ear with one hand and your toes with the other, and you may strain yourself unless you do it properly. That was the general gist of it."

"And shall we come to the Indian soon?" said Lucia.

"Carissima, you have come to him already. I suggest that Mrs Quantock has applied for a teacher and got him. Ecco!"

Mrs Lucas wore a heavily corrugated forehead at this news. Peppino had a wonderful flair in explaining unusual circumstances in the life of Riseholme and his conjectures were generally correct. But if he was right in this instance, it struck Lucia as being a very irregular thing that anyone should have imported a mystical Indian into Riseholme without consulting her. It is true that she had been away, but still there was the medium of the post.

"Ecco indeed!" she said. "It puts me in rather a difficult position, for I must send out my invitations to my garden-party today, and I really don't know whether I ought to be officially aware of this man's existence or not. I can't write to Daisy Quantock and say 'Pray bring your black friend Om or whatever his name proves to be, and on the other hand, if he is the sort of person whom one would be sorry to miss, I should not like to have passed over him."

9

"After all, my dear, you have only been back in Riseholme half an hour," said her husband. "It would have been difficult for Mrs Quantock to have told you yet."

Her face cleared.

"Perhaps Daisy has written to me about him," she said. "I may find a full account of it all when I open my letters."

"Depend upon it you will. She would hardly have been so wanting in proper feeling as not to have told you. I think, too, that her visitor must only have just arrived, or I should have been sure to see him about somewhere."

She rose.

"Well, we will see," she said. "Now I shall be very busy all afternoon, but by tea-time I shall be ready to see anyone who calls. Give me my letters, Caro, and I will find out if Daisy has written to me."

She turned them over as she went to her room, and there among them was a bulky envelope addressed in Mrs Quantock's great sprawling hand, which looked at first sight so large and legible, but on closer examination turned out to be so baffling. You had to hold it at some distance off to make anything out of it, and look at it in an abstracted general manner much as you would look at a view. Treated thus, scattered words began to leap into being, and when you had got a sufficiency of these, like glimpses of the country seen by flashes of lightning, you could hope to get a collective idea of it all. The procedure led to the most promising results as Mrs Lucas sat with the sheets at arm's length, occasionally altering the range to try the effect of a different focus. "Benares" blinked at her, also "Brahmin"; also "highest caste"; "extraordinary sanctity," and "Guru." And when the meaning of this latter was ascertained from the article on "Yoga" in her Encyclopaedia, she progressed very swiftly towards a complete comprehension of the letter.

When fully pieced together it was certainly enough to rivet her whole attention, and make her leave unopened the rest of the correspondence, for such a prelude to adventure had seldom sounded in Riseholme. It appeared, even as her husband had told her at lunch, that Mrs Quantock found her cold too obstinate for all the precepts of Mrs Eddy; the True Statement of Being, however often repeated, only seemed to inflame it further, and one day, when confined to the house, she had taken a book "quite at random" from the shelves in her library, under, she supposed, the influence of some interior compulsion. This then was clearly a "leading."

Mrs Lucas paused a moment as she pieced together these first sentences. She seemed to remember that Mrs Quantock had experienced a similar leading when first she took up Christian Science. It was a leading from the sight of a new church off Sloane Street that day; Mrs Quantock had entered (she scarcely knew why) and had found herself in a Testimony Meeting, where witness after witness declared the miraculous healings they had experienced. One had had a cough, another cancer, another a fractured bone, but all had been cured by the blessed truths conveyed in the Gospel according to Mrs Eddy. However, her memories on this subject were not to the point now; she burned to arrive at the story of the new leading.

Well, the book that Mrs Quantock had taken down in obedience to the last leading proved to be a little handbook of Oriental Philosophies, and it opened, "all of its own accord," at a chapter called Yoga. Instantly she perceived, as by the unclosing of an inward eye, that Yoga was what she wanted and she instantly wrote to the address from which this book was issued asking for any guidance on the subject. She had read in "Oriental Philosophies" that for the successful practice of Yoga, it was necessary to have a teacher, and did they know of any teacher who could give her instruction? A wonderful answer came to that, for two days afterwards her maid came to her and said that an Indian gentleman would like to see her. He was ushered in, and with a profound obeisance said: "Beloved lady, I am the teacher you asked for; I am your Guru. Peace be to this house! Om!"

Mrs Lucas had by this time got her view of Mrs Quantock's letter into perfect focus, and she read on without missing a word. "Is it not wonderful, dearest Lucia," it ran, "that my desire for light should have been so instantly answered? And yet my Guru tells me that it always happens so. I was sent to him, and he was sent to me, just like that! He had been expecting some call when my letter asking for guidance came, and he started at once because he knew he was sent. Fancy! I don't even know his name, and his religion forbids him to tell it me. He is just my Guru, my guide, and he is going to be with me as long as he knows I need him to show me the True Path. He has the spare bedroom and the little room adjoining where he meditates and does Postures and Pranyama which is breathing. If you persevere in them under instruction, you have perfect health and youth, and my cold is gone already. He is a Brahmin of the very highest caste, indeed caste means nothing to him any longer, just as a Baronet and an Honourable must seem about the same thing to the King. He comes from Benares where he used to meditate all day by the Ganges, and I can see for myself that he is a person of the most extraordinary sanctity. But he can meditate just as well in my little room, for he says he was never in any house that had such a wonderful atmosphere. He has no money at all which is so beautiful of him, and looked so pained and disappointed when I asked him if I might not give him some. He doesn't even know how he got here from London; he doesn't think he came by train, so perhaps he was wafted here in some astral manner. He looked so bewildered too when I said the word 'money,' and evidently he had to think what it was, because it is so long since it has meant anything to him. So if he wants anything, I have told him to go into any shop and ask that it shall be put down to me. He has often been without food or sleep for days together when he is meditating. Just think!

"Shall I bring him to see you, or will you come here? He wants to meet you, because he feels you have a beautiful soul and may help him in that way, as well as his helping you. I am helping him too he says, which seems more wonderful than I can believe. Send me a line as soon as you get back. Tante salute!

> "Your own,
> "DAISY."

The voluminous sheets had taken long in reading and Mrs Lucas folded them up slowly and thoughtfully. She felt that she had to make a swift decision that called into play all her mental powers. On the one hand it was "up to her" to return a frigid reply, conveying, without making any bones about the matter, that she had no interest in nameless Gurus who might or might not be Brahmins from Benares and presented themselves at Daisy's doors in a penniless condition without clear knowledge whether they had come by train or not. In favour of such prudent measures was the truly Athenian character of Daisy's mind, for she was always enquiring into "some new thing," which was the secret of life when first discovered, and got speedily relegated to the dust-heap. But against such a course was the undoubted fact that Daisy did occasionally get hold of somebody who subsequently proved to be of interest, and Lucia would never forget to her dying day the advent in Riseholme of a little Welsh attorney, in whom Daisy had discovered a wonderful mentality. Lucia had refused to extend her queenly hospitality to him, or to recognise his existence in any way during the fortnight when he stayed with Daisy, and she was naturally very much annoyed to find him in a prominent position in the Government not many years later. Indeed she had snubbed him so markedly on his first appearance at Riseholme that he had refused on subsequent visits to come to her house at all, though he several times visited Mrs Quantock again, and told her all sorts of political secrets (so she said) which she would not divulge for anything in the world. There must never be a repetition of so fatal an error.

Another thing inclined the wavering balance. She distinctly wanted some fresh element at her court, that should make Riseholme know that she was in residence again. August would soon be here with its languors and absence of stimulus, when it was really rather difficult in the drowsy windless weather to keep the flag of culture flying strongly from her own palace. The Guru had already said that he felt sure she had a beautiful soul, and— The outline of the scheme flashed upon her. She would have Yoga evenings in the hot August weather, at which, as the heat of the day abated, graceful groups should assemble among the mottos in the garden and listen to high talk on spiritual subjects. They would adjourn to delicious moonlit suppers in the pergola, or if the moon was indisposed—she could not be expected to regulate the affairs of the moon as well as of Riseholme—there would be dim seances and sandwiches in the smoking-parlour. The humorous furniture should be put in cupboards, and as they drifted towards the front hall again, when the clocks struck an unexpectedly late hour, little whispered colloquies of "How wonderful he was tonight" would be heard, and there would be faraway looks and sighs, and the notings down of the titles of books that conducted the pilgrim on the Way. Perhaps as they softly assembled for departure, a little music would be suggested to round off the evening, and she saw herself putting down the soft pedal as people rustled into their places, for the first movement of the "Moonlight Sonata." Then at the end there would be silence, and she would get up with a sigh, and someone would say "Lucia mia"! and somebody else "Heavenly Music," and perhaps the Guru would say "Beloved lady," as he had apparently said to poor Daisy Quantock. Flowers, music, addresses from the Guru, soft partings, sense of refreshment.... With the memory of the Welsh attorney in her mind, it seemed clearly wiser to annex rather than to repudiate the Guru. She seized a pen and drew a pile of postcards towards her, on the top of which was printed her name and address.

"Too wonderful," she wrote, "pray bring him yourself to my little garden-party on Friday. There will be only a few. Let me know if he wants a quiet room ready for him."

All this had taken time, and she had but scribbled a dozen postcards to friends bidding them come to her garden party on Friday, when tea was announced. These invitations had the mystic word "Hightum" written at the bottom left hand corner, which conveyed to the enlightened recipient what sort of party it was to be, and denoted the standard of dress. For one of Lucia's quaint ideas was to divide dresses into three classes, "Hightum," "Tightum" and "Scrub." "Hightum" was your very best dress, the smartest and newest of all, and when "Hightum" was written on a card of invitation, it implied that the party was a very resplendent one. "Tightum" similarly indicated a moderately smart party, "Scrub" carried its own significance on the surface. These terms applied to men's dress as well and as regards evening parties: a dinner party "Hightum" would indicate a white tie and a tail coat; a dinner party "Tightum" a black tie and a short coat, and a dinner "Scrub" would mean morning clothes.

With tea was announced also the advent of Georgie Pillson who was her gentleman-in-waiting when she was at home, and her watch-dog when she was not. In order to save subsequent disappointment, it may be at once stated that there never has been, was, or ever would be the smallest approach to a flirtation between them. Neither of them, she with her forty respectable years and he with his blameless forty-five years, had ever flirted, with anybody at all. But it was one of the polite and pleasant fictions of Riseholme that Georgie was passionately attached to her and that it was for her sake that he had settled in Riseholme now some seven years ago, and that for her sake he remained still unmarried. She never, to do her justice, had affirmed anything of the sort, but it is a fact that sometimes when Georgie's name came up in conversation, her eyes wore that "far-away" look that only the masterpieces of art could otherwise call up, and she would sigh and murmur "Dear Georgie"! and change the subject, with the tact that characterized her. In fact their mutual relations were among the most Beautiful Things of Riseholme, and hardly less beautiful was Peppino's attitude towards it all. That large hearted man trusted them both, and his trust was perfectly justified. Georgie was in and out of the house all day, chiefly in; and not only did scandal never rear its hissing head, but it positively had not a head to hiss with, or a foot to stand on. On his side again Georgie had never said that he was in love with her (nor would it have been true if he had), but by his complete silence on the subject coupled with his constancy he seemed to admit the truth of this bloodless idyll. They talked and walked and read the masterpieces of literature and played duets on the piano together. Sometimes (for he was the more brilliant performer, though as he said "terribly lazy about practising," for which she scolded him) he would gently slap the back of her hand, if she played a wrong note, and say "Naughty!" And she would reply in baby language "Me vewy sowwy! Oo naughty too to hurt Lucia!" That was the utmost extent of their carnal familiarities, and with bright eyes fixed on the music they would break into peals of girlish laughter, until the beauty of the music sobered them again.

Georgie (he was Georgie or Mr Georgie, never Pillson to the whole of Riseholme) was not an obtrusively masculine sort of person. Such masculinity as he was possessed of was boyish rather than adult, and the most important ingredients in his nature were womanish. He had, in common with the rest of Riseholme, strong artistic tastes, and in addition to playing the piano, made charming little water-colour sketches, many of which he framed at his own expense and gave to friends, with slightly sentimental titles, neatly printed in gilt letters on the mount. "Golden Autumn Woodland," "Bleak December," "Yellow Daffodils," "Roses of Summer" were perhaps his most notable series, and these he had given to Lucia, on the occasion of four successive birthdays. He did portraits as well in pastel; these were of two types, elderly ladies in lace caps with a row of pearls, and boys in cricket shirts with their sleeves rolled up. He was not very good at eyes, so his sitters always were looking down, but he was excellent at smiles, and the old ladies smiled patiently and sweetly, and the boys gaily. But his finest accomplishment was needlework and his house was full of the creations of his needle, wool-work curtains, petit-point chair seats, and silk embroideries framed and glazed. Next to Lucia he was the hardest worked inhabitant of Riseholme but not being so strong as the Queen, he had often to go away for little rests by the sea-side. Travelling by train fussed him a good deal, for he might not be able to get a corner seat, or somebody with a pipe or a baby might get into his carriage, or the porter might be rough with his luggage, so he always went in his car to some neighbouring watering-place where they knew him. Dicky, his handsome young chauffeur, drove him, and by Dicky's side sat Foljambe, his very pretty parlour-maid who valetted him. If Dicky took the wrong turn his master called "Naughty boy" through the tube, and Foljambe smiled respectfully. For the month of August, his two plain strapping sisters (Hermione and Ursula alas!) always came to stay with him. They liked pigs and dogs and otter-hunting and mutton-chops, and were rather a discordant element in Riseholme. But Georgie had a kind heart, and never even debated whether he should ask Hermy and Ursy or not, though he had to do a great deal of tidying up after they had gone.

There was always a playful touch between the meetings of these two when either of them had been away from Riseholme that very prettily concealed the depth of Georgie's supposed devotion, and when she came out into the garden where her Cavalier and her husband were waiting for their tea under the pergola, Georgie jumped up very nimbly and took a few chassee-ing steps towards her with both hands outstretched in welcome. She caught at his humour, made him a curtsey, and next moment they were treading a little improvised minuet together with hands held high, and pointed toes. Georgie had very small feet, and it was a really elegant toe that he pointed, encased in cloth-topped boots. He had on a suit of fresh white flannels and over his shoulders, for fear of the evening air being chilly after this hot day, he had a little cape of a military cut, like those in which young ladies at music-halls enact the part of colonels. He had a straw-hat on, with a blue riband, a pink shirt and a red tie, rather loose and billowy. His face was pink and round, with blue eyes, a short nose and very red lips. An almost complete absence of eyebrow was made up for by a firm little brown moustache clipped very short, and brushed upwards at its extremities. Contrary to expectation he was quite tall and fitted very neatly into his clothes.

The dance came to an end with a low curtsey on Lucia's part, an obeisance hat in hand from Georgie (this exposure shewing a crop of hair grown on one side of his head and brushed smoothly over the top until it joined the hair on the other side) and a clapping of the hands from Peppino.

"Bravo, bravo," he cried from the tea-table. "Capital!"

Mrs Lucas blew him a kiss in acknowledgment of this compliment and smiled on her partner. "Amico!" she said. "It is nice to see you again. How goes it?"

"Va bene," said Georgie to show he could talk Italian too. "Va very bene now that you've come back."

"Grazie! Now tell us all the news. We'll have a good gossip."

Georgie's face beamed with a "solemn gladness" at the word, like a drunkard's when brandy is mentioned.

"Where shall we begin?" he said. "Such a lot to tell you. I think we must begin with a great bit of news. Something really mysterious."

Lucia smiled inwardly. She felt that she knew for dead certain what the mysterious news was, and also that she knew far more about it than Georgie. This superiority she completely concealed. Nobody could have guessed it.

"Presto, presto!" she said. "You excite me."

"Yesterday morning I was in Rush's," said Georgie, "seeing about some Creme de menthe, which ought to have been sent the day before. Rush is very negligent sometimes—and I was just saying a sharp word about it, when suddenly I saw that Rush was not attending at all, but was looking at something behind my back, and so I looked round. Guess!"

"Don't be tantalising, amico," said she. "How can I guess? A pink elephant with blue spots!"

"No, guess again!"

"A red Indian in full war paint."

"Certainly not! Guess again," said Georgie, with a little sigh of relief. (It would have been awful if she had guessed.) At this moment Peppino suddenly became aware that Lucia had guessed and was up to some game.

"Give me your hand, Georgie," she said, "and look at me. I'm going to read your thoughts. Think of what you saw when you turned round."

She took his hand and pressed it to her forehead, closing her eyes.

"But I do seem to see an Indian," she said. "Ah, not red Indian, other Indian. And—and he has slippers on and brown stockings—no, not brown stockings; it's legs. And there's a beard, and a turban."

She gave a sigh.

"That's all I can see," she said.

"My dear, you're marvellous," said he. "You're quite right."

A slight bubbling sound came from Peppino, and Georgie began to suspect.

"I believe you've seen him!" he said. "How tarsome you are...."

When they had all laughed a great deal, and Georgie had been assured that Lucia really, word of honour, had no idea what happened next, the narrative was resumed.

"So there stood the Indian, bowing and salaaming most politely and when Rush had promised me he would send my Creme de menthe that very morning, I just looked through a wine list for a moment, and the Indian with quantities more bows came up to the counter and said, 'If you will have the great goodness to give me a little brandy bottle.' So Rush gave it him, and instead of paying for it, what do you think he said? Guess."

Mrs Lucas rose with the air of Lady Macbeth and pointed her finger at Georgie.
"He said 'Put it down to Mrs Quantock's account,'" she hissed.

Of course the explanation came now, and Lucia told the two men the contents of Mrs Quantock's letter. With that her cards were on the table, and though the fact of the Brahmin from Benares was news to Georgie, he had got many interesting things to tell her, for his house adjoined Mrs Quantock's and there were plenty of things which Mrs Quantock had not mentioned in her letter, so that Georgie was soon in the position of informant again. His windows overlooked Mrs Quantock's garden, and since he could not keep his eyes shut all day, it followed that the happenings there were quite common property. Indeed that was a general rule in Riseholme: anyone in an adjoining property could say, "What an exciting game of lawn-tennis you had this afternoon!" having followed it from his bedroom. That was part of the charm of Riseholme; it was as if it contained just one happy family with common interests and pursuits. What happened in the house was a more private matter, and Mrs Quantock, for instance, would never look from the rising ground at the end of her garden into Georgie's dining-room or, if she did she would never tell anyone how many places were laid at table on that particular day when she had asked if he could give her lunch, and he had replied that to his great regret his table was full. But nobody could help seeing into gardens from back windows: the "view" belonged to everybody.

Georgie had had wonderful views.

"That very day," he said, "soon after lunch, I was looking for a letter I thought I had left in my bedroom, and happening to glance out, I saw the Indian sitting under Mrs Quantock's pear-tree. He was swaying a little backwards and forwards."

"The brandy!" said Lucia excitedly. "He has his meals in his own room."

"No, amica, it was not the brandy. In fact I don't suppose the brandy had gone to Mrs Quantock's then, for he did not take it from Rush's, but asked that it should be sent...." He paused a moment—"Or did he take it away? I declare I can't remember. But anyhow when he swayed backwards and forwards, he wasn't drunk, for presently he stood on one leg, and crooked the other behind it, and remained there with his hands up, as if he was praying, for quite a long time without swaying at all. So he couldn't have been tipsy. And then he sat down again, and took off his slippers, and held his toes with one hand, while his legs were quite straight out, and put his other hand round behind his head, and grasped his other ear with it. I tried to do it on my bedroom floor, but I couldn't get near it. Then he sat up again and called 'Chela! Chela!' and Mrs Quantock came running out."

"Why did he say 'Chela'?" asked Lucia.

"I wondered too. But I knew I had some clue to it, so I looked through some books by Rudyard Kipling, and found that Chela meant 'Disciple.' What you have told me just now about 'Guru' being 'teacher,' seems to piece the whole thing together."

"And what did Daisy do?" asked Mrs Lucas breathlessly.

"She sat down too, and put her legs out straight in front of her like the Guru, and tried to hold the toe of her shoe in her fingers, and naturally she couldn't get within yards of it. I got nearer than she did. And he said, 'Beloved lady, not too far at first.'"

"So you could hear too," said Lucia.

"Naturally, for my window was open, and as you know Mrs Quantock's pear-tree is quite close to the house. And then he told her to stop up one nostril with her finger and inhale through the other, and then hold her breath, while he counted six. Then she breathed it all out again, and started with the other side. She repeated that several times and he was very much pleased with her. Then she said, 'It is quite wonderful; I feel so light and vigorous.'"

"It would be very wonderful indeed if dear Daisy felt light," remarked Lucia. "What next?"
"Then they sat and swayed backwards and forwards again and muttered something that sounded like Pom!"

"That would be 'Om', and then?"

"I couldn't wait any longer for I had some letters to write."

She smiled at him.

"I shall give you another cup of tea to reward you for your report," she said. "It has all been most interesting. Tell me again about the breathing in and holding your breath."

Georgie did so, and illustrated in his own person what had happened. Next moment Lucia was imitating him, and Peppino came round in order to get a better view of what Georgie was doing. Then they all sat, inhaling through one nostril, holding their breath, and then expelling it again.

"Very interesting," said Lucia at the end. "Upon my word, it does give one a sort of feeling of vigour and lightness. I wonder if there is something in it."

Chapter THREE

Though "The Hurst" was, as befitted its Chatelaine, the most Elizabethanly complete abode in Riseholme, the rest of the village in its due degree, fell very little short of perfection. It had but its one street some half mile in length but that street was a gem of mediaeval domestic architecture. For the most part the houses that lined it were blocks of contiguous cottages, which had been converted either singly or by twos and threes into dwellings containing the comforts demanded by the twentieth century, but externally they preserved the antiquity which, though it might be restored or supplemented by bathrooms or other conveniences, presented a truly Elizabethan appearance. There were, of course, accretions such as old inn signs above front-doors and old bell-pulls at their sides, but the doors were uniformly of inconveniently low stature, roofs were of stone slabs or old brick, in which a suspiciously abundant crop of antirrhinums and stone crops had anchored themselves, and there was hardly a garden that did not contain a path of old paving-stones, a mulberry-tree and some yews cut into shape.

Nothing in the place was more blatantly mediaeval than the village green, across which Georgie took his tripping steps after leaving the presence of his queen. Round it stood a row of great elms, and in its centre was the ducking-pond, according to Riseholme tradition, though perhaps in less classical villages it might have passed merely for a duck-pond. But in Riseholme it would have been rank heresy to dream, even in the most pessimistic moments, of its being anything but a ducking-pond. Close by it stood a pair of stocks, about which there was no doubt whatever, for Mr Lucas had purchased them from a neighbouring iconoclastic village, where they were going to be broken up, and, after having them repaired, had presented them to the village-green, and chosen their site close to the ducking pond. Round the green were grouped the shops of the village, slightly apart from the residential street, and at the far end of it was that undoubtedly Elizabethan hostelry, the Ambermere Arms, full to overflowing of ancient tables and bible-boxes, and fire-dogs and fire-backs, and bottles and chests and settles. These were purchased in large quantities by the American tourists who swarmed there during the summer months, at a high profit to the nimble proprietor, who thereupon purchased fresh antiquities to take their places. The Ambermere Arms in fact was the antique furniture shop of the place, and did a thriving trade, for it was much more interesting to buy objects out of a real old Elizabethan inn, than out of a shop.

Georgie had put his smart military cape over his arm for his walk, and at intervals applied his slim forefinger to one nostril, while he breathed in through the other, continuing the practice which he had observed going on in Mrs Quantock's garden. Though it made him a little dizzy, it certainly produced a sort of lightness, but soon he remembered the letter from Mrs Quantock which Lucia had read out, warning her that these exercises ought to be taken under instruction, and so desisted. He was going to deliver Lucia's answer at Mrs Quantock's house, and with a view to possibly meeting the Guru, and being introduced to him, he said over to himself "Guru, Guru, Guru" instead of doing deep breathing, in order to accustom himself to the unusual syllables.

It would, of course, have been very strange and un-Riseholme-like to have gone to a friend's door, even though the errand was so impersonal a one as bearing somebody else's note, without enquiring whether the friend was in, and being instantly admitted if she was, and as a matter of fact, Georgie caught a glimpse, when the knocker was answered (Mrs Quantock did not have a bell at all), through the open door of the hall, of Mrs Quantock standing in the middle of the lawn on one leg. Naturally, therefore, he ran out into the garden without any further formality. She looked like a little round fat stork, whose legs had not grown, but who preserved the habits of her kind.

"Dear lady, I've brought a note for you," he said, "it's from Lucia."

The other leg went down, and she turned on him the wide firm smile that she had learned in the vanished days of Christian Science.

"Om," said Mrs Quantock, expelling the remainder of her breath. "Thank you, my dear Georgie. It's extraordinary what Yoga has done for me already. Cold quite gone. If ever you feel out of sorts, or depressed or cross you can cure yourself at once. I've got a visitor staying with me."

"Have you indeed?" asked Georgie, without alluding to the thrilling excitements which had trodden so close on each other's heels since yesterday morning when he had seen the Guru in Rush's shop.

"Yes; and as you've just come from dear Lucia's perhaps she may have said something to you about him, for I wrote to her about him. He's a Guru of extraordinary sanctity from Benares, and he's teaching me the Way. You shall see him too, unless he's meditating. I will call to him; if he's meditating he won't hear me, so we shan't be interrupting him. He wouldn't hear a railway accident if he was meditating."

She turned round towards the house.

"Guru, dear!" she called.

There was a moment's pause, and the Indian's face appeared at a window.

"Beloved lady!" he said.

"Guru dear, I want to introduce a friend of mine to you," she said. "This is Mr Pillson, and when you know him a little better you will call him Georgie."

"Beloved lady, I know him very well indeed. I see into his clear white soul. Peace be unto you, my friend."

"Isn't he marvellous? Fancy!" said Mrs Quantock, in an aside.

Georgie raised his hat very politely.

"How do you do?" he said. (After his quiet practice he would have said "How do you do Guru?" but it rhymed in a ridiculous manner and his red lips could not frame the word.)

"I am always well," said the Guru, "I am always young and well because I follow the Way."

18

"Sixty at least he tells me," said Mrs Quantock in a hissing aside, probably audible across the channel, "and he thinks more, but the years make no difference to him. He is like a boy. Call him 'Guru.'"

"Guru,—" began Georgie.

"Yes, my friend."

"I am very glad you are well," said Georgie wildly. He was greatly impressed, but much embarrassed. Also it was so hard to talk at a second-story window with any sense of ease, especially when you had to address a total stranger of extraordinary sanctity from Benares.

Luckily Mrs Quantock came to the assistance of his embarrassment.

"Guru dear, are you coming down to see us?" she asked.

"Beloved lady, no!" said the level voice. "It is laid on me to wait here. It is the time of calm and prayer when it is good to be alone. I will come down when the guides bid me. But teach our dear friend what I have taught you. Surely before long I will grasp his earthly hand, but not now. Peace! Peace! and Light!"

"Have you got some Guides as well?" asked Georgie when the Guru disappeared from the window. "And are they Indians too?"

"Oh, those are his spiritual guides," said Mrs Quantock, "He sees them and talks to them, but they are not in the body."

She gave a happy sigh.

"I never have felt anything like it," she said. "He has brought such an atmosphere into the house that even Robert feels it, and doesn't mind being turned out of his dressing-room. There, he has shut the window. Isn't it all marvellous?"

Georgie had not seen anything particularly marvellous yet, except the phenomenon of Mrs Quantock standing on one leg in the middle of the lawn, but presumably her emotion communicated itself to him by the subtle infection of the spirit.

"And what does he do?" he asked.

"My dear, it is not what he does, but what he is," said she. "Why, even my little bald account of him to Lucia has made her ask him to her garden-party. Of course I can't tell whether he will go or not. He seems so very much—how shall I say it?—so very much sent to Me. But I shall of course ask him whether he will consent. Trances and meditation all day! And in the intervals such serenity and sweetness. You know, for instance, how tiresome Robert is about his food. Well, last night the mutton, I am bound to say, was a little underdone, and Robert was beginning to throw it about his plate in the way he has. Well, my Guru got up and just said, 'Show me the way to kitchen'—he leaves out little words sometimes, because they don't matter—and I took him down, and he said 'Peace!' He told me to leave him there, and in ten minutes he was up again with a little plate of curry and rice and what had been underdone mutton, and you never ate anything so good. Robert had most of it and I had the rest, and my Guru was so pleased at seeing Robert pleased. He said Robert had a pure white soul, just like you, only I wasn't to tell him, because for him the Way ordained that he must find it out

19

for himself. And today before lunch again, the Guru went down in the kitchen, and my cook told me he only took a pinch of pepper and a tomato and a little bit of mutton fat and a sardine and a bit of cheese, and he brought up a dish that you never saw equalled. Delicious! I shouldn't a bit wonder if Robert began breathing-exercises soon. There is one that makes you lean and young and exercises the liver."

This sounded very entrancing.

"Can't you teach me that?" asked Georgie eagerly. He had been rather distressed about his increasing plumpness for a year past, and about his increasing age for longer than that. As for his liver he always had to be careful.

She shook her head.

"You cannot practise it except under tuition from an expert," she said.

Georgie rapidly considered what Hermy's and Ursy's comments would be if, when they arrived tomorrow, he was found doing exercises under the tuition of a Guru. Hermy, when she was not otter-hunting, could be very sarcastic, and he had a clear month of Hermy in front of him, without any otter-hunting, which, so she had informed him, was not possible in August. This was mysterious to Georgie, because it did not seem likely that all otters died in August, and a fresh brood came in like caterpillars. If Hermy was here in October, she would otter-hunt all morning and snore all afternoon, and be in the best of tempers, but the August visit required more careful steering. Yet the prospect of being lean and young and internally untroubled was wonderfully tempting.

"But couldn't he be my Guru as well?" he asked.

Quite suddenly and by some demoniac possession, a desire that had been only intermittently present in Mrs Quantock's consciousness took full possession of her, a red revolutionary insurgence hoisted its banner. Why with this stupendous novelty in the shape of a Guru shouldn't she lead and direct Riseholme instead of Lucia? She had long wondered why darling Lucia should be Queen of Riseholme, and had, by momentary illumination, seen herself thus equipped as far more capable of exercising supremacy. After all, everybody in Riseholme knew Lucia's old tune by now, and was in his secret consciousness quite aware that she did not play the second and third movements of the Moonlight Sonata, simply because they "went faster," however much she might cloak the omission by saying that they resembled eleven o'clock in the morning and 3 p.m. And Mrs Quantock had often suspected that she did not read one quarter of the books she talked about, and that she got up subjects in the Encyclopaedia, in order to make a brave show that covered essential ignorance. Certainly she spent a good deal of money over entertaining, but Robert had lately made twenty times daily what Lucia spent annually, over Roumanian oils. As for her acting, had she not completely forgotten her words as Lady Macbeth in the middle of the sleep-walking scene?

But here was Lucia, as proved by her note, and her A. D. C. Georgie, wildly interested in the Guru. Mrs Quantock conjectured that Lucia's plan was to launch the Guru at her August parties, as her own discovery. He would be a novelty, and it would be Lucia who gave Om-parties and breathing-parties and standing-on-one-leg parties, while she herself, Daisy Quantock, would be bidden to these as a humble guest, and Lucia would get all the credit, and, as likely as not, invite the discoverer, the inventress, just now and then. Mrs Quantock's Guru would become Lucia's Guru and all Riseholme would flock hungrily for light and leading to The Hurst. She had written to Lucia in all sincerity, hoping that she would extend the hospitality of her garden-parties to the Guru, but now the very warmth of Lucia's reply caused her to suspect this ulterior motive. She had been too precipitate, too rash, too ill-advised, too sudden, as Lucia would say. She ought to have known that Lucia, with her August parties coming on, would have jumped at a Guru, and withheld him for her own parties, taking the wind out of Lucia's August sails. Lucia had already suborned Georgie to leave this note, and begin to filch the Guru away. Mrs Quantock saw it all now, and clearly this was not to be borne. Before she answered, she steeled herself with the triumph she had once scored in the matter of the Welsh attorney.

"Dear Georgie," she said, "no one would be more delighted than I if my Guru consented to take you as a pupil. But you can't tell what he will do, as he said to me today, apropos of myself, 'I cannot come unless I'm sent.' Was not that wonderful? He knew at once he had been sent to me."

By this time Georgie was quite determined to have the Guru. The measure of his determination may be gauged from the fact that he forgot all about Lucia's garden-party.

"But he called me his friend," he said. "He told me I had a clean white soul."

"Yes; but that is his attitude towards everybody," said Mrs Quantock.
"His religion makes it impossible for him to think ill of anybody."
"But he didn't say that to Rush," cried Georgie, "when he asked for some brandy, to be put down to you."

Mrs Quantock's expression changed for a moment, but that moment was too short for Georgie to notice it. Her face instantly cleared again.

"Naturally he cannot go about saying that sort of thing," she observed.
"Common people—he is of the highest caste—would not understand him."
Georgie made the direct appeal.

"Please ask him to teach me," he said.

For a moment Mrs Quantock did not answer, but cocked her head sideways in the direction of the pear-tree where a thrush was singing. It fluted a couple of repeated phrases and then was silent again.

Mrs Quantock gave a great smile to the pear-tree.

"Thank you, little brother," she said.

She turned to Georgie again.

"That comes out of St. Francis," she said, "but Yoga embraces all that is true in every religion. Well, I will ask my Guru whether he will take you as a pupil, but I can't answer for what he will say."

"What does he—what does he charge for his lesson?" asked Georgie.

The Christian Science smile illuminated her face again.

"The word 'money' never passes his lips," she said. "I don't think he really knows what it means. He proposed to sit on the green with a beggar's bowl but of course I would not permit that, and for the present I just give him all he wants. No doubt when he goes away, which I hope will not be for many weeks yet, though no one can tell when he will have another call, I shall slip something suitably generous into his hand, but I don't think about that. Must you be going? Good night, dear Georgie. Peace! Om!"

His last backward glance as he went out of the front door revealed her standing on one leg again, just as he had seen her first. He remembered a print of a fakir at Benares, standing in that attitude; and if the stream that flowed into the Avon could be combined with the Ganges, and the garden into the burning ghaut, and the swooping swallows into the kites, and the neat parlour-maid who showed him out, into a Brahmin, and the Chinese gong that was so prominent an object in the hall into a piece of Benares brassware, he could almost have fancied himself as standing on the brink of the sacred river. The marigolds in the garden required no transmutation....

Georgie had quite "to pull himself together," as he stepped round Mrs Quantock's mulberry tree, and ten paces later round his own, before he could recapture his normal evening mood, on those occasions when he was going to dine alone. Usually these evenings were very pleasant and much occupied, for they did not occur very often in this whirl of Riseholme life, and it was not more than once a week that he spent a solitary evening, and then, if he got tired of his own company, there were half a dozen houses, easy of access where he could betake himself in his military cloak, and spend a post-prandial hour. But oftener than not when these occasions occurred, he would be quite busy at home, dusting a little china, and rearranging ornaments on his shelves, and, after putting his rings and handkerchief in the candle-bracket of the piano, spending a serious hour (with the soft pedal down, for fear of irritating Robert) in reading his share of such duets as he would be likely to be called upon to play with Lucia during the next day or two. Though he read music much better than she did, he used to "go over" the part alone first, and let it be understood that he had not seen it before. But then he was sure that she had done precisely the same, so they started fair. Such things whiled away very pleasantly the hours till eleven, when he went to bed, and it was seldom that he had to set out Patience-cards to tide him over the slow minutes.

But every now and then—and tonight was one of those occasions—there occurred evenings when he never went out to dinner even if he was asked, because he "was busy indoors." They occurred about once a month (these evenings that he was "busy indoors")—and even an invitation from Lucia would not succeed in disturbing them. Ages ago Riseholme had decided what made Georgie "busy indoors" once a month, and so none of his friends chatted about the nature of his engagements to anyone else, simply because everybody else knew. His business indoors, in fact, was a perfect secret, from having been public property for so long.

June had been a very busy time, not "indoors," but with other engagements, and as Georgie went up to his bedroom, having been told by Foljambe that the hair-dresser was waiting for him, and had been waiting "this last ten minutes," he glanced at his hair in the Cromwellian mirror that hung on the stairs, and was quite aware that it was time he submitted himself to Mr Holroyd's ministrations. There was certainly an undergrowth of grey hair visible beneath his chestnut crop, that should have been attended to at least a fortnight ago. Also there was a growing thinness in the locks that crossed his head; Mr Holroyd had attended to that before, and had suggested a certain remedy, not in the least inconvenient, unless Georgie proposed to be athletic without a cap, in a high wind, and even then not necessarily so. But as he had no intention of being athletic anywhere, with or without a cap, he determined as he went up the stairs that he would follow Mr Holroyd's advice. Mr Holroyd's procedure, without this added formula, entailed sitting "till it dried," and after that he would have dinner, and then Mr Holroyd would begin again. He was a very clever person with regard to the face and the hands and the feet. Georgie had been conscious of walking a little lamely lately; he had been even more conscious of the need of hot towels on his face and the "tap-tap" of Mr Holroyd's fingers, and the stretchings of Mr Holroyd's thumb across rather slack surfaces of cheek and chin. In the interval between the hair and the face, Mr Holroyd should have a good supper downstairs with Foljambe and the cook. And tomorrow morning, when he met Hermy and Ursy, Georgie would be just as spick and span and young as ever, if not more so.

Georgie (happy innocent!) was completely unaware that the whole of Riseholme knew that the smooth chestnut locks which covered the top of his head, were trained like the tendrils of a grapevine from the roots, and flowed like a river over a bare head, and consequently when Mr Holroyd explained the proposed innovation, a little central wig, the edges of which would mingle in the most natural manner with his own hair, it seemed to Georgie that nobody would know the difference. In addition he would be spared those risky moments when he had to take off his hat to a friend in a high wind, for there was always the danger of his hair blowing away from the top of his head, and hanging down, like the tresses of a Rhine-maiden over one shoulder. So Mr Holroyd was commissioned to put that little affair in hand at once, and when the greyness had been attended to, and Georgie had had his dinner, there came hot towels and tappings on his face, and other ministrations. All was done about half past ten, and when he came downstairs again for a short practice at the bass part of Beethoven's fifth symphony, ingeniously arranged for two performers on the piano, he looked with sincere satisfaction at his rosy face in the Cromwellian mirror, and his shoes felt quite comfortable again, and his nails shone like pink stars, as his hands dashed wildly about the piano in the quicker passages. But all the time the thought of the Guru next door, under whose tuition he might be able to regain his youth without recourse to those expensive subterfuges (for the price of the undetectable toupet astonished him) rang in his head with a melody more haunting than Beethoven's. What he would have liked best of all would have been to have the Guru all to himself, so that he should remain perpetually young, while all the rest of Riseholme, including Hermy and Ursy, grew old. Then, indeed, he would be king of the place, instead of serving the interests of its queen.

He rose with a little sigh, and after adjusting the strip of flannel over the keys, shut his piano and busied himself for a little with a soft duster over his cabinet of bibelots which not even Foljambe was allowed to touch. It was generally understood that he had inherited them, though the inheritance had chiefly passed to him through the medium of curiosity shops, and there were several pieces of considerable value among them. There were a gold Louis XVI snuff box, a miniature by Karl Huth, a silver toy porringer of the time of Queen Anne, a piece of Bow china, an enamelled cigarette case by Faberge. But tonight his handling of them was not so dainty and delicate as usual, and he actually dropped the porringer on the floor as he was dusting it, for his mind still occupied itself with the Guru and the practices that led to permanent youth. How quick Lucia had been to snap him up for her garden-party. Yet perhaps she would not get him, for he might say he was not sent. But surely he would be sent to Georgie, whom he knew, the moment he set eyes on him to have a clean white soul....

The clock struck eleven, and, as usual on warm nights Georgie opened the glass door into his garden and drew in a breath of the night air. There was a slip of moon in the sky which he most punctiliously saluted, wondering (though he did not seriously believe in its superstition) how Lucia could be so foolhardy as to cut the new moon. She had seen it yesterday, she told him, in London, and had taken no notice whatever of it.... The heavens were quickly peppered with pretty stars, which Georgie after his busy interesting day enjoyed looking at, though if he had had the arrangement of them, he would certainly have put them into more definite patterns. Among them was a very red planet, and Georgie with recollections of his classical education, easily remembered that Mars, the God of War, was symbolized in the heavens by a red star. Could that mean anything to peaceful Riseholme? Was internal warfare, were revolutionary movements possible in so serene a realm?

Chapter FOUR

Pink irascible Robert, prone to throw his food about his plate, if it did not commend itself to him, felt in an extremely good natured mood that same night after dinner, for the Guru had again made a visit to the kitchen with the result that instead of a slab of pale dead codfish being put before him after he had eaten some tepid soup, there appeared a delicious little fish-curry. The Guru had behaved with great tact; he had seen the storm gathering on poor Robert's face, as he sipped the cool effete concoction and put down his spoon again with a splash in his soup plate, and thereupon had bowed and smiled and scurried away to the kitchen to intercept the next abomination. Then returning with the little curry he explained that it was entirely for Robert, since those who sought the Way did not indulge in hot sharp foods, and so he had gobbled it up to the very last morsel.

In consequence when the Guru salaamed very humbly, and said that with gracious permission of beloved lady and kind master he would go and meditate in his room, and had shambled away in his red slippers, the discussion which Robert had felt himself obliged to open with his wife, on the subject of having an unknown Indian staying with them for an indefinite period, was opened in a much more amicable key than it would have been on a slice of codfish.

"Well, now, about this Golliwog—haha—I should say Guru, my dear," he began, "what's going to happen?"

Daisy Quantock drew in her breath sharply and winced at this irreverence, but quickly remembered that she must always be sending out messages of love, north, east, south, and west. So she sent a rather spiky one in the direction of her husband who was sitting due east, so that it probably got to him at once, and smiled the particular hard firm smile which was an heirloom inherited from her last rule of life.

"No one knows," she said brightly. "Even the Guides can't tell where and when a Guru may be called."

"Then do you propose he should stop here till he's called somewhere else?"

She continued smiling.

"I don't propose anything," she said. "It's not in my hands."

Under the calming influence of the fish curry, Robert remained still placid.

"He's a first-rate cook anyhow," he said. "Can't you engage him as that? Call to the kitchen, you know."

"Darling!" said Mrs Quantock, sending out more love. But she had a quick temper, and indeed the two were outpoured together, like hot and cold taps turned on in a bath. The pellucid stream of love served to keep her temper moderately cool.

24

"Well, ask him," suggested Mr Quantock, "as you say, you never can tell where a Guru may be called. Give him forty pounds a year and beer money."

"Beer!" began Mrs Quantock, when she suddenly remembered Georgie's story about Rush and the Guru and the brandy-bottle, and stopped.

"Yes, dear, I said 'beer,'" remarked Robert a little irritably, "and in any case I insist that you dismiss your present cook. You only took her because she was a Christian Scientist, and you've left that little sheep-fold now. You used to talk about false claims I remember. Well her claim to be a cook is the falsest I ever heard of. I'd sooner take my chance with an itinerant organ grinder. But that fish-curry tonight and that other thing last night, that's what I mean by good eating."

The thought even of good food always calmed Robert's savage breast; it blew upon him as the wind on an AEolian harp hung in the trees, evoking faint sweet sounds.

"I'm sure, my dear," he said, "that I shall be willing to fall in with any pleasant arrangement about your Guru, but it really isn't unreasonable in me to ask what sort of arrangement you propose. I haven't a word to say against him, especially when he goes to the kitchen; I only want to know if he is going to stop here a night or two or a year or two. Talk to him about it tomorrow with my love. I wonder if he can make bisque soup."

Daisy Quantock carried quite a quantity of material for reflection upstairs with her, then she went to bed, pausing a moment opposite the Guru's door, from inside of which came sounds of breathing so deep that it sounded almost like snoring. But she seemed to detect a timbre of spirituality about it which convinced her that he was holding high communion with the Guides. It was round him that her thoughts centred, he was the tree through the branches of which they scampered chattering.

Her first and main interest in him was sheer Guruism, for she was one of those intensely happy people who pass through life in ecstatic pursuit of some idea which those who do not share it call a fad. Well might poor Robert remember the devastation of his home when Daisy, after the perusal of a little pamphlet which she picked up on a book-stall called "The Uric Acid Monthly," came to the shattering conclusion that her buxom frame consisted almost entirely of waste-products which must be eliminated. For a greedy man the situation was frankly intolerable, for when he continued his ordinary diet (this was before the cursed advent of the Christian Science cook) she kept pointing to his well-furnished plate, and told him that every atom of that beef or mutton and potatoes, turned from the moment he swallowed it into chromogens and toxins, and that his apparent appetite was merely the result of fermentation. For herself her platter was an abominable mess of cheese and protein-powder and apples and salad-oil, while round her, like saucers of specimen seeds were ranged little piles of nuts and pine-branches, which supplied body-building material, and which she weighed out with scrupulous accuracy, in accordance with the directions of the "Uric Acid Monthly." Tea and coffee were taboo, since they flooded the blood with purins, and the kitchen boiler rumbled day and night to supply the rivers of boiling water with which (taken in sips) she inundated her system. Strange gaunt females used to come down from London, with small parcels full of tough food that tasted of travelling-bags and contained so much nutrition that a port-manteau full of it would furnish the daily rations of any army. Luckily even her iron constitution could not stand the strain of such ideal living for long, and her growing anaemia threatened to undermine a constitution seriously impaired by the precepts of perfect health. A course of beef-steaks and other substantial viands loaded with uric acid restored her to her former vigour.

Thus reinforced, she plunged with the same energy as she had devoted to repelling uric acid into the embrace of Christian Science. The inhumanity of that sect towards both herself and others took complete possession of her, and when her husband complained on a bitter January morning that his smoking-room was like an icehouse, because the housemaid had forgotten to light the fire, she had no touch of pity for him, since she knew that there was no such thing as cold or heat or pain, and therefore you could not feel cold. But now, since, according to the new creed, such things as uric acid, chromogens and purins had no existence, she could safely indulge in decent viands again. But her unhappy husband was not a real gainer in this respect, for while he ate, she tirelessly discoursed to him on the new creed, and asked him to recite with her the True Statement of Being. And on the top of that she dismissed the admirable cook, and engaged the miscreant from whom he suffered still, though Christian Science, which had allowed her cold to make so long a false claim on her, had followed the uric-acid fad into the limbo of her discarded beliefs.

But now once more she had temporarily discovered the secret of life in the teachings of the Guru, and it was, as has been mentioned, sheer Guruism that constituted the main attraction of the new creed. That then being taken for granted, she turned her mind to certain side-issues, which to a true Riseholmite were of entrancing interest. She felt a strong suspicion that Lucia contemplated annexing her Guru altogether, for otherwise she would not have returned so enthusiastic a response to her note, nor have sent Georgie to deliver it, nor have professed so violent an interest in the Guru. What then was the correctly diabolical policy to pursue? Should Daisy Quantock refuse to take him to Mrs Lucas altogether, with a message of regret that he did not feel himself sent? Even if she did this, did she feel herself strong enough to throw down the gauntlet (in the shape of the Guru) and, using him as the attraction, challenge darling Lucia to mutual combat, in order to decide who should be the leader of all that was advanced and cultured in Riseholme society? Still following that ramification of this policy, should she bribe Georgie over to her own revolutionary camp, by promising him instruction from the Guru? Or following a less dashing line, should she take darling Lucia and Georgie into the charmed circle, and while retaining her own right of treasure trove, yet share it with them in some inner ring, dispensing the Guru to them, if they were good, in small doses?

Mrs Quantock's mind resembled in its workings the manoeuvres of a moth distracted by the glory of several bright lights. It dashed at one, got slightly singed, and forgetting all about that turned its attention to the second, and the third, taking headers into each in turn, without deciding which, on the whole, was the most enchanting of those luminaries. So, in order to curb the exuberance of these frenzied excursions she got a half sheet of paper, and noted down the alternatives that she must choose from.

"(I) Shall I keep him entirely to myself?

"(II) Shall I run him for all he is worth, and leave out L?

"(III) Shall I get G on my side?

"(IV) Shall I give L and G bits?"

She paused a moment: then remembering that he had voluntarily helped her very pretty housemaid to make the beds that morning, saying that his business (like the Prince of Wales's) was to serve, she added:

"(V) Shall I ask him to be my cook?"

For a few seconds the brightness of her eager interest was dimmed as the unworthy suspicion occurred to her that perhaps the prettiness of her housemaid had something to do with his usefulness in the bedrooms, but she instantly dismissed it. There was the bottle of brandy, too, which he had ordered from Rush's. When she had begged him to order anything he wanted and cause it to be put down to her account, she had not actually contemplated brandy. Then remembering that one of the most necessary conditions for progress in Yoga, was that the disciple should have complete confidence in the Guru, she chased that also out of her mind. But still, even when the lines of all possible policies were written down, she could come to no decision, and putting her paper by her bed, decided to sleep over it. The rhythmical sounds of hallowed breathing came steadily from next door, and she murmured "Om, Om," in time with them.

The hours of the morning between breakfast and lunch were the time which the inhabitants of Riseholme chiefly devoted to spying on each other. They went about from shop to shop on household businesses, occasionally making purchases which they carried away with them in little paper parcels with convenient loops of string, but the real object of these excursions was to see what everybody else was doing, and learn what fresh interests had sprung up like mushrooms during the night. Georgie would be matching silks at the draper's, and very naturally he would carry them from the obscurity of the interior to the door in order to be certain about the shades, and keep his eye on the comings and goings in the street, and very naturally Mr Lucas on his way to the market gardener's to enquire whether he had yet received the bulbs from Holland, would tell him that Lucia had received the piano-arrangement of the Mozart trio. Georgie for his part would mention that Hermy and Ursy were expected that evening, and Peppino enriched by this item would "toddle on," as his phrase went, to meet and exchange confidences with the next spy. He had noticed incidentally that Georgie carried a small oblong box with hard corners, which, perfectly correctly, he conjectured to be cigarettes for Hermy and Ursy, since Georgie never smoked.

"Well, I must be toddling on," he said, after identifying Georgie's box of cigarettes, and being rather puzzled by a bulge in Georgie's pocket. "You'll be looking in some time this morning, perhaps."

Georgie had not been quite sure that he would (for he was very busy owing to the arrival of his sisters, and the necessity of going to Mr Holroyd's, in order that that artist might accurately match the shade of his hair with a view to the expensive toupet), but the mention of the arrival of the Mozart now decided him. He intended anyhow before he went home for lunch to stroll past The Hurst, and see if he did not hear—to adopt a mixed metaphor—the sound of the diligent practice of that classical morsel going on inside. Probably the soft pedal would be down, but he had marvellously acute hearing, and he would be very much surprised if he did not hear the recognisable chords, and even more surprised if, when they came to practise the piece together, Lucia did not give him to understand that she was reading it for the first time. He had already got a copy, and had practised his part last night, but then he was in the superior position of not having a husband who would inadvertently tell on him! Meantime it was of the first importance to get that particular shade of purple silk that had none of that "tarsome" magenta-tint in it. Meantime also, it was of even greater importance to observe the movements of Riseholme.

Just opposite was the village green, and as nobody was quite close to him Georgie put on his spectacles, which he could whisk off in a moment. It was these which formed that bulge in his pocket which Peppino had noticed, but the fact of his using spectacles at all was a secret

27

that would have to be profoundly kept for several years yet. But as there was no one at all near him, he stealthily adjusted them on his small straight nose. The morning train from town had evidently come in, for there was a bustle of cabs about the door of the Ambermere Arms, and a thing that thrilled him to the marrow was the fact that Lady Ambermere's motor was undoubtedly among them. That must surely mean that Lady Ambermere herself was here, for when poor thin Miss Lyall, her companion, came in to Riseholme to do shopping, or transact such business as the majestic life at The Hall required, she always came on foot, or in very inclement weather in a small two-wheeled cart like a hip-bath. At this moment, steeped in conjecture, who should appear, walking stiffly, with her nose in the air, as if suspecting, and not choosing to verify, some faint unpleasant odour, but Lady Ambermere herself, coming from the direction of The Hurst.... Clearly she must have got there after Peppino had left, or he would surely have mentioned the fact that Lady Ambermere had been at The Hurst, if she had been at The Hurst. It is true that she was only coming from the direction of The Hurst, but Georgie put into practice, in his mental processes Darwin's principle, that in order to observe usefully, you must have a theory. Georgie's theory was that Lady Ambermere had been at The Hurst just for a minute or two, and hastily put his spectacles in his pocket. With the precision of a trained mind he also formed the theory that some business had brought Lady Ambermere into Riseholme, and that taking advantage of her presence there, she had probably returned a verbal answer to Lucia's invitation to her garden-party, which she would have received by the first post this morning. He was quite ready to put his theory to the test when Lady Ambermere had arrived at the suitable distance for his conveniently observing her, and for taking off his hat. She always treated him like a boy, which he liked. The usual salutation passed.

"I don't know where my people are," said Lady Ambermere majestically. "Have you seen my motor?"

"Yes, dear lady, it's in at your own arms," said Georgie brightly.

"Happy motor!"

If Lady Ambermere unbent to anybody, she unbent to Georgie. He was of quite good family, because his mother had been a Bartlett and a second cousin of her deceased husband. Sometimes when she talked to Georgie she said "we," implying thereby his connection with the aristocracy, and this gratified Georgie nearly as much as did her treatment of him as being quite a boy still. It was to him, as a boy still, that she answered.

"Well, the happy motor, you little rascal, must come to my arms instead of being at them," she said with the quick wit for which Riseholme pronounced her famous. "Fancy being able to see my motor at that distance. Young eyes!"

It was really young spectacles, but Georgie did not mind that. In fact, he would not have corrected the mistake for the world.

"Shall I run across and fetch it for you?" he asked.

"In a minute. Or whistle on your fingers like a vulgar street boy," said Lady Ambermere. "I'm sure you know how to."

Georgie had not the slightest idea, but with the courage of youth, presuming, with the prudence of middle-age, that he would not really be called upon to perform so unimaginable a feat, he put two fingers up to his mouth.

"Here goes then!" he said, greatly daring. (He knew perfectly well that the dignity of Lady Ambermere would not permit rude vulgar whistling, of which he was hopelessly incapable, to summon her motor. She made a feint of stopping her ears with her hands.)

"Don't do anything of the kind," she said. "In a minute you shall walk with me across to the Arms, but tell me this first. I have just been to say to our good Mrs Lucas that very likely I will look in at her garden-party on Friday, if I have nothing else to do. But who is this wonderful creature she is expecting? Is it an Indian conjurer? If so, I should like to see him, because when Ambermere was in Madras I remember one coming to the Residency who had cobras and that sort of thing. I told her I didn't like snakes, and she said there shouldn't be any. In fact, it was all rather mysterious, and she didn't at present know if he was coming or not. I only said, 'No snakes: I insist on no snakes.'"

Georgie relieved her mind about the chance of there being snakes, and gave a short precis of the ascertained habits of the Guru, laying special stress on his high-caste.

"Yes, some of these Brahmins are of very decent family," admitted Lady Ambermere. "I was always against lumping all dark-skinned people together and calling them niggers. When we were at Madras I was famed for my discrimination."

They were walking across the green as Lady Ambermere gave vent to these liberal sentiments, and Georgie even without the need of his spectacles could see Peppino, who had spied Lady Ambermere from the door of the market-gardener's, hurrying down the street, in order to get a word with her before "her people" drove her back to The Hall.

"I came into Riseholme today to get rooms at the Arms for Olga
Bracely," she observed.
"The prima-donna?" asked Georgie breathless with excitement.

"Yes; she is coming to stay at the Arms for two nights with Mr
Shuttleworth."
"Surely—" began Georgie.

"No, it is all right, he is her husband, they were married last week," said Lady Ambermere. "I should have thought that Shuttleworth was a good enough name, as the Shuttleworths are cousins of the late lord, but she prefers to call herself Miss Bracely. I don't dispute her right to call herself what she pleases: far from it, though who the Bracelys were, I have never been able to discover. But when George Shuttleworth wrote to me saying that he and his wife were intending to stay here for a couple of days, and proposing to come over to The Hall to see me, I thought I would just look in at the Arms myself, and see that they were promised proper accommodation. They will dine with me tomorrow. I have a few people staying, and no doubt Miss Bracely will sing afterwards. My Broadwood was always considered a remarkably fine instrument. It was very proper of George Shuttleworth to say that he would be in the neighbourhood, and I daresay she is a very decent sort of woman."

They had come to the motor by this time—the rich, the noble motor, as Mr Pepys would have described it—and there was poor Miss Lyall hung with parcels, and wearing a faint sycophantic smile. This miserable spinster, of age so obvious as to be called not the least uncertain, was Lady Ambermere's companion, and shared with her the glories of The Hall, which had been left to Lady Ambermere for life. She was provided with food and lodging and the use of the cart like a hip-bath when Lady Ambermere had errands for her to do in Riseholme, so what could a woman want more? In return for these bounties, her only duty was to devote herself body and mind to her patroness, to read the paper aloud, to set Lady Ambermere's patterns for needlework, to carry the little Chinese dog under her arm, and wash him once a week, to accompany Lady Ambermere to church, and never to have a fire in her bedroom. She had a melancholy wistful little face: her head was inclined with a backward slope on her neck, and her mouth was invariably a little open shewing long front teeth, so that she looked rather like a roast hare sent up to table with its head on. Georgie always had a joke ready for Miss Lyall, of the sort that made her say, "Oh, Mr Pillson!" and caused her to blush. She thought him remarkably pleasant.

Georgie had his joke ready on this occasion.

"Why, here's Miss Lyall!" he said. "And what has Miss Lyall been doing while her ladyship and I have been talking? Better not ask, perhaps."

"Oh, Mr Pillson!" said Miss Lyall, as punctually as a cuckoo clock when the hands point to the hour.

Lady Ambermere put half her weight onto the step of the motor, causing it to creak and sway.

"Call on the Shuttleworths, Georgie," she said. "Say I told you to.
Home!"
Miss Lyall effaced herself on the front seat of the motor, like a mouse hiding in a corner, after Lady Ambermere had got in, and the footman mounted onto the box. At that moment Peppino with his bag of bulbs, a little out of breath, squeezed his way between two cabs by the side of the motor. He was just too late, and the motor moved off. It was very improbable that Lady Ambermere saw him at all.

Georgie felt very much like a dog with a bone in his mouth, who only wants to get away from all the other dogs and discuss it quietly. It is safe to say that never in twenty-four hours had so many exciting things happened to him. He had ordered a toupet, he had been looked on with favour by a Guru, all Riseholme knew that he had had quite a long conversation with Lady Ambermere and nobody in Riseholme, except himself, knew that Olga Bracely was going to spend two nights here. Well he remembered her marvellous appearance last year at Covent Garden in the part of Brunnhilde. He had gone to town for a rejuvenating visit to his dentist, and the tarsomeness of being betwixt and between had been quite forgotten by him when he saw her awake to Siegfried's line on the mountain-top. "Das ist keine mann," Siegfried had said, and, to be sure, that was very clever of him, for she looked like some slim beardless boy, and not in the least like those great fat Fraus at Baireuth, whom nobody could have mistaken for a man as they bulged and heaved even before the strings of the breastplate were uncut by his sword. And then she sat up and hailed the sun, and Georgie felt for a moment that he had quite taken the wrong turn in life, when he settled to spend his years in this boyish, maidenly manner with his embroidery and his china-dusting at Riseholme. He ought to have been Siegfried.... He had brought a photograph of her in her cuirass and helmet, and often looked at it when he was not too busy with something else. He had even championed his goddess against Lucia, when she pronounced that Wagner was totally lacking in knowledge of dramatic effects. To be sure she had never seen any Wagner opera, but she had heard the overture to Tristram performed at the Queen's Hall, and if that was Wagner, well——

Already, though Lady Ambermere's motor had not yet completely vanished up the street, Riseholme was gently closing in round him, in order to discover by discreet questions (as in the game of Clumps) what he and she had been talking about. There was Colonel Boucher with his two snorting bull-dogs closing in from one side, and Mrs Weston in her bath-chair being wheeled relentlessly towards him from another, and the two Miss Antrobuses sitting playfully in the stocks, on the third, and Peppino at close range on the fourth. Everyone knew, too, that he did not lunch till half past one, and there was really no reason why he should not stop and chat as usual. But with the eye of the true general, he saw that he could most easily break the surrounding cordon by going off in the direction of Colonel Boucher, because Colonel Boucher always said "Haw, hum, by Jove," before he descended into coherent speech, and thus Georgie could forestall him with "Good morning, Colonel," and pass on before he got to business. He did not like passing close to those slobbering bull-dogs, but something had to be done … Next moment he was clear and saw that the other spies by their original impetus were still converging on each other and walked briskly down towards Lucia's house, to listen for any familiar noises out of the Mozart trio. The noises were there, and the soft pedal was down just as he expected, so, that business being off his mind, he continued his walk for a few hundred yards more, meaning to make a short circuit through fields, cross the bridge, over the happy stream that flowed into the Avon, and regain his house by the door at the bottom of the garden. Then he would sit and think … the Guru, Olga Bracely … What if he asked Olga Bracely and her husband to dine, and persuaded Mrs Quantock to let the Guru come? That would be three men and one woman, and Hermy and Ursy would make all square. Six for dinner was the utmost that Foljambe permitted.

He had come to the stile that led into the fields, and sat there for a moment. Lucia's tentative melodies were still faintly audible, but soon they stopped, and he guessed that she was looking out of the window. She was too great to take part in the morning spying that went on round about the Green, but she often saw a good deal from her window. He wondered what Mrs Quantock was meaning to do. Apparently she had not promised the Guru for the garden-party, or else Lady Ambermere would not have said that Lucia did not know whether he was coming or not. Perhaps Mrs Quantock was going to run him herself, and grant him neither to Lucia nor Georgie. In that case he would certainly ask Olga Bracely and her husband to dine, and should he or should he not ask Lucia?

The red star had risen in Riseholme: Bolshevism was treading in its peaceful air, and if Mrs Quantock was going to secrete her Guru, and set up her own standard on the strength of him, Georgie felt much inclined to ask Olga Bracely to dinner, without saying anything whatever to Lucia about it, and just see what would happen next. Georgie was a Bartlett on his mother's side, and he played the piano better than Lucia, and he had twenty-four hours' leisure every day, which he could devote to being king of Riseholme.… His nature flared up, burning with a red revolutionary flame, that was fed by his secret knowledge about Olga Bracely. Why should Lucia rule everyone with her rod of iron? Why, and again why?

Suddenly he heard his name called in the familiar alto, and there was
Lucia in her Shakespeare's garden.
"Georgino! Georgino mio!" she cried. "Gino!"

Out of mere habit Georgie got down from his stile, and tripped up the road towards her. The manly seething of his soul's insurrection rebuked him, but unfortunately his legs and his voice surrendered. Habit was strong.…

"Amica!" he answered. "Buon Giorno." ("And why do I say it in Italian?" he vainly asked himself.)

"Geordie, come and have ickle talk," she said. "Me want 'oo wise man to advise ickle Lucia."

"What 'oo want?" asked Georgie, now quite quelled for the moment.

"Lots-things. Here's pwetty flower for button-holie. Now tell me about black man. Him no snakes have? Why Mrs Quantock say she thinks he no come to poo' Lucia's party-garden?"

"Oh, did she?" asked Georgie relapsing into the vernacular.

"Yes, oh, and by the way there's a parcel come which I think must be the Mozart trio. Will you come over tomorrow morning and read it with me? Yes? About half-past eleven, then. But never mind that."

She fixed him with her ready, birdy eye.

"Daisy asked me to ask him," she said, "and so to oblige poor Daisy I did. And now she says she doesn't know if he'll come. What does that mean? Is it possible that she wants to keep him to herself? She has done that sort of thing before, you know."

This probably represented Lucia's statement of the said case about the Welsh attorney, and Georgie taking it as such felt rather embarrassed. Also that bird-like eye seemed to gimlet its way into his very soul, and divine the secret disloyalty that he had been contemplating. If she had continued to look into him, he might not only have confessed to the gloomiest suspicions about Mrs Quantock, but have let go of his secret about Olga Bracely also, and suggested the possibility of her and her husband being brought to the garden-party. But the eye at this moment unscrewed itself from him again and travelled up the road.

"There's the Guru," she said. "Now we will see!"

Georgie, faint with emotion, peered out between the form of the peacock and the pine-apple on the yew-hedge, and saw what followed. Lucia went straight up to the Guru, bowed and smiled and clearly introduced herself. In another moment he was showing his white teeth and salaaming, and together they walked back to The Hurst, where Georgie palpitated behind the yew-hedge. Together they entered and Lucia's eye wore its most benignant aspect.

"I want to introduce to you, Guru," she said without a stumble, "a great friend of mine. This is Mr Pillson, Guru; Guru, Mr Pillson. The Guru is coming to tiffin with me, Georgie. Cannot I persuade you to stop?"

"Delighted!" said Georgie. "We met before in a sort of way, didn't we?"

"Yes, indeed. So pleased," said the Guru.

"Let us go in," said Lucia, "It is close on lunch-time."

Georgie followed, after a great many bowings and politenesses from the Guru. He was not sure if he had the makings of a Bolshevist. Lucia was so marvellously efficient.

Chapter FIVE

One of Lucia's greatnesses lay in the fact that when she found anybody out in some act of atrocious meanness, she never indulged in any idle threats of revenge: it was sufficient that she knew, and would take suitable steps on the earliest occasion. Consequently when it appeared, from the artless conversation of the Guru at lunch that the perfidious Mrs Quantock had not even asked him whether he would like to go to Lucia's garden party or not (pending her own decision as to what she was meaning to do with him) Lucia received the information with the utmost good-humour, merely saying, "No doubt dear Mrs Quantock forgot to tell you," and did not announce acts of reprisal, such as striking Daisy off the list of her habitual guests for a week or two, just to give her a lesson. She even, before they sat down to lunch, telephoned over to that thwarted woman to say that she had met the Guru in the street, and they had both felt that there was some wonderful bond of sympathy between them, so he had come back with her, and they were just sitting down to tiffin. She was pleased with the word "tiffin," and also liked explaining to Daisy what it meant.

Tiffin was a great success, and there was no need for the Guru to visit the kitchen in order to make something that could be eaten without struggle. He talked quite freely about his mission here, and Lucia and Georgie and Peppino who had come in rather late, for he had been obliged to go back to the market-gardener's about the bulbs, listened entranced.

"Yes, it was when I went to my friend who keeps the book-shop," he said, "that I knew there was English lady who wanted Guru, and I knew I was called to her. No luggage, no anything at all: as I am. Such a kind lady, too, and she will get on well, but she will find some of the postures difficult, for she is what you call globe, round."

"Was that postures when I saw her standing on one leg in the garden?" asked Georgie, "and when she sat down and tried to hold her toes?"

"Yes, indeed, quite so, and difficult for globe. But she has white soul."

He looked round with a smile.

"I see many white souls here," he said. "It is happy place, when there are white souls, for to them I am sent."

This was sufficient: in another minute Lucia, Georgie and Peppino were all accepted as pupils, and presently they went out into the garden, where the Guru sat on the ground in a most complicated attitude which was obviously quite out of reach of Mrs Quantock.

"One foot on one thigh, other foot on other thigh," he explained. "And the head and back straight: it is good to meditate so."

Lucia tried to imagine meditating so, but felt that any meditation so would certainly be on the subject of broken bones.

"Shall I be able to do that?" she asked. "And what will be the effect?"

"You will be light and active, dear lady, and ah—here is other dear lady come to join us."

Mrs Quantock had certainly made one of her diplomatic errors on this occasion. She had acquiesced on the telephone in her Guru going to tiffin with Lucia, but about the middle of her lunch, she had been unable to resist the desire to know what was happening at The Hurst. She could not bear the thought that Lucia and her Guru were together now, and her own note, saying that it was uncertain whether the Guru would come to the garden party or not filled her with the most uneasy apprehensions. She would sooner have acquiesced in her Guru going to fifty garden-parties, where all was public, and she could keep an eye and a control on him, rather than that Lucia should have "enticed him in,"—that was her phrase—like this to tiffin. The only consolation was that her own lunch had been practically inedible, and

Robert had languished lamentably for the Guru to return, and save his stomach. She had left him glowering over a little mud and water called coffee. Robert, at any rate, would welcome the return of the Guru.

She waddled across the lawn to where this harmonious party was sitting, and at that moment Lucia began to feel vindictive. The calm of victory which had permeated her when she brought the Guru in to lunch, without any bother at all, was troubled and broken up, and darling Daisy's note, containing the outrageous falsity that the Guru would not certainly accept an invitation which had never been permitted to reach him at all, assumed a more sinister aspect. Clearly now Daisy had intended to keep him to herself, a fact that she already suspected and had made a hostile invasion.

"Guru, dear, you naughty thing," said Mrs Quantock playfully, after the usual salutations had passed, "why did you not tell your Chela you would not be home for tiffin?"

The Guru had unwound his legs, and stood up.

"But see, beloved lady," he said, "how pleasant we all are! Take not too much thought, when it is only white souls who are together."

Mrs Quantock patted his shoulder.

"It is all good and kind Om," she said. "I send out my message of love.
There!"
It was necessary to descend from these high altitudes, and Lucia proceeded to do so, as in a parachute that dropped swiftly at first, and then floated in still air.

"And we're making such a lovely plan, dear Daisy," she said. "The Guru is going to teach us all. Classes! Aren't you?"

He held his hands up to his head, palms outwards, and closed his eyes.

"I seem to feel call," he said. "I am sent. Surely the Guides tell me there is a sending of me. What you call classes? Yes? I teach: you learn. We all learn…. I leave all to you. I will walk a little way off to arbour, and meditate, and then when you have arranged, you will tell Guru, who is your servant. Salaam! Om!"

With the Guru in her own house, and with every intention to annex him, it was no wonder that Lucia took the part of chairman in this meeting that was to settle the details of the esoteric brotherhood that was to be formed in Riseholme. Had not Mrs Quantock been actually present, Lucia in revenge for her outrageous conduct about the garden-party invitation would probably have left her out of the classes altogether, but with her sitting firm and square in a basket chair, that creaked querulously as she moved, she could not be completely ignored. But Lucia took the lead throughout, and suggested straightaway that the smoking-parlour would be the most convenient place to hold the classes in.

"I should not think of invading your house, dear Daisy," she said, "and here is the smoking-parlour which no one ever sits in, so quiet and peaceful. Yes. Shall we consider that settled, then?"

She turned briskly to Mrs Quantock.

"And now where shall the Guru stay?" she said. "It would be too bad, dear Daisy, if we are all to profit by his classes, that you should have all the trouble and expense of entertaining him, for in your sweet little house he must be a great inconvenience, and I think you said that your husband had given up his dressing room to him."

Mrs Quantock made a desperate effort to retain her property.

"No inconvenience at all," she said, "quite the contrary in fact, dear. It is delightful having him, and Robert regards him as a most desirable inmate."

Lucia pressed her hand feelingly.

"You and your husband are too unselfish," she said. "Often have I said, 'Daisy and Mr Robert are the most unselfish people I know.' Haven't I, Georgie? But we can't permit you to be so crowded. Your only spare room, you know, and your husband's dressing room! Georgie, I know you agree with me; we must not permit dear Daisy to be so unselfish."

The bird-like eye produced its compelling effect on Georgie. So short a time ago he had indulged in revolutionary ideas, and had contemplated having the Guru and Olga Bracely to dinner, without even asking Lucia: now the faint stirrings of revolt faded like snow in summer. He knew quite well what Lucia's next proposition would be: he knew, too, that he would agree to it.

"No, that would never do," he said. "It is simply trespassing on Mrs Quantock's good-nature, if she is to board and lodge him, while he teaches all of us. I wish I could take him in, but with Hermy and Ursy coming tonight, I have as little room as Mrs Quantock."

"He shall come here," said Lucia brightly, as if she had just that moment thought of it. "There are Hamlet and Othello vacant"—all her rooms were named after Shakespearian plays—"and it will not be the least inconvenient. Will it, Peppino? I shall really like having him here. Shall we consider that settled, then?"

Daisy made a perfectly futile effort to send forth a message of love to all quarters of the compass. Bitterly she repented of having ever mentioned her Guru to Lucia: it had never occurred to her that she would annex him like this. While she was cudgelling her brains as to how she could arrest this powerful offensive, Lucia went sublimely on.

"Then there's the question of what we shall pay him," she said. "Dear Daisy tells us that he scarcely knows what money is, but I for one could never dream of profiting by his wisdom, if I was to pay nothing for it. The labourer is worthy of his hire, and so I suppose the teacher is. What if we pay him five shillings each a lesson: that will make a pound a lesson. Dear me! I shall be busy this August. Now how many classes shall we ask him to give us? I should say six to begin with, if everybody agrees. One every day for the next week except Sunday. That is what you all wish? Yes? Then shall we consider that settled?"

Mrs Quantock, still impotently rebelling, resorted to the most dire weapon in her armoury, namely, sarcasm.

"Perhaps, darling Lucia," she said, "it would be well to ask my Guru if he has anything to say to your settlings. England is a free country still, even if you happen to have come from India."

35

Lucia had a deadlier weapon than sarcasm, which was the apparent unconsciousness of there having been any. For it is no use plunging a dagger into your enemy's heart, if it produces no effect whatever on him. She clapped her hands together, and gave her peal of silvery laughter.

"What a good idea!" she said. "Then you would like me to go and tell him what we propose? Just as you like. I will trot away, shall I, and see if he agrees. Don't think of stirring, dear Daisy, I know how you feel the heat. Sit quiet in the shade. As you know, I am a real salamander, the sun is never troppo caldo for me."

She tripped off to where the Guru was sitting in that wonderful position. She had read the article in the encyclopaedia about Yoga right through again this morning, and had quite made up her mind, as indeed her proceedings had just shown, that Yoga was, to put it irreverently, to be her August stunt. He was still so deep in meditation that he could only look dreamily in her direction as she approached, but then with a long sigh he got up.

"This is beautiful place," he said. "It is full of sweet influences and
I have had high talk with Guides."
Lucia felt thrilled.

"Ah, do tell me what they said to you," she exclaimed.

"They told me to follow where I was led: they said they would settle everything for me in wisdom and love."

This was most encouraging, for decidedly Lucia had been settling for him, and the opinion of the Guides was thus a direct personal testimonial. Any faint twitchings of conscience (they were of the very faintest) that she had grabbed dear Daisy's property were once and for ever quieted, and she proceeded confidently to unfold the settlements of wisdom and love, which met with the Guru's entire approval. He shut his eyes a moment and breathed deeply.

"They give peace and blessing," he said. "It is they who ordered that it should be so. Om!"

He seemed to sink into profound depths of meditation, and Lucia hurried back to the group she had left.

"It is all too wonderful," she said. "The Guides have told him that they were settling everything for him in wisdom and love, so we may be sure we were right in our plans. How lovely to think that we have been guided by them! Dear Daisy, how wonderful he is! I will send across for his things, shall I, and I will have Hamlet and Othello made ready for him!"

Bitter though it was to part with her Guru, it was impious to rebel against the ordinances of the Guides, but there was a trace of human resentment in Daisy's answer.

"Things!" she exclaimed. "He hasn't got a thing in the world. Every material possession chains us down to earth. You will soon come to that, darling Lucia."

It occurred to Georgie that the Guru had certainly got a bottle of brandy, but there was no use in introducing a topic that might lead to discord, and indeed, even as Lucia went indoors to see about Hamlet and Othello, the Guru himself having emerged from meditation, joined them and sat down by Mrs Quantock.

"Beloved lady," he said, "all is peace and happiness. The Guides have spoken to me so lovingly of you, and they say it is best your Guru should come here. Perhaps I shall return later to your kind house. They smiled when I asked that. But just now they send me here: there is more need of me here, for already you have so much light."

Certainly the Guides were very tactful people, for nothing could have soothed Mrs Quantock so effectually as a message of that kind, which she would certainly report to Lucia when she returned from seeing about Hamlet and Othello.

"Oh, do they say I have much light already, Guru, dear?" she asked.
"That is nice of them."
"Surely they said it, and now I shall go back to your house, and leave sweet thoughts there for you. And shall I send sweet thoughts to the home of the kind gentleman next door?"

Georgie eagerly welcomed this proposition, for with Hermy and Ursy coming that evening, he felt that he would have plenty of use for sweet thoughts. He even forebore to complete in his own mind the conjecture that was forming itself there, namely, that though the Guru would be leaving sweet thoughts for Mrs Quantock, he would probably be taking away the brandy bottle for himself. But Georgie knew he was only too apt to indulge in secret cynicisms and perhaps there was no brandy to take away by this time ... and lo and behold, he was being cynical again.

The sun was still hot when, half an hour afterwards, he got into the open cab which he had ordered to take him to the station to meet Hermy and Ursy, and he put up his umbrella with its white linen cover, to shield him from it. He did not take the motor, because either Hermy or Ursy would have insisted on driving it, and he did not choose to put himself in their charge. In all the years that he had lived at Riseholme, he never remembered a time when social events—"work," he called it—had been so exciting and varied. There were Hermy and Ursy coming this evening, and Olga Bracely and her husband (Olga Bracely and Mr Shuttleworth sounded vaguely improper: Georgie rather liked that) were coming tomorrow, and there was Lucia's garden-party the day after, and every day there was to be a lesson from the Guru, so that God alone knew when Georgie would have a moment to himself for his embroidery or to practise the Mozart trio. But with his hair chestnut-coloured to the very roots, and his shining nails, and his comfortable boots, he felt extremely young and fit for anything. Soon, under the influence of the new creed with its postures and breathings, he would feel younger and more vigorous yet.

But he wished that it had been he who had found this pamphlet on Eastern philosophies, which had led Mrs Quantock to make the inquiries that had resulted in the epiphany of the Guru. Of course when once Lucia had heard about it, she was certain to constitute herself head and leader of the movement, and it was really remarkable how completely she had done that. In that meeting in the garden just now she had just sailed through Mrs Quantock as calmly as a steamer cuts through the waters of the sea, throwing her off from her penetrating bows like a spent wave. But baffled though she was for the moment, Georgie had been aware that Mrs Quantock seethed with revolutionary ideas: she deeply resented this confiscation of what was certainly her property, though she was impotent to stop it, and Georgie knew just what she felt. It was all very well to say that Lucia's schemes were entirely in accord with the purposes of the Guides. That might be so, but Mrs Quantock would not cease to think that she had been robbed....

Yet nothing mattered if all the class found themselves getting young and active and loving and excellent under this tuition. It was that notion which had taken such entire command of them all, and for his part Georgie did not really care who owned the Guru, so to speak, if only he got the benefit of his teachings. For social purposes Lucia had annexed him, and doubtless with him in the house she could get little instructions and hints that would not count as a lesson, but after all, Georgie had still got Olga Bracely to himself, for he had not breathed a word of her advent to Lucia. He felt rather like one who, when revolutionary ideas are in the air, had concealed a revolver in his pocket. He did not formulate to himself precisely what he was going to do with it, but it gave him a sense of power to know it was there.

The train came in, but he looked in vain for his sisters. They had distinctly said they were arriving by it, but in a couple of minutes it was perfectly clear that they had done nothing of the kind, for the only person who got out was Mrs Weston's cook, who as all the world knew went into Brinton every Wednesday to buy fish. At the rear of the train, however, was an immense quantity of luggage being taken out, which could not all be Mrs Weston's fish, and indeed, even at that distance there was something familiar to Georgie about a very large green hold-all which was dumped there. Perhaps Hermy and Ursy had travelled in the van, because "it was such a lark," or for some other tomboy reason, and he went down the platform to investigate. There were bags of golf clubs, and a dog, and portmanteaux, and even as the conviction dawned on him that he had seen some of these objects before, the guard, to whom Georgie always gave half-a-crown when he travelled by this train, presented him with a note scrawled in pencil. It ran—

"Dearest Georgie,

"It was such a lovely day that when we got to Paddington Ursy and I decided to bicycle down instead, so for a lark we sent our things on, and we may arrive tonight, but probably tomorrow. Take care of Tiptree: and give him plenty of jam. He loves it.

"Yours,
"HERMY.
"P.S.—Tipsipoozie doesn't really bite: it's only his fun."

Georgie crumpled up this odious epistle, and became aware that Tipsipoozie, a lean Irish terrier, was regarding him with peculiar disfavour, and shewing all his teeth, probably in fun. In pursuance of this humorous idea, he then darted towards Georgie, and would have been extremely funny, if he had not been handicapped by the bag of golf-clubs to which he was tethered. As it was, he pursued him down the platform, towing the clubs after him, till he got entangled in them and fell down.

Georgie hated dogs at any time, though he had never hated one so much as Tipsipoozie, and the problems of life became more complicated than ever. Certainly he was not going to drive back with Tipsipoozie in his cab, and it became necessary to hire another for that abominable hound and the rest of the luggage. And what on earth was to happen when he arrived home, if Tipsipoozie did not drop his fun and become serious? Foljambe, it is true, liked dogs, so perhaps dogs liked her … "But it is most tarsome of Hermy!" thought Georgie bitterly. "I wonder what the Guru would do." There ensued a very trying ten minutes, in which the station-master, the porters, Georgie and Mrs Weston's maid all called Tipsipoozie a good dog as he lay on the ground snapping promiscuously at those who praised him. Eventually a valiant porter picked up the bag of clubs, and by holding them out in front of him at the extreme length of his arms, in the manner of a fishing rod, with Tipsipoozie on a short chain at the other end of the bag, like a savage fish, cursing and swearing, managed to propel him into the cab, and there was another half-crown gone. Georgie thereupon got into his cab and sped homewards in order to arrive there first, and consult with Foljambe. Foljambe usually thought of something.

Foljambe came out at the noise of the arriving wheels and Georgie explained the absence of his sisters and the advent of an atrocious dog.

"He's very fierce," he said, "but he likes jam."

Foljambe gave that supreme smile which sometimes Georgie resented. Now he hailed it, as if it was "an angel-face's smile."

"I'll see to him, sir," she said. "I've brought up your tea."

"But you'll take care, Foljambe won't you?" he asked.

"I expect he'd better take care," returned the intrepid woman.

Georgie, as he often said, trusted Foljambe completely, which must explain why he went into his drawing-room, shut the door, and looked out of the window when the second cab arrived. She opened the door, put her arms inside, and next moment emerged again with Tipsipoozie on the end of the chain, making extravagant exhibitions of delight. Then to Georgie's horror, the drawing-room door opened, and in came Tipsipoozie without any chain at all. Rapidly sending a message of love in all directions like a S. O. S. call, Georgie put a small chair in front of him, to shield his legs. Tipsipoozie evidently thought it was a game, and hid behind the sofa to rush out again from ambush.

"Just got snappy being tied to those golf-clubs," remarked Foljambe.

But Georgie, as he put some jam into his saucer, could not help wondering whether the message of love had not done it.

He dined alone, for Hermy and Ursy did not appear, and had a great polishing of his knick-knacks afterwards, while waiting for them. No one ever felt anxious at the non-arrival of those sisters, for they always turned up from their otter-hunting or their golf sooner or later, chiefly later, in the highest spirits at the larks they had had, with amazingly dirty hands and prodigious appetite. But when twelve o'clock struck, he decided to give up all idea of their appearance that night, and having given Tipsipoozie some more jam and a comfortable bed in the woodshed, he went upstairs to his room. Though he knew it was still possible that he might be roused by wild "Cooees!" and showers of gravel at his window, and have to come down and minister to their gross appetites, the prospect seemed improbable and he soon went to sleep.

Georgie awoke with a start some hours later, wondering what had disturbed him. There was no gravel rattling on his window, no violent ringing of bicycle bells, nor loud genial shouts outraging the decorous calm of Riseholme, but certainly he had heard something. Next moment, the repeated noise sent his heart leaping into his throat, for quite distinctly he heard a muffled sound in the room below, which he instantly diagnosed with fatal certainty as burglars. The first emotion that mingled itself with the sheer terror, was a passionate regret that Hermy and Ursy had not come. They would have thought it tremendous larks, and would have invented some wonderful offensive with fire-irons and golf-clubs and dumb-bells. Even Tipsipoozie, the lately-abhorred, would have been a succour in this crisis, and why, oh why, had not Georgie had him to sleep in his bedroom instead of making him cosy in the woodshed? He would have let Tipsipoozie sleep on his lovely blue quilt for the remainder of his days, if only Tipsipoozie could have been with him now, ready to have fun with the burglar below. As it was, the servants were in the attics at the top of the house, Dicky slept out, and Georgie was all alone, with the prospect of having to defend his property at risk of his life. Even at this moment, as he sat up in bed, blanched with terror, these miscreants might be putting his treasure into their pockets. The thought of the Faberge cigarette case, and the Louis XVI snuff box, and the Queen Anne toy-porringer which he had inherited all these years, made even life seem cheap, for life would be intolerable without them, and he sprang out of bed, groped for his slippers, since until he had made a plan it was wiser not to shew a light, and shuffled noiselessly towards the door.

Chapter SIX

The door-handle felt icy to fingers already frozen with fright, but he stood firmly grasping it, ready to turn it noiselessly when he had quite made up his mind what to do. The first expedient that suggested itself with an overpowering sweetness of relief, was that of locking his door, going back to bed again, and pretending that he had heard nothing. But apart from the sheer cowardice of that, which he did not mind so much, as nobody else would ever know his guilt, the thought of the burglar going off quite unmolested with his property was intolerable. Even if he could not summon up enough courage to get downstairs with his life and a poker in his hand, he must at least give them a good fright. They had frightened him, and so he would frighten them. They should not have it all their own way, and if he decided not to attack them (or him) single-handed, he could at least thump on the floor, and call out "Burglars!" at the top of his voice, or shout "Charles! Henry! Thomas!" as if summoning a bevy of stalwart footmen. The objection to this course, however, would be that Foljambe or somebody else might hear him, and in this case, if he did not then go downstairs to mortal combat, the knowledge of his cowardice would be the property of others beside himself…. And all the time he hesitated, they were probably filling their pockets with his dearest possessions.

He tried to send out a message of love, but he was totally unable to do so.

Then the little clock in his mantelpiece struck two, which was a miserable hour, sundered so far from dawn.

Though he had lived through years of agony since he got out of bed, the actual passage of time, as he stood frozen to the door-handle, was but the duration of a few brief seconds, and then making a tremendous call on his courage he felt his way to his fireplace, and picked up the poker. The tongs and shovel rattled treacherously, and he hoped that had not been heard, for the essence of his plan (though he had yet no idea what that plan was) must be silence till some awful surprise broke upon them. If only he could summon the police, he could come rushing downstairs with his poker, as the professional supporters of the law gained an entrance to his house, but unfortunately the telephone was downstairs, and he could not reasonably hope to carry on a conversation with the police station without being overheard by the burglars.

He opened his door with so masterly a movement that there was no sound either from the hinges nor from the handle as he turned it, and peered out. The hall below was dark, but a long pencil of light came from the drawing room, which showed where the reckless brutes must be, and there, too, alas! was his case of treasures. Then suddenly he heard the sound of a voice, speaking very low, and another voice answered it. At that Georgie's heart sank, for this proved that there must be at least two burglars, and the odds against him were desperate. After that came a low, cruel laugh, the unmistakable sound of the rattle of knives and forks, and the explosive uncorking of a bottle. At that his heart sank even lower yet, for he had read that cool habitual burglars always had supper before they got to work, and therefore he was about to deal with a gang of professionals. Also that explosive uncorking clearly indicated champagne, and he knew that they were feasting on his best. And how wicked of them to take their unhallowed meal in his drawing-room, for there was no proper table there, and they would be making a dreadful mess over everything.

A current of cool night air swept up the stairs, and Georgie saw the panel of light from the open drawing-room door diminish in width, and presently the door shut with a soft thud, leaving him in the dark. At that his desperation seemed pressed and concentrated into a moment of fictitious courage, for he unerringly reasoned that they had left the drawing-room window open, and that perhaps in a few moments now they would have finished their meal and with bulging pockets would step forth unchallenged into the night. Why had he never had bolts put on his shutters, like Mrs Weston, who lived in nightly terror of burglars? But it was too late to think of that now, for it was impossible to ask them to step out till he had put bolts up, and then when he was ready begin again.

He could not let them go gorged with his champagne and laden with his treasures without reprisals of some sort, and keeping his thoughts steadily away from revolvers and clubs and sandbags, walked straight downstairs, threw open the drawing-room door, and with his poker grasped in his shaking hand, cried out in a faint, thin voice:

"If you move I shall fire."

There was a moment of dead silence, and a little dazzled with the light he saw what faced him.

At opposite ends of his Chippendale sofa sat Hermy and Ursy. Hermy had her mouth open and held a bun in her dirty hands. Ursy had her mouth shut and her cheeks were bulging. Between them was a ham and a loaf of bread, and a pot of marmalade and a Stilton cheese, and on the floor was the bottle of champagne with two brimming bubbling tea cups full of wine. The cork and the wire and the tin-foil they had, with some show of decency, thrown into the fireplace.

Hermy put down her bun, and gave a great shout of laughter; Ursy's mouth was disgustingly full and she exploded. Then they lay back against the arms of the sofa and howled.

Georgie was very much vexed.

"Upon my word, Hermy!" he said, and then found it was not nearly a strong enough expression. And in a moment of ungovernable irritation he said:

"Damn it all!"

Hermy showed signs of recovery first, and as Georgie came back after shutting the window, could find her voice, while Ursy collected small fragments of ham and bread which she had partially chewed.

"Lord! What a lark!" she said. "Georgie, it's the most ripping lark."

Ursy pointed to the poker.

41

"He'll fire if we move," she cried. "Or poke the fire, was it?"

"Ask another!" screamed Hermy. "Oh, dear, he thought we were burglars, and came down with a poker, brave boy! It's positively the limit. Have a drink, Georgie."

Suddenly her eyes grew round and awestruck, and pointing with her finger to Georgie's shoulder, she went off into another yell of laughter.

"Ursy! His hair!" she said, and buried her face in a soft cushion.

Naturally Georgie had not put his hair in order when he came downstairs, for nobody thinks about things like that when he is going to encounter burglars single-handed, and there was his bald pate and his long tresses hanging down one side.

It was most annoying, but when an irremediable annoyance has absolutely occurred, the only possible thing for a decent person to do is to take it as lightly as possible. Georgie rose gallantly to the occasion, gave a little squeal and ran from the room.

"Down again presently," he called out, and had a heavy fall on the stairs, as he went up to his bedroom. There he had a short argument with himself. It was possible to slam his door, go to bed, and be very polite in the morning. But that would never do: Hermy and Ursy would have a joke against him forever. It was really much better to share in the joke, identifying himself with it. So he brushed his hair in the orthodox fashion, put on a very smart dressing-gown, and came tripping downstairs again.

"My dears, what fun!" he said. "Let's all have supper. But let's move into the dining-room, where there's a table, and I'll get another bottle of wine, and some glasses, and we'll bring Tipsipoozie in. You naughty girls, fancy arriving at a time like this. I suppose your plan was to go very quietly to bed, and come down to breakfast in the morning, and give me a fine surprise. Tell me about it now."

So presently Tipsipoozie was having his marmalade, which did just as well as jam, and they were all eating slices off the ham, and stuffing them into split buns.

"Yes, we thought we might as well do it all in one go," said Hermy, "and it's a hundred and twenty miles, if it's a yard. And then it was so late when we got here, we thought we wouldn't disturb you, specially as the drawing-room window wasn't bolted."

"Bicycles outside," said Ursy, "they'll just have to be out at grass till morning. Oh, Tipsi-ipsi-poozie-woozy, how is you? Hope he behaved like the good little Tiptree that he is, Georgie?"

"O yes, we made great friends," said Georgie sketchily. "He was wee bit upset at the station, but then he had a good tea with his Uncle Georgie and played hide and seek."

Rather rashly, Georgie made a face at Tiptree, the sort of face which amuses children. But it didn't amuse Tiptree, who made another face, in which teeth played a prominent part.

"Fool-dog," said Hermy, carelessly smacking him across the nose.
"Always hit him if he shows his teeth, Georgie. Pass the fizz."
"Well, so we got through the drawing-room window," continued Ursy, "and golly, we were hungry. So we foraged, and there we were! Jolly plucky of you, Georgie, to come down and beard us."

"Real sport," said Hermy. "And how's old Fol-de-rol-de-ray? Why didn't she come down and fight us, too?"

Georgie guessed that Hermy was making a humourous allusion to Foljambe, who was the one person in Riseholme whom his two sisters seemed to hold in respect. Ursy had once set a booby-trap for Georgie, but the mixed biscuits and Brazil nuts had descended on Foljambe instead. On that occasion Foljambe, girt about in impenetrable calm, had behaved as if nothing had happened and trod on biscuits and Brazil nuts without a smile, unaware to all appearance that there was anything whatever crunching and exploding beneath her feet. That had somehow quelled the two, who, as soon as she left the room again, swept up the mess, and put the uninjured Brazil nuts back into the dessert dish…. It would never do if Foljambe lost her prestige and was alluded to by some outrageously slangy name.

"If you mean Foljambe," said Georgie icily, "it was because I didn't think it worth while to disturb her."

In spite of their ride, the indefatigable sisters were up early next morning, and the first thing Georgie saw out of his bathroom window was the pair of them practising lifting shots over the ducking pond on the green till breakfast was ready. He had given a short account of last night's adventure to Foljambe when she called him, omitting the episode about his hair, and her disapproval was strongly indicated by her silence then, and the studied contempt of her manner to the sisters when they came in to breakfast.

"Hullo, Foljambe," said Hermy. "We had a rare lark last night."

"So I understand, miss," said Foljambe.

"Got in through the drawing-room window," said Hermy, hoping to make her smile.

"Indeed, miss," said Foljambe. "Have you any orders for the car, sir?"

"Oh, Georgie, may we run over to the links this morning?" asked Hermy.
"Mayn't Dickie-bird take us there?"
She glanced at Foljambe to see whether this brilliant wit afforded her any amusement. Apparently it didn't.

"Tell Dicky to be round at half-past ten," said Georgie.

"Yes, sir."

"Hurrah!" said Ursy. "Come, too, Foljambe, and we'll have a three-ball match."

"No, thank you, miss," said Foljambe, and sailed from the room, looking down her nose.

"Golly, what an iceberg!" said Hermy when the door was quite shut.

Georgie was not sorry to have the morning to himself, for he wanted to have a little quiet practice at the Mozart trio, before he went over to Lucia's at half-past eleven, the hour when she had arranged to run through it for the first time. He would also have time to do a few posturing exercises before the first Yoga-class, which was to take place in Lucia's smoking-parlour at half-past twelve. That would make a pretty busy morning, and as for the afternoon,

43

there would be sure to be some callers, since the arrival of his sisters had been expected, and after that he had to go to the Ambermere Arms for his visit to Olga Bracely…. And what was he to do about her with regard to Lucia? Already he had been guilty of disloyalty, for Lady Ambermere had warned him of the prima-donna's arrival yesterday, and he had not instantly communicated that really great piece of news to Lucia. Should he make such amends as were in his power for that omission, or, greatly daring, should he keep her to himself, as Mrs Quantock so fervently wished that she had done with regard to the Guru? After the adventure of last night, he felt he ought to be able to look any situation in the face, but he found himself utterly unable to conceive himself manly and erect before the bird-like eyes of the Queen, if she found out that Olga Bracely had been at Riseholme for the day of her garden-party, and that Georgie, knowing it and having gone to see her, had not informed the Court of that fact.

The spirit of Bolshevism, the desire to throw off all authority and act independently, which had assailed him yesterday returned now with redoubled force. If he had been perfectly certain that he would not be found out, there is no doubt he would have kept it from her, and yet, after all, what was the glory of going to see Olga Bracely (and perhaps even entertaining her here) if all Riseholme did not turn green with jealousy? Moreover there was every chance of being found out, for Lady Ambermere would be at the garden party tomorrow, and she would be sure to wonder why Lucia had not asked Olga. Then it would come out that Lucia didn't know of that eminent presence, and Lady Ambermere would be astonished that Georgie had not told her. Thus he would be in the situation which his imagination was unable to face, although he had thrown the drawing room door open in the middle of the night, and announced that he would fire with his poker.

No; he would have to tell Lucia, when he went to read the Mozart trio with her for the first time, and very likely she would call on Olga Bracely herself, though nobody had asked her to, and take all the wind out of Georgie's sails. Sickening though that would be, he could not face the alternative, and he opened his copy of the Mozart trio with a sigh. Lucia did push and shove, and have everything her own way. Anyhow he would not tell her that Olga and her husband were dining at The Hall tonight; he would not even tell her that her husband's name was Shuttleworth, and Lucia might make a dreadful mistake, and ask Mr and Mrs Bracely. That would be jam for Georgie, and he could easily imagine himself saying to Lucia, "My dear, I thought you must have known that she had married Mr Shuttleworth and kept her maiden name! How tarsome for you! They are so touchy about that sort of thing."

Georgie heard the tinkle of the treble part of the Mozart trio (Lucia always took the treble, because it had more tune in it, though she pretended that she had not Georgie's fine touch, which made the bass effective) as he let himself in to Shakespeare's garden a few minutes before the appointed time. Lucia must have seen him from the window, for the subdued noise of the piano ceased even before he had got as far as Perdita's garden round the sundial, and she opened the door to him. The far-away look was in her eyes, and the black undulations of hair had encroached a little on her forehead, but, after all, others besides Lucia had trouble with their hair, and Georgie only sympathized.

"Georgino mio!" she said. "It is all being so wonderful. There seems a new atmosphere about the house since my Guru came. Something holy and peaceful; do you not notice it?"

"Delicious!" said Georgie, inhaling the pot-pourri. "What is he doing now?"

"Meditating, and preparing for our class. I do hope dear Daisy will not bring in discordant elements."

"Oh, but that's not likely, is it?" said Georgie. "I thought he said she had so much light."

"Yes, he did. But now he is a little troubled about her, I think. She did not want him to go away from her house, and she sent over here for some silk pyjamas belonging to her husband, which he thought she had given him. But Robert didn't think so at all. The Guru brought them across yesterday after he had left good thoughts for her in her house. But it was the Guides who wished him to come here; they told him so distinctly. It would have been very wrong of me not to do as they said."

She gave a great sigh.

"Let us have an hour with Mozart," she said "and repel all thought of discord. My Guru says that music and flowers are good influences for those who are walkers on the Way. He says that my love for both of them which I have had all my life will help me very much."

For one moment the mundane world obtruded itself into the calm peace.

"Any news in particular?" she asked. "I saw you drive back from the station yesterday afternoon, for I happened to be looking out of the window, in a little moment of leisure—the Guru says I work too hard, by the way—and your sisters were not with you. And yet there were two cabs, and a quantity of luggage. Did they not come?"

Georgie gave a respectably accurate account of all that had happened, omitting the fact of his terror when first he awoke, for that was not really a happening, and had had no effect on his subsequent proceedings. He also omitted the adventure about his hair, for that was quite extraneous, and said what fun they had all had over their supper at half past two this morning.

"I think you were marvellously brave, Georgie," said she, "and most good natured. You must have been sending out love, and so were full of it yourself, and that casts out fear."

She spread the music open.

"Anything else?" she asked.

Georgie took his seat and put his rings on the candle-bracket.

"Oh yes," he said, "Olga Bracely, the prima-donna, you know, and her husband are arriving at the Ambermere Arms this afternoon for a couple of days."

The old fire kindled.

"No!" exclaimed Lucia. "Then they'll be here for my party tomorrow. Fancy if she would come and sing for us! I shall certainly leave cards today, and write later in the evening, asking her."

"I have been asked to go and see her," said Georgie, not proudly.

The music rest fell down with a loud slap, but Lucia paid no attention.

"Let us go together then," she said. "Who asked you to call on her?"

"Lady Ambermere," said he.

"When she was in here yesterday? She never mentioned it to me. But she would certainly think it very odd of me not to call on friends of hers, and be polite to them. What time shall we go?"

Georgie made up his mind that wild horses should not drag from him the fact that Olga's husband's name was Shuttleworth, for here was Lucia grabbing at his discovery, just as she had grabbed at Daisy's discovery who was now "her Guru." She should call him Mr Bracely then.

"Somewhere about six, do you think?" said he, inwardly raging.

He looked up and distinctly saw that sharp foxy expression cross Lucia's face, which from long knowledge of her he knew to betoken that she had thought of some new plan. But she did not choose to reveal it and re-erected the music-rest.

"That will do beautifully," she said. "And now for our heavenly Mozart. You must be patient with me, Georgie, for you know how badly I read. Caro! How difficult it looks. I am frightened! Lucia never saw such a dwefful thing to read!"

And it had been those very bars, which Georgie had heard through the open window just now.

"Georgie's is much more dwefful!" he said, remembering the double sharp that came in the second bar. "Georgie fwightened too at reading it. O-o-h," and he gave a little scream. "Cattivo Mozart to wite anything so dwefful diffy!"

It was quite clear at the class this morning that though the pupils were quite interested in the abstract messages of love which they were to shoot out in all directions, and in the atmosphere of peace with which they were to surround themselves, the branch of the subject which thrilled them to the marrow was the breathing exercises and contortions which, if persevered in, would give them youth and activity, faultless digestions and indefatigable energy. They all sat on the floor, and stopped up alternate nostrils, and held their breath till Mrs Quantock got purple in the face, and Georgie and Lucia red, and expelled their breath again with sudden puffs that set the rushes on the floor quivering, or with long quiet exhalations. Then there were certain postures to be learned, in one of which, entailing the bending of the body backwards, two of Georgie's trouser-buttons came off with a sharp snap and he felt the corresponding member of his braces, thus violently released, spring up to his shoulder. Various other embarrassing noises issued from Lucia and Daisy that sounded like the bursting of strings and tapes, but everybody pretended to hear nothing at all, or covered up the report of those explosions with coughings and clearings of the throat. But apart from these discordances, everything was fairly harmonious indeed, so far from Daisy introducing discords, she wore a fixed smile, which it would have been purely cynical to call superior, when Lucia asked some amazingly simple question with regard to Om. She sighed too, at intervals, but these sighs were expressive of nothing but patience and resignation, till Lucia's ignorance of the most elementary doctrines was enlightened, and though she rather pointedly looked in any direction but hers, and appeared completely unaware of her presence, she had not, after all, come here to look at Lucia, but to listen to her own (whatever Lucia might say) Guru.

At the end Lucia, with her far-away look, emerged, you might say, in a dazed condition from hearing about the fastness of Thibet, where the Guru had been in commune with the Guides, whose wisdom he interpreted to them.

"I feel such a difference already," she said dreamily. "I feel as if I could never be hasty or worried any more at all. Don't you experience that, dear Daisy?"

"Yes, dear," said she. "I went through all that at my first lesson.
Didn't I, Guru dear?"
"I felt it too," said Georgie, unwilling not to share in these benefits, and surreptitiously tightening his trouser-strap to compensate for the loss of buttons. "And am I to do that swaying exercise before every meal?"

"Yes, Georgie," said Lucia, saving her Guru from the trouble of answering. "Five times to the right and five times to the left and then five times backwards and forwards. I felt so young and light just now when we did it that I thought I was rising into the air. Didn't you, Daisy?"

Daisy smiled kindly.

"No, dear, that is levitation," she said, "and comes a very long way on."

She turned briskly towards her Guru.

"Will you tell them about that time when you levitated at Paddington Station?" she said. "Or will you keep that for when Mrs Lucas gets rather further on? You must be patient, dear Lucia; we all have to go through the early stages, before we get to that."

Mrs Quantock spoke as if she was in the habit of levitating herself, and it was but reasonable, in spite of the love that was swirling about them all, that Lucia should protest against such an attitude. Humility, after all, was the first essential to progress on the Way.

"Yes, dear," she said. "We will tread these early stages together, and encourage each other."

Georgie went home, feeling also unusually light and hungry, for he had paid special attention to the exercise that enabled him to have his liver and digestive organs in complete control, but that did not prevent him from devoting his mind to arriving at that which had made Lucia look so sharp and foxy during their conversation about Olga Bracely. He felt sure that she was meaning to steal a march on him, and she was planning to draw first blood with the prima-donna, and, as likely as not, claim her for her own, with the same odious greed as she was already exhibiting with regard to the Guru. All these years Georgie had been her faithful servant and coadjutor; now for the first time the spirit of independence had begun to seethe within him. The scales were falling from his eyes, and just as he turned into shelter of his mulberry-tree, he put on his spectacles to see how Riseholme was getting on without him to assist at the morning parliament. His absence and Mrs Quantock's would be sure to evoke comment, and since the Yoga classes were always to take place at half-past twelve, the fact that they would never be there, would soon rise to the level of a first-class mystery. It would, of course, begin to leak out that they and Lucia were having a course of Eastern philosophy that made its pupils young and light and energetic, and there was a sensation!

Like all great discoveries, the solution of Lucia's foxy look broke on him with the suddenness of a lightning-flash, and since it had been settled that she should call for him at six, he stationed himself in the window of his bathroom, which commanded a perfect view of the village green and the entrance to the Ambermere Arms at five. He had brought up with him a pair of opera-glasses, with the intention of taking them to bits, so he had informed Foljambe, and washing their lenses, but he did not at once proceed about this, merely holding them ready to hand for use. Hermy and Ursy had gone back to their golf again after lunch, and so callers would be told that they were all out. Thus he could wash the lenses, when he chose to do so, uninterrupted.

The minutes passed on pleasantly enough, for there was plenty going on. The two Miss Antrobuses frisked about the green, jumping over the stocks in their playful way, and running round the duck-pond in the eternal hope of attracting Colonel Boucher's attention to their pretty nimble movements. For many years past, they had tried to gain Georgie's serious attention, without any result, and lately they had turned to Colonel Boucher. There was Mrs Antrobus there, too, with her ham-like face and her ear-trumpet, and Mrs Weston was being pushed round and round the asphalt path below the elms in her bath-chair. She hated going slow, and her gardener and his boy took turns with her during her hour's carriage exercise, and propelled her, amid streams of perspiration, at a steady four miles an hour. As she passed Mrs Antrobus she shouted something at her, and Mrs Antrobus returned her reply, when next she came round.

Suddenly all these interesting objects vanished completely from Georgie's ken, for his dark suspicions were confirmed, and there was Lucia in her "Hightum" hat and her "Hightum" gown making her gracious way across the green. She had distinctly been wearing one of the "Scrub" this morning at the class, so she must have changed after lunch, which was an unheard of thing to do for a mere stroll on the green. Georgie knew well that this was no mere stroll; she was on her way to pay a call of the most formal and magnificent kind. She did not deviate a hair-breadth from her straight course to the door of the Arms, she just waggled her hand to Mrs Antrobus, blew a kiss to her sprightly daughters, made a gracious bow to Colonel Boucher, who stood up and took his hat off, and went on with the inexorability of the march of destiny, or of fate knocking at the door in the immortal fifth symphony. And in her hand she carried a note. Through his glasses Georgie could see it quite plainly, and it was not a little folded-up sheet, such as she commonly used, but a square thick envelope. She disappeared in the Arms and Georgie began thinking feverishly. A great deal depended on how long she stopped there.

A few little happenings beguiled the period of waiting. Mrs Weston desisted from her wild career, and came to anchor on the path just opposite the door into the Arms, while the gardener's boy sank exhausted on to the grass. It was quite easy to guess that she proposed to have a chat with Lucia when she came out. Similarly the Miss Antrobuses who had paid no attention to her at all before, ceased from their pretty gambolings, and ran up to talk to her, so they wanted a word too. Colonel Boucher, a little less obviously, began throwing sticks into the ducking-pond for his bull-dog (for Lucia would be obliged to pass the ducking-pond) and Mrs Antrobus examined the stocks very carefully, as if she had never seen them before.

And then, before a couple of minutes had elapsed Lucia came out. She had no longer the note in her hand, and Georgie began taking his opera-glasses to bits, in order to wash the lenses. For the present they had served their purpose. "She has left a note on Olga Bracely," said Georgie quite aloud, so powerful was the current of his thoughts. Then as a corollary came the further proposition which might be considered as proved, "But she had not seen her."

The justice of this conclusion was soon proved, for Lucia had hardly disengaged herself from the group of her subjects, and traversed the green on her way back to her house, when a motor passed Georgie's bathroom window, closely followed by a second; both drew up at the entrance to the Ambermere Arms. With the speed of a practised optician Georgie put his opera glass together again, and after looking through the wrong end of it in his agitation was in time to see a man get out of the second car, and hold the carriage-door open for the occupants of the first. A lady got out first, tall and slight in figure, who stood there unwinding her motor veil, then she turned round again, and with a thump of his heart that surprised Georgie with its violence, he beheld the well-remembered features of his Brunnhilde.

Swiftly he passed into his bedroom next door, and arrayed himself in his summer Hightums; a fresh (almost pearly) suit of white duck, a mauve tie with an amethyst pin in it, socks, tightly braced up, of precisely the same colour as the tie, so that an imaginative beholder might have conjectured that on this warm day the end of his tie had melted and run down his legs; buckskin shoes with tall slim heels and a straw hat completed this pretty Hightum. He had meant to wear it for the first time at Lucia's party tomorrow, but now, after her meanness, she deserved to be punished. All Riseholme should see it before she did.

The group round Mrs Weston's chair was still engaged in conversation when Georgie came up, and he casually let slip what a bore it was to pay calls on such a lovely day, but he had promised to visit Miss Olga Bracely, who had just arrived. So there was another nasty one for Lucia, since now all Riseholme would know of her actual arrival before Lucia did.

"And who, Mr Georgie," asked Mrs Antrobus presenting her trumpet to him in the manner in which an elephant presents its trunk to receive a bun, "who was that with her?"

"Oh, her husband, Mr Shuttleworth," said Georgie. "They have just been married, and are on their honeymoon." And if that was not another staggerer for Lucia, it is diffy, as Georgie would say, to know what a staggerer is. For Lucia would be last of all to know that this was not Mr Bracely.

"And will they be at Mrs Lucas's party tomorrow?" asked Mrs Weston.

"Oh, does she know them?" asked Georgie.

"Haw, haw, by Jove!" began Colonel Boucher. "Very handsome woman. Envy you, my boy. Pity it's their honeymoon. Haw!"

Mrs Antrobus's trumpet was turned in his direction at this moment, and she heard these daring remarks.

"Naughty!" she said, and Georgie, the envied, passed in into the inn.

He sent in his card, on which he had thought it prudent to write "From Lady Ambermere," and was presently led through into the garden behind the building. There she was, tall and lovely and welcoming, and held out a most cordial hand.

"How kind of you to come and see us," she said. "Georgie, this is Mr Pillson. My husband."
"How do you do, Mr Shuttleworth," said Georgie to shew he knew, though his own Christian name had given him quite a start. For the moment he had almost thought she was speaking to him.

"And so Lady Ambermere asked you to come and see us?" Olga went on. "I think that was much kinder of her than to ask us to dinner. I hate going out to dinner in the country almost as much as I hate not going out to dinner in town. Besides with that great hook nose of hers, I'm always afraid that in an absent moment I might scratch her on the head and say 'Pretty Polly.' Is she a great friend of yours, Mr Pillson? I hope so, because everyone likes his best friends being laughed at."

Up till that moment Georgie was prepared to indicate that Lady Ambermere was the hand and he the glove. But evidently that would not impress Olga in the least. He laughed in a most irreverent manner instead.

"Don't let us go," she went on. "Georgie, can't you send a telegram saying that we have just discovered a subsequent engagement and then we'll ask Mr Pillson to show us round this utterly adorable place, and dine with us afterwards. That would be so much nicer. Fancy living here! Oh, and do tell me something, Mr Pillson. I found a note when I arrived half an hour ago, from Mrs Lucas asking me and Mr Shuttleworth to go to a garden-party tomorrow. She said she didn't even hope that I should remember her, but would we come. Who is she? Really I don't think she can remember me very well, if she thinks I am Mrs Bracely. Georgie says I must have been married before, and that I have caused him to commit bigamy. That's pleasant conversation for a honeymoon, isn't it? Who is she?"

"Oh, she's quite an old friend of mine," said Georgie, "though I never knew she had met you before; I'm devoted to her."

"Extremely proper. But now tell me this, and look straight in my face, so that I shall know if you're speaking the truth. Should I enjoy myself more wandering about this heavenly place than at her garden party?"

Georgie felt that poor Lucia was really punished enough by this time.

"You will give her a great deal of pleasure if you go," he began.

"Ah, that's not fair; it is hitting below the belt to appeal to unselfish motives. I have come here simply to enjoy myself. Go on; eyes front."

The candour and friendliness of that beautiful face gave Georgie an impulse of courage. Besides, though no doubt in fun, she had already suggested that it would be much nicer to wander about with him and dine together than spend the evening among the splendours of The Hall.

"I've got a suggestion," he said. "Will you come and lunch with me first, and we'll stroll about, and then we can go to the garden-party, and if you don't like it I'll take you away again?"

"Done!" she said. "Now don't you try to get out of it, because my husband is a witness. Georgie, give me a cigarette."

In a moment Riseholme-Georgie had his cigarette-case open.

"Do take one of mine," he said, "I'm Georgie too."

"You don't say so! Let's send it to the Psychical Research, or whoever those people are who collect coincidences and say it's spooks. And a match please, one of you Georgies. Oh, how

I should like never to see the inside of an Opera House again. Why mayn't I grow on the walls of a garden like this, or better still, why shouldn't I have a house and garden of my own here, and sing on the village-green, and ask for halfpennies? Tell me what happens here! I've always lived in town since the time a hook-nosed Hebrew, rather like Lady Ambermere, took me out of the gutter."

"My dear!" said Mr Shuttleworth.

"Well, out of an orphan-school at Brixton and I would much prefer the gutter. That's all about my early life just now, because I am keeping it for my memoirs which I shall write when my voice becomes a little more like a steam-whistle. But don't tell Lady Ambermere, for she would have a fit, but say you happen to know that I belong to the Surrey Bracelys. So I do; Brixton is on the Surrey side. Oh, my dear, look at the sun. It's behaving like the best sort of Claude! Heile Sonne!"

"I heard you do that last May," said Georgie.

"Then you heard a most second-rate performance," said she. "But really being unlaced by that Thing, that great fat profligate beery Prussian was almost too much for me. And the duet! But it was very polite of you to come, and I will do better next time. Siegfried! Brunnhilde! Siegfried! Miaou! Miaou! Bring on the next lot of cats! Darling Georgie, wasn't it awful? And you had proposed to me only the day before."

"I was absolutely enchanted," said Riseholme-Georgie.

"Yes, but then you didn't have that Thing breathing beer into your innocent face." Georgie rose; the first call on a stranger in Riseholme was never supposed to last more than half an hour, however much you were enjoying it, and never less, however bored you might be, and he felt sure he had already exceeded this.

"I must be off," he said. "Too delightful to think that you and Mr Shuttleworth will come to lunch with me tomorrow. Half past one, shall we say?"

"Excellent; but where do you live?"

"Just across the green. Shall I call for you?" he asked.

"Certainly not. Why should you have that bother?" she said. "Ah, let me come with you to the inn-door, and perhaps you will shew me from there."

She passed through the hall with him, and they stood together in the sight of all Riseholme, which was strolling about the green at this as at most other hours. Instantly all faces turned round in their direction, like so many sunflowers following the sun, while Georgie pointed out his particular mulberry tree. When everybody had had a good look, he raised his hat.

"A domani then," she said. "So many thanks."

And quite distinctly she kissed her hand to him as he turned away....

"So she talks Italian too," thought Georgie, as he dropped little crumbs of information to his friends on his way to his house. "Domani, that means tomorrow. Oh yes; she was meaning lunch."

It is hardly necessary to add that on the table in his hall there was one of Lucia's commoner kinds of note, merely a half sheet folded together in her own manner. Georgie felt that it was scarcely more necessary to read it, for he felt quite sure that it contained some excuse for not coming to his house at six in order to call on Mr and Mrs Bracely. But he gave a glance at it before he rolled it up in a ball for Tipsipoozie to play with, and found its contents to be precisely what he expected, the excuse being that she had not done her practising. But the post-script was interesting, for it told him that she had asked Foljambe to give her his copy of Siegfried....

Georgie strolled down past The Hurst before dinner. Mozart was silent now, but there came out of the open windows the most amazing hash of sound, which he could just recognise as being the piano arrangement of the duet between Brunnhilde and Siegfried at the end. He would have been dull indeed if he had not instantly guessed what that signified.

Chapter SEVEN

A fresh thrill went through an atmosphere already super-saturated with excitement, when next morning all Lucia's friends who had been bidden to the garden-party (Tightum) were rung up on the telephone and informed that the party was Hightum. That caused a good deal of extra work, because the Tightum robes had to be put away again, and the Hightums aired and brushed and valetted. But it was well worth it, for Riseholme had not the slightest difficulty in conjecturing that Olga Bracely was to be among the guests. For a cultured and artistic centre the presence of a star that blazed so regally in the very zenith of the firmament of art absolutely demanded the Hightum which the presence of poor Lady Ambermere (though she would not have liked that) had been powerless to bring out of their cupboards. And these delightful anticipations concentrated themselves into one rose-coloured point of joy, when no less than two independent observers, without collusion, saw the piano-tuner either entering or leaving The Hurst, while a third, an ear-witness, unmistakably heard the tuning of the piano actually going on. It was thus clear to all penetrating minds that Olga Bracely was going to sing. It was further known that something was going on between her and Georgie, for she had been heard by one Miss Antrobus to ask for Georgie's number at the telephone in the Ambermere Arms. Etiquette forbade her actually to listen to what passed, but she could not help hearing Olga laugh at something (presumably) that Georgie said. He himself took no part in the green-parliament that morning, but had been seen to dash into the fruiterer's and out again, before he went in a great hurry to The Hurst, shortly after twelve-thirty. Classes on Eastern philosophy under the tuition of Mrs Quantock's Indian, were already beginning to be hinted at, but today in the breathless excitement about the prima-donna nobody cared about that; they might all have been taking lessons in cannibalism, and nobody would have been interested. Finally about one o'clock one of the motors in which the party had arrived yesterday drew up at the door of the Ambermere Arms, and presently Mr Bracely,—no, dear, Mr Shuttleworth got in and drove off alone. That was very odd conduct in a lately-married bridegroom, and it was hoped that there had been no quarrel.

Olga had, of course, been given no directions as to Hightum or Tightum, and when she walked across to Georgie's house shortly after half-past one only Mrs Weston who was going back home to lunch at top speed was aware that she was dressed in a very simple dark blue morning frock, that would almost have passed for Scrub. It is true that it was exceedingly well cut, and had not the look of having been rolled up in a ball and hastily ironed out again that usually distinguished Scrub, and she also wore a string of particularly fine pearls round her neck, the sort of ornament that in Riseholme would only be seen in an evening Hightum, even if anybody in Riseholme had owned such things. Lucia, not long ago had expressed the opinion that jewels were vulgar except at night, and for her part she wore none at all, preferring one Greek cameo of uncertain authenticity.

Georgie received Olga alone, for Hermy and Ursy were not yet back from their golf.

"It is good of you to let me come without my husband," she said. "His excuse is toothache and he has driven into Brinton—"

"I'm very sorry," said Georgie.

"You needn't be, for now I'll tell you his real reason. He thought that if he lunched with you he would have to come on to the garden party, and that he was absolutely determined not to do. You were the thin edge of the wedge, in fact. My dear, what a delicious house. All panelled, with that lovely garden behind. And croquet—may we play croquet after lunch? I always try to cheat, and if I'm found out I lose my temper. Georgie won't play with me, so I play with my maid."

"This Georgie will," said he.

"How nice of him! And do you know what we did this morning, before the toothache didn't begin? We went all over that house three doors away, which is being done up. It belongs to the proprietor of the Ambermere Arms. And—oh, I wonder if you can keep a secret?"

"Yes," said Georgie. He probably had never kept one yet, but there was no reason why he shouldn't begin now.

"Well, I'm absolutely determined to buy it, only I daren't tell my husband until I've done it. He has an odd nature. When a thing is done, settled, and there's no help for it, he finds it adorable, but he also finds fatal objections to doing it at all, if he is consulted about it before it is done. So not a word! I shall buy it, make the garden, furnish it, down to the minutest detail, and engage the servants, and then he'll give it me for a birthday present. I had to tell somebody or I should burst."

Georgie nearly swooned with fervour and admiration.

"But what a perfect plan!" he said. "You really like our little Riseholme?"
"It's not a question of liking; it's a mere detail of not being able to do without it. I don't like breathing, but I should die if I didn't. I want some delicious, hole-in-the-corner, lazy backwater sort of place, where nothing ever happens, and nobody ever does anything. I've been observing all the morning, and your habits are adorable. Nothing ever happens here, and that will precisely suit me, when I get away from my work."

Georgie was nearer swooning than ever at this. He could hardly believe his ears when she talked of Riseholme being a lazy backwater, and almost thought she must have been speaking of London, where, as Lucia had acutely observed, people sat in the Park all morning and talked of each other's affairs, and spent the afternoon at picture-galleries, and danced all night. There was a flippant, lazy existence.

But she was far too much absorbed in her project to notice his stupefaction.

53

"But if you breathe a word," she said, "everything will be spoilt. It has to burst on Georgie. Oh, and there's another mulberry-tree in your garden as well as the one in front. It's too much."

Her eyes followed Foljambe out of the door.

"And I know your parlour-maid is called Paravicini or Grosvenor," she said.

"No, she is Foljambe," said Georgie.

She laughed.

"I knew I was right," she said. "It's practically the same thing. Oh, and last night! I never had such an awful evening. Why didn't you warn me, and my husband should have had toothache then instead of this morning."

"What happened?" asked he.

"But the woman's insane, that Ambermere parrot, I mean. Georgie and I were ten minutes late, and she had a jet tiara on, and why did she ask us to dine at a quarter to eight, if she meant a quarter to eight, instead of saying half-past-seven? They were actually going into dinner when we came, a mournful procession of three moth-eaten men and three whiskered women. Upon which the procession broke up, as if we had been the riot act, and was arranged again, as a funeral procession, and Georgie with Lady Ambermere was the hearse. We dined in the family vault and talked about Lady Ambermere's pug. She talked about you, too, and said you were of county family, and that Mrs Lucas was a very decent sort of woman, and that she herself was going to look in on her garden-party today. Then she looked at my pearls, and asked if they were genuine. So I looked at her teeth, and there was no need to ask about them."

"Don't miss out a moment," said Georgie greedily.

"Whenever Lady Ambermere spoke, everybody else was silent. I didn't grasp that at first, for no one had explained the rules. So she stopped in the middle of a sentence and waited till I had finished. Then she went on again, precisely where she had left off. Then when we came into the drawing room, the whiskered ladies and I, there a little woman like a mouse sitting there, and nobody introduced her. So naturally I went to talk to her, before which the great parrot said, 'Will you kindly fetch my wool-work, Miss Lyall?' and Miss Lyall took a sack out of the corner, and inside was the sacred carpet. And then I waited for some coffee and cigarettes, and I waited, and I waited, and I am waiting still. The Parrot said that coffee always kept her awake, and that was why. And then Georgie came in with the others, and I could see by his face that he hadn't had a cigarette either. It was then half-past nine. And then each man sat down between two women, and Pug sat in the middle and looked for fleas. Then Lady Ambermere got up, and came across the charmed circle to me. She said: 'I hope you have brought your music, Mrs Shuttleworth. Kindly open the piano, Miss Lyall. It was always considered a remarkably fine instrument.'"

Olga waved the fork on which was impaled a piece of the pineapple which Georgie had purchased that morning at the fruiterer's.

"The stupendous cheek!" she said. "I thought it must be a joke, and laughed with the greatest politeness. But it wasn't! You'll hardly believe it, but it wasn't! One of the whiskered ones said, 'That will be a great treat,' and another put on the face that everyone wears at concerts. And I was so stunned that I sang, and Lady Ambermere beat time, and Pug barked."

She pointed a finger at Georgie.

"Never till the day of judgment," she said, "when Lady Ambermere gnashes her beautiful teeth for ever and ever, will I set foot in that house again. Nor she in my house. I will set fire to it sooner. There! My dear, what a good lunch you have given me. May we play croquet at once?"

Lucia's garden-parties were scheduled from four to seven and half-an-hour before the earliest guest might be expected, she was casting an eagle eye over the preparations which today were on a very sumptuous scale. The bowls were laid out in the bowling alley, not because anybody in Hightums dresses was the least likely to risk the stooping down and the strong movements that the game entailed, but because bowls were Elizabethan. Between the alley and the lawn nearer to the house was a large marquee, where the commoner crowd—though no crowd could be really common in Riseholme—would refresh itself. But even where none are common there may still be degrees in rarity, and by the side of this general refreshment room was a smaller tent carpeted with Oriental rugs, and having inside it some half-dozen chairs, and two seats which can only be described as thrones, for Lady Ambermere or Olga Bracely, while Lucia's Guru, though throneworthy, would very kindly sit in one of his most interesting attitudes on the floor. This tent was designed only for high converse, and common guests (if they were good) would be led into it and introduced to the great presences, while for the refreshment of the presences, in intervals of audience, a more elaborate meal, with peaches and four sorts of sandwiches was laid in the smoking-parlour. Thus those guests for whom audiences were not provided, could have the felicity of seeing the great ones pass across the lawn on their excursions for food, and possibly trip over the croquet hoops, which had been left up to give an air of naturalness to the lawn. In the smoking-parlour an Elzevir or two were left negligently open, as if Mr and Mrs Lucas had been reading the works of Persius and Juvenal when the first guests arrived. In the music-room, finally, which was not usually open on these occasions, there were fresh flowers: the piano, too, was open, and if you had not seen the Elzevirs in the smoking-parlour, it would have been reasonable for the early guests, if they penetrated here, to imagine that Mrs Lucas had been running over the last act of Siegfried a minute before.

In this visit of final inspection Lucia was accompanied by her Guru, for he was part of the domestic dramatis personae, and she wanted him to be "discovered" in the special tent. She pointed out the site of his proposed "discovery" to him.

"Probably the first person I shall bring in here," she said, "will be Lady Ambermere, for she is noted for her punctuality. She is so anxious to see you, and would it not be exciting if you found you had met before? Her husband was Governor of Madras, and she spent many years in India."

"Madras, gracious lady?" asked the Guru. "I, too, know Madras: there are many dark spirits in Madras. And she was at English Residency?"

"Yes. She says Mr Kipling knows nothing about India. You and she will have much to talk about. I wish I could sit on the floor, too, and listen to what you say to each other."

"It will be great treat," said the Guru thoughtfully, "I love all who love my wonderful country."

Suddenly he stopped, and put his hands up to his head, palms outward.

"There are wonderful vibrations today," he said. "All day I feel that some word is on way from the Guides, some great message of light."

"Oh, wouldn't it be wonderful if it came to you in the middle of my garden party?" said Lucia enthusiastically.

"Ah, gracious lady, the great word comes not so. It comes always in solitude and quiet. Gracious lady knows that as well as Guru."

Pure Guruism and social pre-eminence struggled together in Lucia. Guruism told her that she ought to be ecstatic at the idea of a great message coming and should instantly smile on his desire for solitude and quiet, while social pre-eminence whispered to her that she had already dangled the presence of a high-caste mystic from Benares before the eyes of Lady Ambermere, who only came from Madras. On the other hand Olga Bracely was to be an even more resplendent guest than either Lady Ambermere or the Guru; surely Olga Bracely was enough to set this particular garden-party on the giddiest of pinnacles. And an awful consequence lurked as a possibility if she attempted to force her Guru not to immune himself in solitude and quiet, which was that conceivably he might choose to go back to the pit whence he was digged, namely the house of poor Daisy Quantock. The thought was intolerable, for with him in her house, she had seen herself as dispenser of Eastern Mysteries, and Mistress of Omism to Riseholme. In fact the Guru was her August stunt; it would never do to lose him before the end of July, and rage to see all Riseholme making pilgrimages to Daisy. There was a thin-lipped firmness, too, about him at this moment: she felt that under provocation he might easily defy or desert her. She felt she had to yield, and so decided to do so in the most complete manner.

"Ah, yes," she said. "I know how true that is. Dear Guru, go up to Hamlet: no one will disturb you there. But if the message comes through before Lady Ambermere goes away, promise me you will come back."

He went back to the house, where the front door was already open to admit Lady Ambermere, who was telling "her people" when to come back for her, and fled with the heels of his slippers tapping on the oak stairs up to Hamlet. Softly he shut out the dark spirits from Madras, and made himself even more secure by turning the key in his door. It would never do to appear as a high caste Brahmin from Benares before anyone who knew India with such fatal intimacy, for he might not entirely correspond with her preconceived notions of such a person.

Lady Ambermere's arrival was soon followed by that of other guests, and instead of going into the special tent reserved for the lions, she took up a commanding position in the middle of the lawn, where she could examine everybody through her tortoiseshell handled lorgnette. She kept Peppino by her, who darted forward to shake hands with his wife's guests, and then darted back again to her. Poor Miss Lyall stood behind her chair, and from time to time as ordered, gave her a cape, or put up her parasol, or adjusted her footstool for her, or took up Pug or put him down as her patroness required. Most of the time Lady Ambermere kept up a majestic monologue.

"You have a pretty little garden here, Mr Lucas," she said, "though perhaps inconveniently small. Your croquet lawn does not look to me the full size, and then there is no tennis-court. But I think you have a little strip of grass somewhere, which you use for bowls, have you not?

56

Presently I will walk around with you and see your domain. Put Pug down again, please, Miss Lyall, and let him run about. See, he wants to play with one of those croquet balls. Put it in motion for him, and he will run with it. Bless me, who is that coming up the path at such a tremendous speed in a bath-chair? Oh, I see, it is Mrs Weston. She should not go as fast as that. If Pug was to stray on to the path he would be run over. Better pick up Pug again, Miss Lyall, till she has gone by. And here is Colonel Boucher. If he had brought his bull-dogs, I should have asked him to take them away again. I should like a cup of tea, Miss Lyall, with plenty of milk in it, and not too strong. You know how I like my tea. And a biscuit or something for Pug, with a little cream in a saucer or anything that's handy."

"Won't you come into the smoking-parlour, and have tea there, Lady Ambermere?" asked Peppino.
"The smoking-parlour?" asked she. "How very strange to lay tea in a smoking-room."

Peppino explained that nobody had in all probability used the smoking-parlour to smoke in for five or six years.

"Oh, if that is so, I will come," said she. "Better bring Pug along, too, Miss Lyall. There is a croquet-hoop. I am glad I saw it or I should have stumbled over it perhaps. Oh, this is the smoking-parlour, is it? Why do you have rushes on the floor? Put Pug in a chair, Miss Lyall, or he may prick his paws. Books, too, I see. That one lying open is an old one. It is Latin poetry. The library at The Hall is very famous for its classical literature. The first Viscount collected it, and it numbers many thousands of volumes."

"Indeed, it is the most wonderful library," said Peppino. "I can never tear myself away from it, when I am at The Hall."

"I do not wonder. I am a great student myself and often spend a morning there, do I not, Miss Lyall? You should have some new glass put in those windows, Mr Lucas. On a dark day it must be very difficult to see here. By the way, your good wife told me that there would probably be a very remarkable Indian at her party, a Brahmin from Benares, she said. I should like to have a talk with him while I am having my tea. Kindly prepare a peach for me, Miss Lyall."

Peppino had heard about the retirement of the Guru, in consequence of a message from the Guides being expected, and proceeded to explain this to Lady Ambermere, who did not take the slightest notice, as she was looking at the peaches through her lorgnette.

"That one nearest me looks eatable," she said. "And then I do not see Miss Olga Bracely, though I distinctly told her I should be here this afternoon, and she said Mrs Lucas had asked her. She sang to us yesterday evening at The Hall, and very creditably indeed. Her husband, Mr Shuttleworth, is a cousin of the late lord's."

Lucia had come into the smoking-parlour during this speech, and heard these fatal words. At the moment she would gladly have recalled her invitation to Olga Bracely altogether, sooner than have alluded therein to Mr Bracely. But that was one of the irremediable things of life, and since it was no use wasting regret on that, she was only the more eager for Olga to come, whatever her husband's name was. She braced herself up to the situation.

"Peppino, are you looking after Lady Ambermere?" she said. "Dear Lady Ambermere, I hope they are all taking care of you."

"A very decent peach," said Lady Ambermere. "The south wall of my garden is covered with them, and they are always of a peculiarly delicious flavour. The Hall is famed for its peaches. I understood that Miss Bracely was going to be here, Mrs Lucas. I cannot imagine what makes her so late. I was always famed for my punctuality myself. I have finished my tea."

The lawn outside was now growing thick with people all in their Hightums, and Lady Ambermere as she emerged from the smoking-parlour again viewed the scene with marked disfavour. The two Miss Antrobuses had just arrived, and skipped up to their hostess with pretty cries.

"We are dreadfully late," said the eldest, "but it was all Piggy's fault."

"No, Goosie, it was yours," said the other. "How can you be so naughty as to say it was mine? Dear Mrs Lucas, what a lovely party it's being, and may we go and play bowls?"

Lady Ambermere regarded their retreating backs, as they raced off with arms intertwined to the bowling green.

"And who are those young ladies?" she asked. "And why Piggy and Goosie? Miss Lyall, do not let Pug go to the bowls. They are very heavy." Elsewhere Mrs Antrobus was slowly advancing from group to group, with her trumpet violently engaged in receiving refreshment. But conversation was not quite so varied as usual, for there was an attitude of intense expectation about with regard to the appearance of Miss Bracely, that made talk rather jerky and unconnective. Then also it had gone about that the mysterious Indian, who had been seen now and then during the last week, was actually staying with Mrs Lucas, and why was he not here? More unconjecturable yet, though not so thrillingly interesting, was the absence of Mr Georgie. What could have happened to him, that he was not flitting about on his hostess's errands, and being the life and soul of the party? It was in vain that Mrs Antrobus plodded on her methodical course, seeking answers to all these riddles, and that Mrs Weston in her swifter progression dashed about in her bath-chair from group to group, wherever people seemed to be talking in an animated manner. She could learn nothing, and Mrs Antrobus could learn nothing, in fact the only information to be had on the subject was what Mrs Weston herself supplied. She had a very high-coloured handsome face, and an extremely impressive manner, as if she was imparting information of the very highest importance. She naturally spoke in a loud, clear voice, so that she had not got to raise it much even when she addressed Mrs Antrobus. Her wealth of discursive detail was absolutely unrivalled, and she was quite the best observer in Riseholme.

"The last I saw of Miss Bracely," she said exactly as if she had been told to describe something on oath in the witness-box, "was a little after half-past one today. It must have been after half-past because when I got home it was close on a quarter to two, and I wasn't a hundred yards from my house when I saw her. As soon as I saw her I said to my gardener boy, Henry Luton, who was pushing me—he's the son of old Mrs Luton who kept the fish shop, and when she died last year, I began to get my fish from Brinton, for I didn't fancy the look of the new person who took on the business, and Henry went to live with his aunt. That was his father's sister, not his mother's, for Mrs Luton never had a sister, and no brothers either. Well, I said to Henry, 'You can go a bit slower, Henry, as we're late, we're late, and a minute or two more doesn't make any difference.' 'No, ma'am,' said Henry touching his cap, so we went slower. Miss Bracely was just opposite the ducking-pond then, and presently she came out between the elms. She had just an ordinary morning frock on; it was dark-blue, about the same shade as your cape, Mrs Antrobus, or perhaps a little darker, for the sunshine brightened it up. Quite simple it was, nothing grand. And she looked at the watch on her wrist, and she seemed to me to walk a little quicker after that, as if she was a bit late, just as I was. But slower than I was going, I could not go, for I was crawling along, and before she got off the grass, I had come to the corner of Church Lane, and though I turned my head round sharp, like that, at the very last moment, so as to catch the last of her, she hadn't more than stepped off the grass onto the road before the laurestinus at the corner of Colonel Boucher's garden—no, of the Vicar's garden—hid her from me. And if you ask me——"

Mrs Weston stopped for a moment, nodding her head up and down, to emphasize the importance of what she had said, and to raise the expectations of Mrs Antrobus to the highest pitch, as to what was coming.

"And if you ask me where I think she was going and what she was going to do," she said, "I believe she was going out to lunch and that she was going to one of those houses there, just across the road, for she made a bee-line across the green towards them. Well, there are three houses there: there's Mrs Quantock's, and it couldn't have been that, or else Mrs Quantock would have had some news of her, or Colonel Boucher's, and it wouldn't have been that, for the Colonel would have had news of her, and we all know whose the third house just there is."

Mrs Antrobus had not completely followed this powerful reasoning.

"But Colonel Boucher and Mrs Quantock are both here, eh?" said she.

Mrs Weston raised her voice a little.

"That's what I'm saying," she announced, "but who isn't here whom we should expect to see, and where's his house?"

It was generally felt that Mrs Weston had hit the nail on the head. What that nail precisely was no one knew, because she had not explained why both Olga Bracely and Georgie were absentees. But now came the climax, bang on the top of the nail, a shrewd straight stroke.

"So there she was having her lunch with Mr Georgie," said Mrs Weston, now introducing this name for the first time, with the highest dramatic art, "and they would be seeing round his house afterwards. And then when it was time to come here, Mr Georgie would have remembered that the party was Hightum not Tightum, and there was Miss Bracely not in Hightum at all, nor even Tightum, in my opinion, but Scrub. No doubt she said to him, 'Is it a very grand sort of party, Mr Pillson?' and he couldn't do other than reply, for we all received notice that it was Hightum—mine came about twelve—he couldn't do other than reply, 'Yes, Miss Bracely, it is.' 'Good gracious me,' she would say, 'and I've only got this old rag on. I must go back to the Ambermere Arms, and tell my maid—for she brought a maid in that second motor—and tell my maid to put me out something tidy.' 'But that will be a great bother for you,' he would say, or something of that sort, for I don't pretend to know what he actually did say, and she would reply, 'Oh Mr Pillson, but I must put on something tidy, and it would be so kind of you, if you would wait for me, while I do that, and let us go together.' That's what she said."

Mrs Weston made a sign to her gardener to proceed, wishing to leave the stage at the moment of climax.

"And that's why they're both late," she said, and was whirled away in the direction of the bowling-green.

The minutes went on, and still nobody appeared who could possibly have accounted for the three-lined whip of Hightums, but by degrees Lucia, who had utterly failed to decoy Lady Ambermere into the place of thrones, began to notice a certain thinning on her lawns. Her guests, it would seem, were not in process of dispersal, for it was a long way off seven o'clock yet, and also none would be so ill-mannered as to leave without shaking hands and saying what a delicious afternoon they had spent. But certainly the lawns grew emptier, and she was utterly unable to explain this extraordinary phenomenon, until she happened to go close to the windows of her music-room. Then, looking in, she saw that not only was every chair there occupied, but people were standing about in expectant groups. For a moment, her heart beat high…. Could Olga have arrived and by some mistake have gone straight in there? It was a dreamlike possibility, but it burst like a ray of sunshine on the party that was rapidly becoming a nightmare to her,—for everyone, not Lady Ambermere alone, was audibly wondering when the Guru was coming, and when Miss Bracely was going to sing.

At the moment as she paused, a window in the music-room was opened, and Piggy's odious head looked out.
"Oh, Mrs Lucas," she said. "Goosie and I have got beautiful seats, and Mamma is quite close to the piano where she will hear excellently. Has she promised to sing Siegfried? Is Mr Georgie going to play for her? It's the most delicious surprise; how could you be so sly and clever as not to tell anybody?"

Lucia cloaked her rage under the most playful manner, as she ran into the music-room through the hall.

"You naughty things!" she said. "Do all come into the garden! It's a garden party, and I couldn't guess where you had all gone. What's all this about singing and playing? I know nothing of it."

She herded the incredulous crowd out into the garden again, all in their Hightums, every one of them, only to meet Lady Ambermere with Pug and Miss Lyall coming in.

"Better be going, Miss Lyall," she said. "Kindly run out and find my people. Oh, here's Mrs Lucas. Been very pleasant indeed, thank you, good-bye. Your charming garden. Yes."

"Oh, but it's very early," said Lucia. "It's hardly six yet."

"Indeed!" said Lady Ambermere. "Been so charming," and she marched out after Miss Lyall out into Shakespeare's garden.

It was soon terribly evident that other people were sharing Lady Ambermere's conclusion about the delights of the afternoon, and the necessity of getting home. Colonel Boucher had to take his bull-dogs for a run and walk off the excitement of the party; Piggy and Goosie explained to their mother that nobody was going to sing, and by silvery laughter tried to drown her just indignation, and presently Lucia had the agony of seeing Mrs Quantock seated on one of the thrones, that had been designed for much worthier ends, and Peppino sitting in the other, while a few guests drifted about the lawn with all the purposelessness of autumn leaves. What with the Guru, presumably meditating upstairs still, and with Olga Bracely most conspicuously absent, she had hardly nervous energy left to wonder what could have become of Georgie. Never in all the years of his ministry had he failed to be at her elbow through the entire duration of her garden-parties, flying about on her errands like a tripping Hermes, herding her flocks if she wanted them in one part of the garden rather than another, like a sagacious sheep-dog, and coming back to heel again ready for further tasks. But today Georgie was mysteriously away, for he had neither applied for leave nor given any explanation, however improbable, of his absence. He at least would have prevented Lady Ambermere, the only cornerstone of the party, from going away in what must be called a huff, and have continued to tell Lucia how marvellous she was, and what a beautiful party they were having. With the prospect of two other much more magnificent cornerstones, Lucia had not provided any further entertainment for her guests: there was not the conjurer from Brinton, nor the three young ladies who played banjo-trios, nor even the mild performing doves which cooed so prettily, and walked up their mistress's outstretched fingers according to order, if they felt disposed. There was nothing to justify Hightums, there was scarcely even sufficient to warrant Tightums. Scrub was written all over "the desert's dusty face."

It was about half-past six when the miracles began, and without warning the Guru walked out into the garden. Probably he had watched the departure of the great motor with its chauffeur and footman, and Miss Lyall and Lady Ambermere and Pug, and with his intuitive sagacity had conjectured that the danger from Madras was over. He wore his new red slippers, a wonderful turban and an ecstatic smile. Lucia and Daisy met him with cries of joy, and the remaining guests, those drifting autumn leaves, were swept up, as it were, by some compelling broom and clustered in a heap in front of him. There had been a Great Message, a Word of Might, full of Love and Peace. Never had there been such a Word....

And then, even before they had all felt the full thrill of that, once more the door from the house opened, and out came Olga Bracely and Georgie. It is true that she had still her blue morning frock, which Mrs Weston had designated as Scrub, but it was a perfectly new Scrub, and if it had been completely covered with Paris labels, they would not have made its provenance one whit clearer. "Dear Mrs Lucas," she said, "Mr Georgie and I are terribly late, and it was quite my fault. There was a game of croquet that wouldn't come to an end, and my life has been guided by only one principle, and that is to finish a game of croquet whatever happens. I missed six trains once by finishing a game of croquet. And Mr Georgie was so unkind: he wouldn't give me a cup of tea, or let me change my frock, but dragged me off to see you. And I won!"

The autumn leaves turned green and vigorous again, while Georgie went to get refreshment for his conqueror, and they were all introduced. She allowed herself to be taken with the utmost docility—how unlike Somebody—into the tent with the thrones: she confessed to having stood on tiptoe and looked into Mrs Quantock's garden and wanted to see it so much from the other side of the wall. And this garden, too—might she go and wander all over this garden when she had finished the most delicious peach that the world held? She was so glad she had not had tea with Mr Georgie: he would never have given her such a good peach....

Now the departing guests in their Hightums, lingering on the village green a little, and being rather sarcastic about the utter failure of Lucia's party, could hardly help seeing Georgie and Olga emerge from his house and proceed swiftly in the direction of The Hurst, and Mrs Antrobus who retained marvellous eyesight as compensation for her defective hearing, saw them go in, and simultaneously thought that she had left her parasol at The Hurst. Next moment she was walking thoughtfully away in that direction. Mrs Weston had been the next to realize what had happened, and though she had to go round by the road in her bath-chair, she passed Mrs Antrobus a hundred yards from the house, her pretext for going back being that Lucia had promised to lend her the book by Antonio Caporelli (or was it Caporelto?).

So once more the door into the garden opened, and out shot Mrs Weston. Olga by this time had made her tour of the garden, and might she see the house? She might. There was a pretty music-room. At this stage, just as Mrs Weston was poured out in the garden, as with the floodgates being unopened, the crowd that followed her came surging into Shakespeare's garden, and never had the mermaid's tail behind which was secreted the electric bell, experienced such feverish usage. Pressure after pressure invoked its aid, and the pretexts for re-admission were soon not made at all, or simply disregarded by the parlour-maid. Colonel Boucher might have left a bull-dog, and Mrs Antrobus an ear trumpet, or Miss Antrobus (Piggy) a shoe lace, and the other Miss Antrobus (Goosie) a shoe-horn: but in brisk succession the guests who had been so sarcastic about the party on the village-green, jostled each other in order to revisit the scenes of their irony. Miss Olga Bracely had been known to enter the portals, and as many of them who entered after her, found a Guru as well.

Olga was in the music-room when the crowd had congested the hall. People were introduced to her, and sank down into the nearest chairs. Mrs Antrobus took up her old place by the keyboard of the piano. Everybody seemed to be expecting something, and by degrees the import of their longing was borne in upon Olga. They waited, and waited and waited, much as she had waited for a cigarette the evening before. She looked at the piano, and there was a comfortable murmur from her audience. She looked at Lucia, who gave a great gasp, and said nothing at all. She was the only person present who was standing now except her hostess, and Mrs Weston's gardener, who had wheeled his mistress's chair into an admirable position for hearing. She was not too well pleased, but after all....

"Would you like me to sing?" she asked Lucia. "Yes? Ah, there's a copy of Siegfried. Do you play?"

Lucia could not smile any more than she was smiling already.

"Is it very diffy?" she asked. "Could I read it, Georgie? Shall I try?"

She slid onto the music-stool.

"Me to begin?" she asked, finding that Olga had opened the book at the salutation of Brunnhilde, which Lucia had practised so diligently all the morning.

She got no answer. Olga standing by her, had assumed a perfectly different aspect. For her gaiety, her lightness was substituted some air of intense concentrated seriousness which Lucia did not understand at all. She was looking straight in front of her, gathering herself in, and paying not the smallest attention to Lucia or anybody else.

"One, two," said Lucia. "Three. Now," and she plunged wildly into a sea of demi-semi-quavers. Olga had just opened her mouth, but shut it again.

"No," she said. "Once more," and she whistled the motif.

"Oh! it's so diffy!" said Lucia beginning again. "Georgie! Turn over!"

Georgie turned over, and Lucia counting audibly to herself made an incomparable mess all over the piano.

Olga turned to her accompanist.

"Shall I try?" she said.

She sat down at the piano, and made some sort of sketch of the accompaniment, simplifying, and yet retaining the essence. And then she sang.

Chapter EIGHT

Throughout August, Guruism reigned supreme over the cultured life of Riseholme, and the priestess and dispenser of its mysteries was Lucia. Never before had she ruled from so elate a pinnacle, nor wielded so secure a supremacy. None had access to the Guru but through her: all his classes were held in the smoking-parlour and he meditated only in Hamlet or in the sequestered arbour at the end of the laburnum walk. Once he had meditated on the village green, but Lucia did not approve of that and had led him, still rapt, home by the hand.

The classes had swelled prodigiously, for practically all Riseholmites now were at some stage of instruction, with the exception of Hermy and Ursy, who pronounced the whole thing "piffle," and, as gentle chaff for Georgie, sometimes stood on one leg in the middle of the lawn and held their breath. Then Hermy would say One, Two, Three, and they shouted "Om" at the tops of their discordant voices. Now that the Guru was practically interned in The Hurst, they had actually never set eyes on him, for they had not chosen to come to the Hightum garden-party, preferring to have a second round of golf, and meeting Lucia next day had been distinctly irreverent on the subject of Eastern philosophy. Since then she had not been aware of their existence.

Lucia now received special instruction from the Guru in a class all by herself so prodigious was her advance in Yoga, for she could hold her breath much longer than anybody else, and had mastered six postures, while the next class which she attended also consisted of the other original members, namely Daisy Quantock, Georgie and Peppino. They had got on very well, too, but Lucia had quite shot away from them, and now if the Guru had other urgent spiritual claims on him, she gave instruction to a less advanced class herself. For this purpose she habited herself in a peculiarly becoming dress of white linen, which reached to her feet and had full flowing sleeves like a surplice. It was girdled with a silver cord with long tassels, and had mother-of-pearl buttons and a hood at the back lined with white satin which came over her head. Below its hem as she sat and taught in a really rather advanced posture showed the toes of her white morocco slippers, and she called it her "Teacher's Robe." The class which she taught consisted of Colonel Boucher, Piggy Antrobus and Mrs Weston: sometimes the Colonel brought his bull-dogs with him, who lay and snorted precisely as if they were doing breathing exercises, too. A general air of joyful mystery and spiritual endeavour blew balmily round them all, and without any doubt the exercises and the deep breathing were extremely good for them.

One evening, towards the end of the month, Georgie was sitting in his garden, for the half hour before dressing-time, thinking how busy he was, and yet how extraordinarily young and fresh he felt. Usually this month when Hermy and Ursy were with him was very fatiguing, and in ordinary years he would have driven away with Foljambe and Dicky on the day after their departure, and had a quiet week by the seaside. But now, though his sisters were going away tomorrow morning, he had no intention of taking a well-earned rest, in spite of the fact that not only had he been their host all this time, but had done an amazing quantity of other things as well. There had been the daily classes to begin with, which entailed much work in the way of meditation and exercises, as well as the actual learning, and also he had had another job which might easily have taxed his energies to the utmost any other year. For Olga Bracely had definitely bought that house without which she had felt that life was not worth living, and Georgie all this month had at her request been exercising a semi-independent supervision over its decoration and furnishing. She had ordered the general scheme herself and had sent down from London the greater part of the furniture, but Georgie was commissioned to report on any likely pieces of old stuff that he could find, and if expedition was necessary to act on his own responsibility and buy them. But above all secrecy was still necessary till the house was so complete that her Georgie might be told, and by the end of the month Riseholme generally was in a state of prostration following on the violent and feverish curiosity as to who had taken the house. Georgie had gone so far as to confess that he knew, but the most pathetic appeals as to the owner's identity had fallen on obdurate, if not deaf, ears. Not the smallest hint would he give on the subject, and though those incessant visits to the house, those searchings for furniture, the bestowal of it in suitable places, the superintendence of the making of the garden, the interviewings of paperhangers, plumbers, upholsterers, painters, carpenters and so forth occupied a great deal of time, the delicious mystery about it all, and the fact that he was doing it for so adorable a creature, rendered his exertions a positive refreshment. Another thing which, in conjunction with this and his youth-giving studies, made him feel younger than ever was the discreet arrival and perfect success of his toupet. No longer was there any need to fear the dislocation of his espaliered locks. He felt so secure and undetectable in that regard that he had taken to wearing no hat, and was soon about to say that his hair was growing more thickly than ever in consequence. But it was not quite time for that yet: it would be inartistic to suggest that just a couple of weeks of hatlessness had produced so desirable a result.

As he sat at ease after the labours of the day he wondered how the coming of Olga Bracely to Riseholme would affect the economy of the place. It was impossible to think of her with her beauty, her charm, her fame, her personality as taking any second place in its life. Unless she was really meaning to use Riseholme as a retreat, to take no part in its life at all, it was hard to see what part she would take except the first part. One who by her arrival at Lucia's ever-memorable party had converted it in a moment from the most dire of Scrubs (in a psychical sense) to the Hightumest gathering ever known could not lay aside her distinction and pre-eminence. Never had Lucia "scored" so amazingly as over Olga's late appearance, which had the effect of bringing back all her departed guests with the compulsion of a magnet over iron-filings, and sending up the whole party like a rocket into the zenith of social success. All Riseholme knew that Olga had come (after playing croquet with Georgie the entire afternoon) and had given them free gratis and for nothing, such a treat as only the wealthiest could obtain with the most staggering fees. Lady Ambermere alone, driving back to The Hall with Pug and poor Miss Lyall, was the only person who had not shared in that, and she knew all about it next day, for Georgie had driven out on purpose to tell her, and met Lucia coming away. How, then, would the advent of Olga affect Riseholme's social working generally, and how would it affect Lucia in particular? And what would Lucia say when she knew on whose behalf Georgie was so busy with plumbers and painters, and with buying so many of the desirable treasures in the Ambermere Arms?

Frankly he could not answer these conundrums: they presupposed inconceivable situations, which yet, though inconceivable, were shortly coming to pass, for Olga's advent might be expected before October, that season of tea-parties that ushered in the multifarious gaieties of the winter. Would Olga form part of the moonlit circle to whom Lucia played the first movement of the Moonlight Sonata, and give a long sigh at the end like the rest of them? And would Lucia when they had all recovered a little from the invariable emotion go to her and say, "Olga mia, just a little bit out of the Valkyrie? It would be so pleasant." Somehow Georgie, with all his imagination, could not picture such a scene. And would Olga take the part of second citizenness or something of the sort when Lucia played Portia? Would Olga join the elementary class of Yoga, and be instructed by Lucia in her Teacher's Robe? Would she sing treble in the Christmas Carols, while Lucia beat time, and said in syllables dictated by the rhythm, "Trebles a little flat! My poor ears!"? Georgie could not imagine any of these things, and yet, unless Olga took no part in the social life of Riseholme at all (and that was equally inconceivable) what was the alternative? True, she had said that she was coming here because it was so ideally lazy a backwater, but Georgie did not take that seriously. She would soon see what Riseholme was when its life poured down in spate, whirling her punt along with it.

And finally, what would happen to him, when Olga was set as a shining star in this firmament? Already he revolved about her, he was aware, like some eager delighted little moon, drawn away from the orbit where it had encircled so contentedly by the more potent planet. And the measure of his detachment from that old orbit might be judged precisely by the fact that the process of detachment which was already taking place was marked by no sense of the pull of opposing forces at all. The great new star sailing into the heavens had just picked him up by force of its superior power of attraction, even as by its momentary conjunction with Lucia at the garden-party it had raised her to a magnitude she had never possessed before. That magnitude was still Lucia's, and no doubt would be until the great star appeared again. Then without effort its shining must surely eclipse every other illumination, just as without effort it must surely attract all the little moons to itself. Or would Lucia manage somehow or other, either by sheer force of will, by desperate and hostile endeavour, or, on the other hand, by some supreme tact and cleverness to harness the great star to her own chariot? He thought the desperate and hostile endeavour was more in keeping with Lucia's methods, and this quiet evening hour represented itself to him as the lull before the storm.

The actual quiet of the moment was suddenly broken into. His front-door banged, and the house was filled with running footsteps and screams of laughter. But it was not uncommon for Hermy and Ursy to make this sort of entrance, and at the moment Georgie had not the slightest idea of how much further-reaching was the disturbance of the tranquillity. He but drew a couple of long breaths, said "Om" once or twice, and was quite prepared to find his deeper calm unshattered.

Hermy and Ursy ran down the steps into the garden where he sat still yelling with laughter, and still Georgie's imagination went no further than to suppose that one of them had laid a stymie for the other at their golf, or driven a ball out of bounds or done some other of these things that appeared to make the game so diverting to them.

"Georgie, you'll never guess!" cried Hermy.

"The Guru: the Om, of high caste and extraordinary sanctity," cried
Ursy.
"The Brahmin from Benares," shrieked Hermy.

"The great Teacher! Who do you think he is?" said Ursy. "We never seen him before—"

"But we recognised him at once—"

"He recognised us, too, and didn't he run?—"

"Into The Hurst and shut the door—"

Georgie's deeper calm suddenly quivered like a jelly.

"My dears, you needn't howl so, or talk quite so loud," he said. "All Riseholme will hear you. Tell me without shouting who it was you thought you recognised."

"There's no think about it," said Hermy. "It was one of the cooks from the Calcutta Restaurant in Bedford Street—"

"Where we often have lunch," said Ursy. "He makes the most delicious curries."

"Especially when he's a little tipsy," said Hermy.

"And is about as much a Brahmin as I am."

"And always said he came from Madras."

"We always tip him to make the curry himself, so he isn't quite ignorant about money."

"O Lord!" said Hermy, wiping her eyes. "If it isn't the limit!"

"And to think of Mrs Lucas and Colonel Boucher and you and Mrs Quantock, and Piggy and all the rest of them sitting round a cook," said Ursy, "and drinking in his wisdom. Mr Quantock was on the right track after all when he wanted to engage him."

Georgie with a fallen heart had first to satisfy himself that this was not one of his sisters' jokes, and then tried to raise his fallen heart by remembering that the Guru had often spoken of the dignity of simple manual work, but somehow it was a blow, if Hermy and Ursy were right, to know that this was a tipsy contriver of curry. There was nothing in the simple manual office of curry-making that could possibly tarnish sanctity, but the amazing tissue of falsehoods with which the Guru had modestly masked his innocent calling was not so markedly in the spirit of the Guides, as retailed by him. It was of the first importance, however, to be assured that his sisters had not at present communicated their upsetting discovery to anybody but himself, and after that to get their promise that they would not do so.

This was not quite so easy, for Hermy and Ursy had projected a round of visits after dinner to every member of the classes with the exception of Lucia, who should wake up next morning to find herself the only illusioned person in the place.

"She wouldn't like that, you know," said Hermy with brisk malice. "We thought it would serve her out for never asking us to her house again after her foolish old garden-party."

"My dear, you never wanted to go," said Georgie.

"I know we didn't, but we rather wanted to tell her we didn't want to go. She wasn't nice. Oh, I don't think we can give up telling everybody. It has made such sillies of you all. I think he's a real sport."

"So do I," said Ursy. "We shall soon have him back at his curry-oven again. What a laugh we shall have with him."

They subsided for just as long as it took Foljambe to come out of the house, inform them that it was a quarter of an hour to dinner-time, and return again. They all rose obediently.

"Well, we'll talk about it at dinner-time," said Georgie diplomatically. "And I'll just go down to the cellar first to see if I can find something you like."

"Good old Georgie," said Hermy. "But if you're going to bribe us, you must bribe us well."

"We'll see," said he.

Georgie was quite right to be careful over his Veuve Clicquot, especially since it was a bottle of that admirable beverage that Hermy and Ursy had looted from his cellar on the night of their burglarious entry. He remembered that well, though he had—chiefly from the desire to keep things pleasant about his hair—joined in "the fun," and had even produced another half-bottle. But tonight, even more than then, there was need for the abolition of all petty economies, for the situation would be absolutely intolerable if Hermy and Ursy spread about Riseholme the fact that the introducers and innermost circle of Yoga philosophers had sat at the feet of no Gamaliel at all, but at those of a curry-cook from some low restaurant. Indeed he brought up a second bottle tonight with a view if Hermy and Ursy were not softened by the first to administer that also. They would then hardly be in a condition to be taken seriously if they still insisted on making a house-to-house visit in Riseholme, and tearing the veil from off the features of the Guru. Georgie was far too upright of purpose to dream of making his sisters drunk, but he was willing to make great sacrifices in order to render them kind. What the inner circle would do about this cook he had no idea; he must talk to Lucia about it, before the advanced class tomorrow morning. But anything was better than letting Hermy and Ursy loose in Riseholme with their rude laughs and discreditable exposures. This evening safely over, he could discuss with Lucia what was to be done, for Hermy and Ursy would have vanished at cock-crow as they were going in for some golf-competition at a safe distance. Lucia might recommend doing nothing at all, and wish to continue enlightening studies as if nothing had happened. But Georgie felt that the romance would have evaporated from the classes as regards himself. Or again they might have to get rid of the Guru somehow. He only felt quite sure that Lucia would agree with him that Daisy Quantock must not be told. She with her thwarted ambitions of being the prime dispenser of Guruism to Riseholme might easily "turn nasty" and let it be widely known that she and Robert had seen through that fraud long ago, and had considered whether they should not offer the Guru the situation of cook in their household, for which he was so much better qualified. She might even add that his leanings towards her pretty housemaid had alone dissuaded her.

The evening went off with a success more brilliant than Georgie had anticipated, and it was quite unnecessary to open the second bottle of champagne. Hermy and Ursy, perhaps under the influence of the first, perhaps from innate good-nature, perhaps because they were starting so very early next morning, and wanted to be driven into Brinton, instead of taking a slower and earlier train at this station, readily gave up their project of informing the whole of Riseholme of their discovery, and went to bed as soon as they had rooked their brother of eleven shillings at cut-throat bridge. They continued to say, "I'll play the Guru," whenever they had to play a knave, but Georgie found it quite easy to laugh at that, so long as the humour of it did not spread. He even himself said, "I'll Guru you, then," when he took a trick with the Knave of Trumps.

The agitation and uncertainty caused him not to sleep very well, and in addition there was a good deal of disturbance in the house, for his sisters had still all their packing in front of them when they went to bed and the doze that preceded sleep was often broken by the sound of the banging of luggage, the clash of golf-clubs and steps on the stairs as they made ready for their departure.

But after a while these disturbances ceased, and it was out of a deep sleep that he awoke with the sense that some noise had awakened him. Apparently they had not finished yet, for there was surely some faint stir of movement somewhere. Anyhow they respected his legitimate desire for quiet, for the noise, whatever it was, was extremely stealthy and subdued. He thought of his absurd lark about burglars on the night of their arrival, and smiled at the notion. His toupet was in a drawer close to his bed, but he had no substantial impulse to put it on, and make sure that the noise was not anything other than his sisters' preparations for their early start. For himself, he would have had everything packed and corded long before dinner, if he was to start next day, except just a suit case that would hold the apparatus of immediate necessities, but then dear Hermy and Ursy were so ramshackle in their ways. Some time he would have bells put on all the shutters as he had determined to do a month ago, and then no sort of noise would disturb him any more....

The Yoga-class next morning was (unusually) to assemble at ten, since Peppino, who would not miss it for anything, was going to have a day's fishing in the happy stream that flowed into the Avon, and he wanted to be off by eleven. Peppino had made great progress lately and had certain curious dizzy symptoms when he meditated which were highly satisfactory.

Georgie breakfasted with his sisters at eight (they had enticed the motor out of him to convey them to Brinton) and when they were gone, Foljambe informed him that the housemaid had a sore throat, and had not "done" the drawing-room. Foljambe herself would "do" it, when she had cleaned the "young ladies'" rooms (there was a hint of scorn in this) upstairs, and so Georgie sat on the window seat of the dining-room, and thought how pleasant peace and quietness were. But just when it was time to start for The Hurst in order to talk over the disclosures of the night before with Lucia before the class, and perhaps to frame some secretive policy which would obviate further exposure, he remembered that he had left his cigarette-case (the pretty straw one with the turquoise in the corner) in the drawing-room and went to find it. The window was open, and apparently Foljambe had just come in to let fresh air into the atmosphere which Hermy and Ursy had so uninterruptedly contaminated last night with their "fags" as they called them, but his cigarette-case was not on the table where he thought he had left it. He looked round, and then stood rooted to the spot.

His glass-case of treasures was not only open but empty. Gone was the Louis XVI snuff-box, gone was the miniature of Karl Huth, gone the piece of Bow China, and gone the Faberge cigarette case. Only the Queen Anne toy-porringer was there, and in the absence of the others, it looked to him, as no doubt it had looked to the burglar, indescribably insignificant.

Georgie gave a little low wailing cry, but did not tear his hair for obvious reasons. Then he rang the bell three times in swift succession, which was the signal to Foljambe that even if she was in her bath, she must come at once. In she came with one of Hermy's horrid woolen jerseys that had been left behind, in her hand.

"Yes, sir, what is it?" she asked, in an agitated manner, for never could she remember Georgie having rung the bell three times except once when a fish-bone had stuck in his throat, and once again when a note had announced to him that Piggy was going to call and hoped to find him alone. For answer Georgie pointed to the rifled treasure-case. "Gone! Burgled!" he said. "Oh, my God!"

At that supreme moment the telephone bell sounded.

"See what it is," he said to Foljambe, and put the Queen Anne toy-porringer in his pocket.

She came hurrying back.

"Mrs Lucas wants you to come around at once," she said.

68

"I can't," said Georgie. "I must stop here and send for the police. Nothing must be moved," and he hastily replaced the toy-porringer on the exact circle of pressed velvet where it had stood before.

"Yes, sir," said Foljambe, but in another moment she returned.

"She would be very much obliged if you would come at once," she said.
"There's been a robbery in the house."
"Well, tell her there's been one in mine," said Georgie irritably. Then good-nature mixed with furious curiosity came to his aid.

"Wait here, then, Foljambe, on this very spot," he said, "and see that nobody touches anything. I shall probably ring up the police from The Hurst. Admit them."

In his agitation he put on his hat, instead of going bareheaded and was received by Lucia, who had clearly been looking out of the music-room window, at the door. She wore her Teacher's Robe.

"Georgie," she said, quite forgetting to speak Italian in her greeting, "someone broke into Philip's safe last night, and took a hundred pounds in bank-notes. He had put them there only yesterday in order to pay in cash for that cob. And my Roman pearls."

Georgie felt a certain pride of achievement.

"I've been burgled, too," he said. "My Louis XVI snuff-box is worth more than that, and there's the piece of Bow china, and the cigarette-case, and the Karl Huth as well."

"My dear! Come inside," said she. "It's a gang. And I was feeling so peaceful and exalted. It will make a terrible atmosphere in the house. My Guru will be profoundly affected. An atmosphere where thieves have been will stifle him. He has often told me how he cannot stop in a house where there have been wicked emotions at play. I must keep it from him. I cannot lose him."

Lucia had sunk down on a spacious Elizabethan settle in the hall. The humorous spider mocked them from the window, the humorous stone fruit from the plate beside the pot-pourri bowl. Even as she repeated, "I cannot lose him," again, a tremendous rap came on the front door, and Georgie, at a sign from his queen, admitted Mrs Quantock.

"Robert and I have been burgled," she said. "Four silver spoons—thank God, most of our things are plate—eight silver forks and a Georgian tankard. I could have spared all but the last."

A faint sign of relief escaped Lucia. If the foul atmosphere of thieves permeated Daisy's house, too, there was no great danger that her Guru would go back there. She instantly became sublime.

"Peace!" she said. "Let us have our class first, for it is ten already, and not let any thought of revenge or evil spoil that for us. If I sent for the police now I could not concentrate. I will not tell my Guru what has happened to any of us, but for poor Peppino's sake I will ask him to give us rather a short lesson. I feel completely calm. Om."

Vague nightmare images began to take shape in Georgie's mind, unworthy suspicions based on his sisters' information the evening before. But with Foljambe keeping guard over the Queen Anne porringer, there was nothing more to fear, and he followed Lucia, her silver cord with tassels gently swinging as she moved, to the smoking-parlour, where Peppino was already sitting on the floor, and breathing in a rather more agitated manner than was usual with the advanced class. There were fresh flowers on the table, and the scented morning breeze blew in from the garden. According to custom they all sat down and waited, getting calmer and more peaceful every moment. Soon there would be the tapping of slippered heels on the walk of broken paving-stones outside, and for the time they would forget all these disturbances. But they were all rather glad that Lucia was to ask the Guru to give them a shorter lesson than usual.

They waited. Presently the hands of the Cromwellian timepiece which was the nearest approach to an Elizabethan clock that Lucia had been able at present to obtain, pointed to a quarter past ten.

"My Guru is a little late," said she.

Two minutes afterwards, Peppino sneezed. Two minutes after that Daisy spoke, using irony.

"Would it not be well to see what has happened to your Guru, dear?" she asked. "Have you seen your Guru this morning?"

"No, dear," said Lucia, not opening her eyes, for she was "concentrating," "he always meditates before a class."

"So do I," said Daisy, "but I have meditated long enough."

"Hush!" said Lucia. "He is coming."

That proved to be a false alarm, for it was nothing but Lucia's Persian cat, who had a quarrel with some dead laurel leaves. Lucia rose.

"I don't like to interrupt him," she said, "but time is getting on."

She left the smoking-parlour with the slow supple walk that she adopted when she wore her Teacher's Robes. Before many seconds had passed, she came back more quickly and with no suppleness.

"His door is locked", she said; "and yet there's no key in it."

"Did you look through the keyhole, Lucia mia?" asked Mrs Quantock, with irrepressible irony.
Naturally Lucia disregarded this.

"I knocked," she said, "and there was no reply. I said, 'Master, we are waiting,' and he didn't answer."

Suddenly Georgie spoke, as with the report of a cork flying out of a bottle.

"My sisters told me last night that he was the curry-cook at the Calcutta restaurant," he said. "They recognised him, and they thought

70

he recognised them. He comes from Madras, and is no more a Brahmin than Foljambe."

Peppino bounded to his feet.

"What?" he said. "Let's get a poker and break in the door! I believe he's gone and I believe he's the burglar. Ring for the police."

"Curry-cook, is he?" said Daisy. "Robert and I were right after all. We knew what your Guru was best fitted for, dear Lucia, but then of course you always know best, and you and he have been fooling us finely. But you didn't fool me. I knew when you took him away from me, what sort of a bargain you had made. Guru, indeed! He's the same class as Mrs Eddy, and I saw through her fast enough. And now what are we to do? For my part, I shall just get home, and ring up for the police, and say that the Indian who has been living with you all these weeks has stolen my spoons and forks and my Georgian tankard. Guru, indeed! Burglaroo, I call him! There!"

Her passion, like Hyperion's, had lifted her upon her feet, and she stood there defying the whole of the advanced class, short and stout and wholly ridiculous, but with some revolutionary menace about her. She was not exactly "terrible as an army with banners," but she was terrible as an elderly lady with a long-standing grievance that had been accentuated by the loss of a Georgian tankard, and that was terrible enough to make Lucia adopt a conciliatory attitude. Bitterly she repented having stolen Daisy's Guru at all, if the suspicions now thickening in the air proved to be true, but after all they were not proved yet. The Guru might still walk in from the arbor on the laburnum alley which they had not yet searched, or he might be levitating with the door key in his pocket. It was not probable but it was possible, and at this crisis possibilities were things that must be clung to, for otherwise you would simply have to submerge, like those U-boats.

They searched all the garden, but found no trace of the curry-cook: they made guarded enquiries of the servants as to whether he had been seen, but nothing whatever could be learned about him. So when Peppino took a ponderous hammer and a stout chisel from his tool chest and led the way upstairs, they all knew that the decisive moment had come. Perhaps he might be meditating (for indeed it was likely that he had a good deal to meditate about), but perhaps—Peppino called to him in his most sonorous tones, and said that he would be obliged to break his lock if no answer came, and presently the house resounded with knockings as terrible as those in Macbeth, and much louder. Then suddenly the lock gave, and the door was open.

The room was empty, and as they had all conjectured by now, the bed was unslept in. They opened the drawers of the wardrobe and they were as empty as the room. Finally, Peppino unlocked the door of a large cupboard that stood in the corner, and with a clinking and crashing of glass there poured out a cataract of empty brandy bottles. Emptiness: that was the key-note of the whole scene, and blank consternation its effect.

"My brandy!" said Mrs Quantock in a strangled voice. "There are fourteen or fifteen bottles. That accounts for the glazed look in his eyes which you, dear Lucia, thought was concentration. I call it distillation."

"Did he take it from your cellar?" asked Lucia, too shattered to feel resentment, but still capable of intense curiosity.

"No: he had a standing order from me to order any little things he might want from my tradesmen. I wish I had my bills sent in every week."

"Yes, dear," said Lucia.

Georgie's eyes sought hers.

"I saw him buy the first bottle," he said. "I remember telling you about it. It was at Rush's."

Peppino gathered up his hammer and chisel.

"Well, it's no use sitting here and thinking of old times," he observed. "I shall ring up the police-station and put the whole matter into their hands, as far as I am concerned. They'll soon lay hands on him, and he can do his postures in prison for the next few years."

"But we don't know that it was he who committed all these burglaries yet," said Lucia.

No one felt it was worth answering this, for the others had all tried and convicted him already.

"I shall do the same," said Georgie.

"My tankard," said Mrs Quantock. Lucia got up.

"Peppino mio," she said, "and you, Georgie, and you, Daisy, I want you before you do anything at all to listen to me for five minutes. Just consider this. What sort of figure shall we all cut if we put the matter into the hands of the police? They will probably catch him, and it will all come out that we have been the dupes of a curry-cook. Think what we have all been doing for this last month, think of our classes, our exercises, our—everything. We have been made fools of, but for my part, I simply couldn't bear that everybody should know I had been made a fool of. Anything but that. What's a hundred pounds compared to that, or a tankard—"

"My Louis XVI snuff-box was worth at least that without the other things," said Georgie, still with a secret satisfaction in being the greatest sufferer.

"And it was my hundred pounds, not yours, carissima," said Peppino. But it was clear that Lucia's words were working within him like leaven.

"I'll go halves with you," she said. "I'll give you a cheque for fifty pounds."

"And who would like to go halves in my tankard?" said Daisy with bitter irony. "I want my tankard."

Georgie said nothing, but his mind was extremely busy. There was Olga soon coming to Riseholme, and it would be awful if she found it ringing with the tale of the Guru, and glancing across to Peppino, he saw a thoughtful and sympathetic look in his eyes, that seemed to indicate that his mind was working on parallel lines. Certainly Lucia had given them all something to meditate upon. He tried to imagine the whole story being shouted into Mrs Antrobus's ear-trumpet on the village-green, and could not endure the idea. He tried to imagine Mrs Weston ever ceasing to talk about it, and could not picture her silence. No doubt they had all been taken in, too, but here in this empty bedroom were the original dupes, who encouraged the rest.

72

After Mrs Quantock's enquiry a dead silence fell.

"What do you propose, then?" asked Peppino, showing signs of surrender.

Lucia exerted her utmost wiles.

"Caro!" she said. "I want 'oo to propose. Daisy and me, we silly women, we want 'oo and Georgie to tell us what to do. But if Lucia must speak, I fink—"

She paused a moment, and observing strong disgust at her playfulness on Mrs Quantock's face, reverted to ordinary English again.
"I should do something of this sort," she said. "I should say that dear Daisy's Guru had left us quite suddenly, and that he has had a call somewhere else. His work here was done; he had established our classes, and set all our feet upon the Way. He always said that something of the sort might happen to him——"

"I believe he had planned it all along," said Georgie. "He knew the thing couldn't last for ever, and when my sisters recognised him, he concluded it was time to bolt."

"With all the available property he could lay hands on," said Mrs Quantock.
Lucia fingered her tassel.

"Now about the burglaries," she said. "It won't do to let it be known that three burglaries were committed in one night, and that simultaneously Daisy's Guru was called away—"

"My Guru, indeed!" said Mrs Quantock, fizzing with indignation at the repetition of this insult.

"That might give rise to suspicion," continued Lucia calmly, disregarding the interruption, "and we must stop the news from spreading. Now with regard to our burglary ... let me think a moment."

She had got such complete control of them all now that no one spoke.

"I have it," she said. "Only Boaler knows, for Peppino told her not to say a word till the police had been sent for. You must tell her, carissimo, that you have found the hundred pounds. That settles that. Now you, Georgie."

"Foljambe knows," said Georgie.

"Then tell her not to say a word about it. Put some more things out in your lovely treasure-case, no one will notice. And you, Daisy."

"Robert is away," said she, quite meekly, for she had been thinking things over. "My maid knows."

"And when he comes back, will he notice the loss of the tankard? Did you often use it?"

"About once in ten years."

"Chance it, then," said Lucia. "Just tell your maid to say nothing about it."

She became deliciously modest again.

"There!" she said. "That's just a little rough idea of mine and now Peppino and Georgie will put their wise heads together, and tell us what to do."

That was easily done: they repeated what she had said, and she corrected them if they went wrong. Then once again she stood fingering the tassels of her Teacher's Robe.

"About our studies," she said. "I for one should be very sorry to drop them altogether, because they made such a wonderful difference to me, and I think you all felt the same. Look at Georgie now: he looks ten years younger than he did a month ago, and as for Daisy, I wish I could trip about as she does. And it wouldn't do, would it, to drop everything just because Daisy's Guru—I mean our Guru—had been called away. It would look as if we weren't really interested in what he taught us, as if it was only the novelty of having a—a Brahmin among us that had attracted us."

Lucia smiled benignly at them all.

"Perhaps we shall find, bye and bye, that we can't progress much all by ourselves," she said, "and it will all drop quietly. But don't let us drop it with a bang. I shall certainly take my elementary class as usual this afternoon."

She paused.

"In my Robe, just as usual," she said.

Chapter NINE

The fish for which Mrs Weston sent to Brinton every week since she did not like the look of the successor to Tommy Luton's mother lay disregarded on the dish, while with fork and fish-slice in her hand, as aids to gesticulation, she was recounting to Colonel Boucher the complete steps that had led up to her remarkable discovery.

"It was the day of Mrs Lucas's garden-party," she said, "when first I began to have my ideas, and you may be sure I kept them to myself, for I'm not one to speak before I'm pretty sure, but now if the King and Queen came to me on their bended knee and said it wasn't so, I shouldn't believe them. Well—as you may remember, we all went back to Mrs Lucas's party again about half-past six, and it was an umbrella that one had left behind, and a stick that another had forgotten, and what not, for me it was a book all about Venice, that I wanted to borrow, most interesting I am sure, but I haven't had time to glance at it yet, and there was Miss Bracely just come!"

Mrs Weston had to pause a moment for her maid, Elizabeth Luton (cousin of Tommy), jogged her elbow with the dishcover in a manner that could not fail to remind her that Colonel Boucher was still waiting for his piece of brill. As she carved it for him, he rapidly ran over in his mind what seemed to be the main points so far, for as yet there was no certain clue as to the purpose of this preliminary matter, he guessed either Guru or Miss Bracely. Then he received his piece of brill, and Mrs Weston laid down her carving implements again.

"You'd better help yourself, ma'am," said Elizabeth discreetly.

"So I had, and I'll give you a piece of advice too, Elizabeth, and that is to give the Colonel a glass of wine. Burgundy! I was only wondering this afternoon when it began to turn chilly, if there was a bottle or two of the old Burgundy left, which Mr Weston used to be so fond of, and there was. He bought it on the very spot where it was made, and he said there wasn't a headache in it, not if you drank it all night. He never did, for a couple of glasses and one more was all he ever took, so I don't know how he knew about drinking it all night, but he was a very fine judge of wine. So I said to Elizabeth, 'A bottle of the old Burgundy, Elizabeth,' Well, on that evening I stopped behind a bit, to have another look at the Guru, and get my book, and when I came up the street again, what should I see but Miss Bracely walking in to the little front garden at 'Old Place.' It was getting dark, I know, and my eyes aren't like Mrs Antrobus's, which I call gimlets, but I saw her plain enough. And if it wasn't the next day, it was the day after that, that they began mending the roof, and since then, there have been plumbers and painters and upholsterers and furniture vans at the door day and night."

"Haw, hum," said the Colonel, "then do you mean that it's Miss Bracely who has taken it?"

Mrs Weston nodded her head up and down.

"I shall ask you what you think when I've told you all," she said. "Well! There came a day, and if today's Friday it would be last Tuesday fortnight, and if today's Thursday, for I get mixed about it this morning, and then I never get it straight till next Sunday, but if today's Thursday, then it would be last Monday fortnight, when the Guru went away very suddenly, and I'm sure I wasn't very sorry, because those breathings made me feel very giddy and yet I didn't like to be out of it all. Mr Georgie's sisters went away the same day, and I've often wondered whether there was any connection between the two events, for it was odd their happening together like that, and I'm not sure we've heard the last of it yet."

Colonel Boucher began to wonder whether this was going to be about the Guru after all and helped himself to half a partridge. This had the effect of diverting Mrs Weston's attention.

"No," she said. "I insist on your taking the whole bird. They are quite small, and I was disappointed when I saw them plucked, and a bit of cold ham and a savoury is all the rest of your dinner. Mary asked me if I wouldn't have an apple tart as well, but I said 'No; the Colonel never touches sweets, but he'll have a partridge, a whole partridge,' I said, 'and he won't complain of his dinner.' Well! On the day that they all went away, whatever the explanation of that was, I was sitting in my chair opposite the Arms, when out came the landlord followed by two men carrying the settle that stood on the right of the fireplace in the hall. So I said, 'Well, landlord, who has ordered that handsome piece?' For handsome it was with its carved arms. And he said, 'Good morning, ma'am no, good afternoon ma'am, it would be—It's for Miss—and then he stopped dead and corrected himself, 'It's for Mr Pillson.'"

Mrs Weston rapidly took a great quantity of mouthfuls of partridge. As soon as possible she went on.

"So perhaps you can tell me where it is now, if it was for Mr Georgie," she said. "I was there only two days ago, and it wasn't in his hall, or in his dining room, or in his drawing room, for though there are changes there, that settle isn't one of them. It's his treasure case that's so altered. The snuff-box is gone, and the cigarette case and the piece of Bow china, and instead there's a rat-tail spoon which he used to have on his dinner-table, and made a great fuss with, and a bit of Worcester china that used to stand on the mantelpiece, and a different cigarette case, and a bead-bag. I don't know where that came from, but if he inherited it, he didn't inherit much that time, I priced it at five shillings. But there's no settle in the treasure-case or out of it, and if you want to know where that settle is, it's in Old Place, because I saw it there myself, when the door was open, as I passed. He bought it—Mr Georgie—on behalf of Miss Bracely, unless you suppose that Mr Georgie is going to live in Old Place one day and his own house the next. No; it's Miss Bracely who is going to live at 'Old Place' and that explains the landlord saying 'Miss' and then stopping. For some reason, and I daresay that won't puzzle me long, now I can give my mind to it, she's making a secret about it, and only Mr Georgie and the landlord of the Arms know. Of course he had to, for 'Old Place' is his, and I wish I had bought it myself now, for he got it for an old song."

"Well, by Jove, you have pieced it together finely," said Colonel Boucher.

"Wait a bit," said Mrs Weston, rising to her climax. "This very day, when Mary, that's my cook as you know, was coming back from Brinton with that bit of brill we've been eating, for they hadn't got an ounce of turbot, which I wanted, a luggage-train was standing at Riseholme station, and they had just taken out of it a case that could have held nothing but a grand piano. And if that's not enough for you, Colonel, there were two big dress-baskets as well, which I think must have contained linen, for they were corded, and it took two men to move each of them, so Mary said, and there's nothing so heavy as linen properly packed, unless it's plate, and there printed on them in black—no, it would be white, because the dress-baskets are black, were two initials, O.B. And if you can point to another O.B. in Riseholme I shall think I've lost my memory."

At this moment of supreme climax, the telephone-bell rang in the hall, shrill through the noise of cracking walnuts, and in came Elizabeth with the news that Mr Georgie wanted to know if he might come in for half-an-hour and chat. If it had been Olga Bracely herself, she could hardly have been more welcome; virtue (the virtue of observation and inference) was receiving its immediate reward.

"Delighted; say I'm delighted, Elizabeth," said Mrs Weston, "and now, Colonel, why should you sit all alone here, and I all alone in the drawing room? Bring your decanter and your glass with you, and you shall spare me half a glass for myself, and if you can't guess what one of the questions that I shall ask Mr Georgie is: well——"

Georgie made haste to avail himself of this hospitality for he was bursting with the most important news that had been his since the night of the burglaries. Today he had received permission to let it be known that Olga was coming to Old Place, for Mr Shuttleworth had been informed of the purchase and furnishing of the house, and had, as expected, presented his wife with it, a really magnificent gift. So now Riseholme might know, too, and Georgie, as eager as Hermes, if not quite so swift, tripped across to Mrs Weston's, on his delightful errand. It was, too, of the nature of just such a punitive expedition as Georgie thoroughly enjoyed, for Lucia all this week had been rather haughty and cold with him for his firm refusal to tell her who the purchaser of Old Place was. He had admitted that he knew, but had said that he was under promise not to reveal that, until permitted and Lucia had been haughty in consequence. She had, in fact, been so haughty that when Georgie rang her up just now, before ringing Mrs Weston up, to ask if he might spend an hour after dinner there, fully intending to tell her the great news, she had replied through her parlour-maid that she was very busy at the piano. Very well, if she preferred the second and third movements of the Moonlight Sonata, which she had seriously taken in hand, to Georgie's company, why, he would offer himself and his great news elsewhere. But he determined not to bring it out at once; that sort of thing must be kept till he said it was time to go away. Then he would bring it out, and depart in the blaze of Success.

He had brought a pretty piece of embroidery with him to occupy himself with, for his work had fallen into sad arrears during August, and he settled himself comfortably down close to the light, so that at the cost of very little eye-strain, he need not put on his spectacles.

"Any news?" he asked, according to the invariable formula. Mrs Weston caught the Colonel's eye. She was not proposing to bring out her tremendous interrogation just yet.

"Poor Mrs Antrobus. Toothache!" she said. "I was in the chemist's this morning and who should come in but Miss Piggy, and she wanted a drop of laudanum and had to say what it was for, and even then she had to sign a paper. Very unpleasant, I call it, to be obliged to let a chemist know that your mother has a toothache. But there it was, tell him she had to, or go away without any laudanum. I don't know whether Mr Doubleday wasn't asking more than he should, just out of inquisitiveness, for I don't see what business it is of his. I know what I should have said: 'Oh, Mr Doubleday, I want it to make laudanum tartlets, we are all so fond of laudanum tartlets.' Something sharp and sarcastic like that, to show him his place. But I expect it did Mrs Antrobus good, for there she was on the green in the afternoon, and her face wasn't swollen for I had a good look at her. Oh, and there was something I wanted to ask you, Mr Georgie, and I had it on the tip of my tongue a moment ago. We talked about it at dinner, the Colonel and I, while we were eating our bit of partridge, and I thought 'Mr Georgie will be sure to be able to tell us,' and if you didn't ring up on the telephone immediately afterwards! That seemed just Providential, but what's the use of that, if I can't remember what it was that I wanted to ask you."

This seemed a good opening for his startling news, but Georgie rejected it, as it was too early yet. "I wonder what it could have been," he said.

"Well, it will come back to me presently, and here's our coffee, and I see Elizabeth hasn't forgotten to bring a drop of something good for you two gentlemen. And I don't say that I won't join you, if Elizabeth will bring another glass. What with a glass of Burgundy at my dinner, and a drop of brandy now, I shall be quite tipsy unless I take care. The Guru now, Mr Georgie, no, that's not what I wanted to ask you about—but has there been any news of the Guru?"

For a moment in this juxtaposition of the topics of brandy and Guru, Georgie was afraid that something might have leaked out about the contents of the cupboard in Othello. But it was evidently a chance combination, for Mrs Weston went straight on without waiting for an answer.

"What a day that was," she said, "when he and Miss Olga Bracely were both at Mrs Lucas' garden-party. Ah, now I've got it; now I know what I wanted to ask. When will Miss Olga Bracely come to live at Old Place? Quite soon now, I suppose."

If Georgie had not put down his embroidery with great expedition, he would undoubtedly have pricked his finger.

"But how on earth did you know she was coming at all?" he said. "I was just going to tell you that she was coming, as a great bit of news. How tarsome! It's spoiled all my pleasure."

"Haw, hum, not a very gallant speech, when you're talking to Mrs Weston," said the Colonel, who hated Georgie's embroidery.

Luckily the pleasure in the punitive part of the expedition remained and Georgie recovered himself. He had some news too; he could answer Mrs Weston's question.

"But it was to have been such a secret until the whole thing was ready," he said. "I knew all along; I have known since the day of the garden-party. No one but me, not even her husband."

He was well rewarded for the recovery of his temper. Mrs Weston put down her glass of something good untasted.

"What?" she said. "Is she going to live here alone in hiding from him?
Have they quarrelled so soon?"
Georgie had to disappoint her about this, and gave the authentic version.

"And she's coming next week, Monday probably," he said.

They were all now extremely happy, for Mrs Weston felt convinced that nobody else had put two and two together with the same brilliant result as herself, and Georgie was in the even superior position of having known the result without having to do any addition at all, and Colonel Boucher enjoyed the first fruits of it all. When they parted, having thoroughly discussed it, the chief preoccupation in the minds of all was the number of Riseholmites that each of them would be the first to pass on the news to, Mrs Weston could tell Elizabeth that night, and Colonel Boucher his bull-dogs, but the first blood was really drawn by Georgie, who seeing a light in Mrs Quantock's drawing room when he returned, dropped in for a moment and scored a right and left by telling Robert who let him in, before going upstairs, and Mrs Quantock when he got there. It was impossible to do any more that night.

Lucia was always very busy of a morning in polishing the sword and shield of Art, in order to present herself daily to her subjects in shining armour, and keep a little ahead of them all in culture, and thus did not as a rule take part in the parliament on the Green. Moreover Georgie usually dropped in before lunch, and her casual interrogation "Any news?" as they sat down to the piano, elicited from him, as in a neat little jug, the cream of the morning's milkings. Today she was attired in her Teacher's Robe, for the elementary class, though not always now in full conclave, gathered at her house on Tuesdays and Fridays. There had been signs of late that the interest of her pupils was on the wane, for Colonel Boucher had not appeared for two meetings, nor had Mrs Weston come to the last, but it was part of Lucia's policy to let Guruism die a natural death without herself facilitating its happy release, and she meant to be ready for her class at the appointed times as long as anybody turned up. Besides the Teacher's Robe was singularly becoming and she often wore it when there was no question of teaching at all.

But today, though she would not have been surprised at the complete absence of pupils, she was still in consultation with her cook over the commissariat of the day, when a succession of tinklings from the mermaid's tail, announced that a full meeting was assembling. Her maid in fact had announced to her without pause except to go to the door and back, though it still wanted a few minutes to eleven, that Colonel Boucher, Mrs Weston, Mrs Antrobus and Piggy were all assembled in the smoking-parlour. Even as she passed through the hall on her way 'there, Georgie came hurrying across Shakespeare's garden, his figure distorted through the wavy glass of the windows, and she opened the door to him herself.

"Georgino mio," she said, "oo not angry with Lucia for saying she was busy last night? And now I'm just going to take my Yoga-class. They all came rather early and I haven't seen any of them yet. Any news?"

Georgie heaved a sigh; all Riseholme knew by this time, and he was going to score one more by telling Lucia.

"My dear, haven't you heard yet?" he asked. "I was going to tell you last night."

"The tenant of Old Place?" asked Lucia unerringly.

"Yes. Guess!" said Georgie tantalizingly. This was his last revelation and he wanted to spin it out.

Lucia decided on a great stroke, involving risks but magnificent if it came off. In a flash she guessed why all the Yoga-class had come so super-punctually; each of them she felt convinced wanted to have the joy of telling her, after everybody else knew, who the new tenant was. On the top of this bitterness was the added acrimony of Georgie, whose clear duty it was to have informed her the moment he knew, wanting to make the same revelation to her, last of all Riseholme. She had already had her suspicions, for she had not forgotten the fact that Olga Bracely and Georgie had played croquet all afternoon when they should have been at her garden-party, and she determined to risk all for the sake of spoiling Georgie's pleasure in telling her. She gave her silvery laugh, that started, so she had ascertained, on A flat above the treble clef.

"Georgino, did all my questions as to who it was really take you in?" she asked. "Just as if I hadn't known all along! Why, Miss Olga Bracely, of course!"

Georgie's fallen face shewed her how completely she had spoiled his pleasure.

"Who told you?" he asked.

She rattled her tassels.

"Little bird!" she said. "I must run away to my class, or they will scold me."

Once again before they settled down to high philosophies, Lucia had the pleasure of disappointing the ambitions of her class to surprise, inform and astonish her.

"Good morning to you all," she said, "and before we settle down I'll give you a little bit of news now that at last I'm allowed to. Dear Miss Olga Bracely, whom I think you all met here, is coming to live at Old Place. Will she not be a great addition to our musical parties? Now, please."

But this splendid bravado was but a scintillation, on a hard and highly polished surface, and had Georgie been able to penetrate into Lucia's heart he would have found complete healing for his recent severe mortification. He did not really believe that Lucia had known all along, like himself, who the new tenant was, for her enquiries had seemed to be pointed with the most piercing curiosity, but, after all, Lucia (when she did not forget her part) was a fine actress, and perhaps all the time he thought he had been punishing her, she had been fooling him. And, in any ease, he certainly had not had the joy of telling her; whether she had guessed or really knew, it was she who had told him, and there was no getting over it. He went back straight home and drew a caricature of her.

But if Georgie was sitting with a clouded brow, Lucia was troubled by nothing less than a raging tornado of agitated thought. Though Olga would undoubtedly be a great addition to the musical talent of Riseholme, would she fall into line, and, for instance, "bring her music" and sing after dinner when Lucia asked her? As regards music, it was possible that she might be almost too great an addition, and cause the rest of the gifted amateurs to sink into comparative insignificance. At present Lucia was high-priestess at every altar of Art, and she could not think with equanimity of seeing anybody in charge of the ritual at any. Again to so eminent an opera-singer there must be conceded a certain dramatic knowledge, and indeed Georgie had often spoken to Lucia of that superb moment when Brunnhilde woke and hailed the sun. Must Lucia give up the direction of dramatic art as well as of music?

Point by point pricked themselves out of the general gloom, and hoisted danger signals; then suddenly the whole was in blaze together. What if Olga took the lead, not in this particular or in that, but attempted to constitute herself supreme in the affairs of Riseholme? It was all very well for her to be a brilliant bird of passage just for a couple of days, and drop so to speak, "a moulted feather, a eagle's feather" on Lucia's party, thereby causing it to shine out from all previous festivities, making it the Hightumest affair that had ever happened, but it was a totally different matter to contemplate her permanent residence here. It seemed possible that then she might keep her feathers to line her own eyrie. She thought of Belshazzar's feast, and the writing of doom on the wall which she was Daniel enough to interpret herself, "Thy kingdom is divided" it said, "and given to the Bracelys or the Shuttleworths."

She rallied her forces. If Olga meant to show herself that sort of woman, she should soon know with whom she had to deal. Not but what Lucia would give her the chance first of behaving with suitable loyalty and obedience; she would even condescend to cooperate with her so long as it was perfectly clear that she aimed at no supremacy. But there was only one lawgiver in Riseholme, one court of appeal, one dispenser of destiny.

Her own firmness of soul calmed and invigorated her, and changing her Teacher's Robe for a walking dress, she went out up the road that led by Old Place, to see what could be observed of the interior from outside.

Chapter TEN
One morning about the middle of October, Lucia was seated at breakfast and frowning over a note she had just received. It began without any formality and was written in pencil.

"Do look in about half-past nine on Saturday and be silly for an hour or two. We'll play games and dance, shall we? Bring your husband of course, and don't bother to reply.

"O.B."
"An invitation," she said icily, as she passed it to her husband.
"Rather short notice."
"We're not doing anything, are we?" he asked.

Peppino was a little imperceptive sometimes.

"No, it wasn't that I meant," she said. "But there's a little more informality about it than one would expect."

"Probably it's an informal party," said he.

"It certainly seems most informal. I am not accustomed to be asked quite like that."

80

Peppino began to be aware of the true nature of the situation.

"I see what you mean, cara," he said. "So don't let us go. Then she will take the hint perhaps."

Lucia thought this over for a moment and found that she rather wanted to go. But a certain resentment that had been slowly accumulating in her mind for some days past began to leak out first, before she consented to overlook Olga's informality.

"It is a fortnight since I called on her," she said, "and she has not even returned the call. I daresay they behave like that in London in certain circles, but I don't know that London is any better for it."

"She has been away twice since she came," said Peppino. "She has hardly been here for a couple of days together yet."

"I may be wrong," said Lucia. "No doubt I am wrong. But I should have thought that she might have spared half-an-hour out of these days by returning my call. However, she thought not."

Peppino suddenly recollected a thrilling piece of news which most unaccountably he had forgotten to tell Lucia.

"Dear me, something slipped my memory," he said. "I met Mrs Weston yesterday afternoon, who told me that half an hour ago Miss Bracely had seen her in her bath-chair and had taken the handles from Tommy Luton, and pushed her twice round the green, positively running."

"That does not seem to me of very prime importance," said Lucia, though she was thrilled to the marrow. "I do not wonder it slipped your memory, caro."

"Carissima, wait a minute. That is not all. She told Mrs Weston that she would have returned her call, but that she hadn't got any calling cards."

"Impossible!" cried Lucia. "They could have printed them at 'Ye olde Booke Shop' in an afternoon."
"That may be so, indeed, if you say so, it is," said Peppino. "Anyhow she said she hadn't got any calling cards, and I don't see why she should lie about it."

"No, it is not the confession one would be likely to make," said she, "unless it was true. Or even if it was," she added.

"Anyhow it explains why she has not been here," said Peppino. "She would naturally like to do everything in order, when she called on you, carissima. It would have been embarrassing if you were out, and she could not hand in her card."

"And about Mr Shuttleworth?" asked she in an absent voice, as if she had no real interest in her question.

"He has not been seen yet at all, as far as I can gather."

"Then shall we have no host, if we drop in tomorrow night?"

"Let us go and see, cara," said he gaily.

Apart from this matter of her call not being returned, Lucia had not as yet had any reason to suspect Olga of revolutionary designs on the throne. She had done odd things, pushing Mrs Weston's chair round the green was one of them, smoking a cigarette as she came back from church on Sunday was another, but these she set down to the Bohemianism and want of polish which might be expected from her upbringing, if you could call an orphan school at Brixton an upbringing at all. This terrific fact Georgie had let slip in his stern determination to know twice as much about Olga as anybody else, and Lucia had treasured it. She had in the last fortnight labelled Olga as "rather common," retaining, however, a certain respect for her professional career, given that that professional career was to be thrown down as a carpet for her own feet. But, after all, if Olga was a bit Bohemian in her way of life, as exhibited by the absence of calling cards, Lucia was perfectly ready to overlook that (confident in the refining influence of Riseholme), and to go to the informal party next day, if she felt so disposed, for no direct answer was asked for.

There was a considerable illumination in the windows of Old Place when she and Peppino set out after dinner next night to go to the "silly" party, kindly overlooking the informality and the absence of a return visit to her call. It had been a sloppy day of rain, and, as was natural, Lucia carried some very smart indoor shoes in a paper-parcel and Peppino had his Russian goloshes on. These were immense snow-boots, in which his evening shoes were completely encased, but Lucia preferred not to disfigure her feet to that extent, and was clad in neat walking-boots which she could exchange for her smart satin footwear in the cloak-room. The resumption of walking-boots when the evening was over was rather a feature among the ladies and was called "The cobbler's at-home." The two started rather late, for it was fitting that Lucia should be the last to arrive.

They had come to the door of the Old Place, and Peppino was fumbling in the dark for the bell, when Lucia gave a little cry of agony and put her hands over her ears, just as if she had been seized with a double-earache of peculiar intensity.

"Gramophone," she said faintly.

There could be no doubt about that. From the window close at hand came out the excruciating strains of a very lusty instrument, and the record was that of a vulgar "catchy" waltz-tune, taken down from a brass-band. All Riseholme knew what her opinion about gramophones was; to the lover of Beethoven they were like indecent and profane language loudly used in a public place. Only one, so far as was known, had ever come to Riseholme, and that was introduced by the misguided Robert Quantock. Once he had turned it on in her presence, but the look of agony which crossed her face was such that he had to stop it immediately. Then the door was opened, and the abominable noise poured out in increased volume.

Lucia paused for a moment in indecision. Would it be the great, the magnificent thing to go home without coming in, trusting to Peppino to let it be widely known what had turned her back from the door? There was a good deal to be said for that, for it would be living up to her own high and immutable standards. On the other hand she particularly wanted to see what standard of entertaining Olga was initiating. The "silly evening" was quite a new type of party, for since she had directed and controlled the social side of things there had been no "silly evenings" of any kind in Riseholme, and it might be a good thing to ensure the failure of this (in case she did not like it) by setting the example of a bored and frosty face. But if she went in, the gramophone must be stopped. She would sit and wince, and Peppino must explain her feeling about gramophones. That would be a suitable exhibition of authority. Or she might tell Olga.

Lucia put on her satin shoes, leaving her boots till the hour of the cobbler's at-home came, and composing her face to a suitable wince was led by a footman on tiptoe to the door of the big music room which Georgie had spoken of.

"If you'll please to step in very quietly, ma'am," he said.

The room was full of people; all Riseholme was there, and since there were not nearly enough chairs (Lucia saw that at once) a large number were sitting on the floor on cushions. At the far end of the room was a slightly-raised dais, to the corner of which the grand piano had been pushed, on the top of which, with its braying trumpet pointing straight at Lucia was an immense gramophone. On the dais was Olga dancing. She was dressed in some white soft fabric shimmering with silver, which left her beautiful arms bare to the shoulder. It was cut squarely and simply about the neck, and hung in straight folds down to just above her ankles. She held in her hands some long shimmering scarf of brilliant red, that floated and undulated as she moved, as if inspired by some life of its own that it drew out of her slim superb vitality. From the cloud of shifting crimson, with the slow billows of silver moving rhythmically round her body, that beautiful face looked out deliciously smiling and brimming with life....

Lucia had hardly entered when with a final bray the gramophone came to the end of its record, and Olga swept a great curtsey, threw down her scarf, and stepped off the dais. Georgie was sitting on the floor close to it, and jumped up, leading the applause. For a moment, though several heads had been turned at Lucia's entrance, nobody took the slightest notice of her, indeed, the first apparently to recognize her presence was her hostess, who just kissed her hand to her, and then continued talking to Georgie. Then Olga threaded her way through the besprinkled floor, and came up to her.

"How wise you were to miss that very poor performance," she said. "But Mr Georgie insisted that I should make a fool of myself."
"Indeed, I am sorry not to have been here for it," said Lucia in her most stately manner. "It seemed to me very far from being a poor performance, very far indeed. Caro mio, you remember Miss Bracely."

"Si, si molto bene," said Peppino, shaking hands.

"Ah, and you talk Italian," said Olga. "Che bella lingua! I wish I knew it."
"You have a very good pronunciation," said Lucia.

"Tante grazie. You know everyone here of course. Now, what shall we do next? Clumps or charades or what? Ah, there are some cigarettes. Won't you have one?"

Lucia gave a little scream of dismay.

"A cigarette for me? That would be a very odd thing," she said. Then relenting, as she remembered that Olga must be excused for her ignorance, she added: "You see I never smoke. Never."

"Oh, you should learn," said Olga. "Now let's play clumps. Does everyone know clumps? If they don't they will find out. Or shall we dance? There's the gramophone to dance to."

Lucia put up her hands in playful petition.

"Oh please, no gramophone!" she said.

"Oh, don't you like it?" said Olga. "It's so horrible that I adore it, as I adore dreadful creatures in an aquarium. But I think we won't dance till after supper. We'll have supper extremely soon, partly because I am dying of famine, and partly because people are sillier afterwards. But just one game of clumps first. Let's see; there are but enough for four clumps. Please make four clumps everybody, and—and will you and two more go out with Mr Georgie, Mrs Lucas? We will be as quick as we can, and we won't think of anything that will make Mr Georgie blush. Oh, there he is! He heard!"

Olga's intense enjoyment of her own party was rapidly galvanizing everybody into a much keener gaiety than was at all usual in Riseholme, where as a rule, the hostess was somewhat anxious and watchful, fearing that her guests were not amusing themselves, and that the sandwiches would give out. There was a sit-down supper when the clumps were over (Mrs Quantock had been the first to guess Beethoven's little toe on his right foot, which made Lucia wince) and there were not enough men and maids to wait, and so people foraged for themselves, and Olga paraded up and down the room with a bottle of champagne in one hand, and a dish of lobster-salad in the other. She sat for a minute or two first at one table and then at another, and asked silly riddles, and sent to the kitchen for a ham, and put out all the electric light by mistake, when she meant to turn on some more. Then when supper was over they all took their seats back into the music-room and played musical chairs, at the end of which Mrs Quantock was left in with Olga, and it was believed that she said "Damn," when Mrs Quantock won. Georgie was in charge of the gramophone which supplied deadly music, quite forgetting that this was agony to Lucia, and not even being aware when she made a sign to Peppino, and went away having a cobbler's at-home all to herself. Nobody noticed when Saturday ended and Sunday began, for Georgie and Colonel Boucher were cock-fighting on the floor, Georgie screaming out "How tarsome" when he was upset, and Colonel Boucher very red in the face saying "Haw, hum. Never thought I should romp again like this. By Jove, most amusing!" Georgie was the last to leave and did not notice till he was half-way home that he had a ham-frill adorning his shirt front. He hoped that it had been Olga who put it there, when he had to walk blind-fold across the floor and try to keep in a straight line.

Riseholme got up rather late next morning, and had to hurry over its breakfast in order to be in time for church. There was a slight feeling of reaction abroad, and a sense of having been young and amused, and of waking now to the fact of church-bells and middle-age. Colonel Boucher singing the bass of "A few more years shall roll," felt his mind instinctively wandering to the cock-fight the evening before, and depressedly recollecting that a considerable number of years had rolled already. Mrs Weston, with her bath-chair in the aisle and Tommy Luton to hand her hymn-book and prayer-book as she required, looked sideways at Mrs Quantock, and thought how strange it was that Daisy, so few hours ago, had been racing round a solitary chair with Georgie's finger on the gramophone, while Georgie, singing tenor by Colonel Boucher's ample side, saw with keen annoyance that there was a stain of tarnished silver on his forefinger, accounted for by the fact that after breakfast he had been cleaning the frame which held the photograph of Olga Bracely and had been astonished to hear the church-bells beginning. Another conducement to depression on his part was the fact that he was lunching with Lucia, and he could not imagine what Lucia's attitude would be towards the party last night. She had come to church rather late, having no use for the General Confession, and sang with stony fervour. She wore her usual church-face, from which nothing whatever could be gathered. A great many stealthy glances right and left from everybody failed to reveal the presence of their hostess of last night. Georgie, in particular, was sorry for this; he would have liked her to show that capacity for respectable seriousness which her presence at church that morning would have implied; while Lucia, in particular, was glad of this, for it confirmed her view that Miss Bracely was not, nor could ever be, a true Riseholmite. She had thought as much last night, and had said so to Peppino. She proposed to say the same to Georgie today.

Then came a stupefying surprise as Mr Rumbold walked from his stall to the pulpit for the sermon. Generally he gave out the number of the short anthem which accompanied this manoeuvre, but today he made no such announcement. A discreet curtain hid the organist from the congregation, and veiled his gymnastics with the stops and his antic dancing on the pedals, and now when Mr Rumbold moved from his stall, there came from the organ the short introduction to Bach's "Mein Glaubige Herz," which even Lucia had allowed to be nearly "equal" to Beethoven. And then came the voice....

The reaction after the romp last night went out like a snuffed candle at this divine singing, which was charged with the joyfulness of some heavenly child. It grew low and soft, it rang out again, it lingered and tarried, it quickened into the ultimate triumph. No singing could have been simpler, but that simplicity could only have sprung from the highest art. But now the art was wholly unconscious; it was part of the singer who but praised God as the thrushes do. She who had made gaiety last night, made worship this morning.

As they sat down for the discourse, Colonel Boucher discreetly whispered to Georgie "By Jove." And Georgie rather more audibly answered "Adorable." Mrs Weston drew a half-a-crown from her purse instead of her usual shilling, to be ready for the offertory, and Mrs Quantock wondered if she was too old to learn to sing.

Georgie found Lucia very full of talk that day at luncheon, and was markedly more Italian than usual. Indeed she put down an Italian grammar when he entered the drawing-room, and covered it up with the essays of Antonio Caporelli. This possibly had some connection with the fact that she had encouraged Olga last night with regard to her pronunciation.

"Ben arrivato, Georgio," she said. "Ho finito il libro di Antonio Caporelli quanta memento. E magnifico!"

Georgie thought she had finished it long ago, but perhaps he was mistaken. The sentence flew off Lucia's tongue as if it was perched there all quite ready.

"Sono un poco fatigata dopo il—dear me how rusty I am getting in Italian for I can't remember the word," she went on. "Anyhow I am a little tired after last night. A delightful little party, was it not? It was clever of Miss Bracely to get so many people together at so short a notice. Once in a while that sort of romp is very well."

"I enjoyed it quite enormously," said Georgie.

"I saw you did, cattivo ragazzo," said she. "You quite forgot about your poor Lucia and her horror of that dreadful gramophone. I had to exert all the calmness that Yoga has given me not to scream. But you were naughty with the gramophone over those musical chairs—unmusical chairs, as I said to Peppino, didn't I, caro?—taking it off and putting it on again so suddenly. Each time I thought it was the end. E pronta la colazione. Andiamo."

Presently they were seated; the menu, an unusual thing in itself at luncheon, was written in Italian, the scribe being clearly Lucia.

"I shall want a lot of Georgino's tempo this week," she said, "for Peppino and I have quite settled we must give a little after dinner party next Saturday, and I want you to help me to arrange some impromptu tableaux. Everything impromptu must just be sketched out first, and I daresay Miss Bracely worked a great deal at her dance last night and I wish I had seen more of it. She was a little awkward in the management of her draperies I thought, but I daresay she does not know much about dancing. Still it was very graceful and effective for an amateur, and she carried it off very well."

"Oh, but she is not quite an amateur," said Georgie. "She has played in Salome."
Lucia pursed her lips.

"Indeed, I am sorry she played in that," she said. "With her undoubtedly great gifts I should have thought she might have found a worthier object. Naturally I have not heard it. I should be very much ashamed to be seen there. But about our tableaux now. Peppino thought we might open with the Execution of Mary Queen of Scots. It is a dreadful thing that I have lost my pearls. He would be the executioner and you the priest. Then I should like to have the awakening of Brunnhilde."

"That would be lovely," said Georgie. "Have you asked Miss Olga if she will?"

"Georgino mio, you don't quite understand," said Lucia. "This party is to be for Miss Bracely. I was her guest last night in spite of the gramophone, and indeed I hope she will find nothing in my house that jars on her as much as her gramophone jarred on me. I had a dreadful nightmare last night—didn't I, Peppino?—in consequence. About the Brunnhilde tableaux, I thought Peppino would be Siegfried—and perhaps you could learn just fifteen or twenty bars of the music and play it while the curtain was up. You can play the same over again if it is encored. Then how about King Cophetua and the beggar-maid. I should be with my back to the audience, and should not turn round at all; it would be quite your tableaux. We will just sketch them out, as I said, and have a grouping or two to make sure we don't get in each other's way, and I will see that there are some dresses of some kind which we can just throw on. The tableaux with a little music, serious music, would be quite sufficient to keep everybody interested."

By this time Georgie had got a tolerable inkling of the import of all this. It was not at present to be war; it was to be magnificent rivalry, a throwing down perhaps of a gauntlet, which none would venture to pick up. To confirm this view, Lucia went on with gathering animation.

"I do not propose to have games, romps shall I call them?" she said, "for as far as I know Riseholme, and perhaps I know it a little better than dear Miss Bracely, Riseholme does not care for that sort of thing. It is not quite in our line; we may be right or wrong, I am sure I do not know, but as a matter of fact, we don't care for that sort of thing. Dear Miss Bracely did her very best last night; I am sure she was prompted only by the most hospitable motives, but how should she know? The supper too. Peppino counted nineteen empty champagne bottles."

"Eighteen, carissima," said Peppino.

"I think you told me nineteen, caro, but it makes very little difference. Eighteen empty champagne bottles standing on the sideboard, and no end to the caviare sandwiches which were left over. It was all too much, though there were not nearly enough chairs, and indeed I never got one at all except just at supper."

Lucia leaned forward over the table, with her hands clasped.

"There was display about it, Georgino, and you know how I hate display," she said. "Shakespeare was content with the most modest scenery for his masterpieces, and it would be a great mistake if we allowed ourselves to be carried away by mere wasteful opulence. In all the years I have lived here, and contributed in my humble way to the life of the place, I have heard no complaints about my suppers or teas, nor about the quality of entertainment which I offer my guests when they are so good as to say 'Si,' to le mie invitazione. Art is not advanced by romping, and we are able to enjoy ourselves without two hundred caviare sandwiches being left over. And such wasteful cutting of the ham; I had to slice the chunk she gave me over and over again before I could eat it."

Georgie felt he could not quite let this pass.

"Well, I had an excellent supper," he said, "and I enjoyed it very much. Besides, I saw Peppino tucking in like anything. Ask him what he thought of it."

Lucia gave her silvery laugh.

"Georgino, you are a boy," she said artfully, "and 'tuck in' as you so vulgarly call it without thinking, I'm saying nothing against the supper, but I'm sure that Peppino and Colonel Boucher would have felt better this morning if they had been wiser last night. But that's not the real point. I want to show Miss Bracely, and I'm sure she will be grateful for it, the sort of entertainment that has contented us at Riseholme for so long. I will frame it on her lines; I will ask all and sundry to drop in with just a few hours' notice, as she did. Everything shall be good, and there shall be about it all something that I seemed to miss last night. There was a little bit—how shall I say it?—a little bit of the footlights about it all. And the footlights didn't seem to me to have been extinguished at church-time this morning. The singing of that very fine aria was theatrical, I can't call it less than theatrical."

She fixed Georgie with her black beady eye, and smoothed her undulated hair.

"Theatrical," she said again. "Now let us have our coffee in the music-room. Shall Lucia play a little bit of Beethoven to take out any nasty taste of gramophone? Me no likey gramophone at all. Nebber!"

Georgie now began to feel himself able to sympathise with that surfeited swain who thought how happy he could be with either, were t'other dear charmer away. Certainly he had been very happy with Lucia all these years, before t'other dear charmer alighted in Riseholme, and now he felt that should Lucia decide, as she had often so nearly decided, to spend the winter on the Riviera, Riseholme would still be a very pleasant place of residence. He never was quite sure how seriously she had contemplated a winter on the Riviera, for the mere mention of it had always been enough to make him protest that Riseholme could not possibly exist without her, but today, as he sat and heard (rather than listened to) a series of slow movements, with a brief and hazardous attempt at the scherzo of the "Moonlight," he felt that if any talk of the Riviera came up, he would not be quite so insistent as to the impossibility of Riseholme continuing to exist without her. He could, for instance, have existed perfectly well this Sunday afternoon if Lucia had been even at Timbuctoo or the Antipodes, for as he went away last night, Olga had thrown a casual intimation to him that she would be at home, if he had nothing better to do, and cared to drop in. Certainly he had nothing better to do but he had something worse to do....

Peppino was sitting in the window-seat, with eyes closed, because he listened to music better so, and with head that nodded occasionally, presumably for the same reason. But the cessation of the slow movement naturally made him cease to listen, and he stirred and gave the sigh with which Riseholme always acknowledged the end of a slow movement. Georgie sighed too, and Lucia sighed; they all sighed, and then Lucia began again. So Peppino closed his eyes again, and Georgie continued his mental analysis of the situation.

At present, so he concluded, Lucia did not mean war. She meant, as by some great armed demonstration, to exhibit the Riseholme spirit in its full panoply, and then crush into dazzled submission any potential rivalry. She meant also to exert an educational influence, for she allowed that Olga had great gifts, and she meant to train and refine those gifts so that they might, when exercised under benign but autocratic supervision, conduce to the strength and splendour of Riseholme. Naturally she must be loyally and ably assisted, and Georgie realized that the tableau of King Cophetua (his tableau as she had said) partook of the nature of a bribe, and, if that word was invidious, of a raising of his pay. It was equally certain that this prolonged recital of slow movements was intended to produce in his mind a vivid consciousness of the contrast between the romp last night and the present tranquil hour, and it did not fail in this respect.

Lucia shut the piano-lid, and almost before they had given their sighs, spoke.

"I think I will have a little dinner-party first," she said. "I will ask Lady Ambermere. That will make us four, with you Georgie, and Miss Bracely and Mr Shuttleworth will make six. The rest I shall ask to come in at nine, for I know Lady Ambermere does not like late hours. And now shall we talk over our tableaux?"

So even Lucia's mind had not been wholly absorbed in Beethoven, though
Georgie, as usual, told her she had never played so divinely.
Chapter ELEVEN
The manoeuvres of the next week became so bewilderingly complicated that by Wednesday Georgie was almost thinking of going away to the seaside with Foljambe and Dicky in sheer despair, and in after years he could not without great mental effort succeed in straightening it all out, and the effort caused quite a buzzing in his head.... That Sunday evening Lucia sent an invitation to Lady Ambermere for "dinner and tableaux," to which Lady Ambermere's "people" replied by telephone on Monday afternoon that her ladyship was sorry to be unable. Lucia therefore gave up the idea of a dinner-party, and reverted to her original scheme of an evening party like Olga's got up on the spur of the moment, with great care and most anxious preparation. The rehearsals for the impromptu tableaux meantime went steadily forward behind closed doors, and Georgie wrestled with twenty bars of the music of the "Awakening of Brunnhilde." Lucia intended to ask nobody until Friday evening, and Olga should see what sort of party Riseholme could raise at a moment's notice.

Early on Tuesday morning the devil entered into Daisy Quantock, probably by means of subconscious telepathy, and she proceeded to go round the green at the morning parliament, and ask everybody to come in for a good romp on Saturday evening, and they all accepted. Georgie, Lucia and Olga were absentees, and so, making a house-to-house visitation she went first to Georgie. He with secret knowledge of the tableaux (indeed he was stitching himself a

88

robe to be worn by King Cophetua at the time and hastily bundling it under the table) regretted that he was already engaged. This was rather mysterious, but he might have planned, for all Mrs Quantock knew, an evening when he would be "busy indoors," and since those evenings were never to be pried upon, she asked no questions, but went off to Lucia's to give her invitation there. There again she was met with a similarly mysterious refusal. Lucia much regretted that she and Peppino were unable to come, and she hoped Daisy would have a lovely party. Even as she spoke, she heard her telephone bell ringing, and hurried off to find that Georgie, faithful lieutenant, was acquainting her with the fact that Mrs Quantock was planning a party for Saturday; he did not know how far she had got. At that moment she had got just half-way to Old Place, walking at unusual speed. Lucia grasped the situation with amazing quickness, and cutting off Georgie with a snap, she abandoned all idea of her party being impromptu, and rang up Olga. She would secure her anyhow....

The telephone was in the hall, and Olga, with her hat on, was just preparing to go out, when the bell sounded. The words of grateful acceptance were on her very lips when her front-door bell rang too, very long and insistently and had hardly left off when it began again. Olga opened the door herself and there was Mrs Quantock on the doorstep with her invitation for Saturday night. She was obliged to refuse, but promised to look in, if she was not very late in getting away from Mrs Lucas's (and pop went the cat out of the bag). Another romp would be lovely.

Already the evils of decentralisation and overlapping were becoming manifest. Lucia rang up house after house, only to find that its inhabitants were already engaged. She had got Olga and Georgie, and could begin the good work of education and the crushing of rivalry, not by force but by pure and refined example, but Mrs Quantock had got everybody else. In the old days this could never have happened for everything devolved round one central body. Now with the appearance of this other great star, all the known laws of gravity and attraction were upset.

Georgie, again summoned to the telephone, recommended an appeal to Mrs Quantock's better nature, which Lucia rejected, doubting whether she had one.

"But what about the tableaux?" asked Georgie. "We three can't very well do tableaux for Miss Olga to look at."

Then Lucia showed herself truly great.

"The merit of the tableaux does not consist in the number of the audience," she said.

She paused a moment.

"Have you got the Cophetua-robe to set properly?" she asked.

"Oh, it'll do," said Georgie dejectedly.

On Tuesday afternoon Olga rang up Lucia again to say that her husband was arriving that day, so might she bring him on Saturday? To this Lucia cordially assented, but she felt that a husband and wife sitting together and looking at another husband and wife doing tableaux would be an unusual entertainment, and not characteristic of Riseholme's best. She began to waver about the tableaux and to consider dinner instead. She also wondered whether she had been wronging dear Daisy, and whether she had a better nature after all. Perhaps Georgie might ascertain.

Georgie was roused from a little fatigued nap by the telephone, for he had fallen asleep over King Cophetua's robe. Lucia explained the situation and delicately suggested that it would be so easy for him to "pop in" to dear Daisy's, and be very diplomatic. There was nobody like Georgie for tact. So with a heavy yawn he popped in.

"You've come about this business on Saturday," said Daisy unerringly. "Haven't you?"
Georgie remembered his character for tact.

"How wonderful of you to guess that!" he said. "I thought we might see if we couldn't arrange something, if we put our heads together. It's such a pity to split up. We—I mean Lucia has got Miss Olga and her husband coming, and———"

"And I've got everybody else," said Daisy brightly. "And Miss Bracely is coming over here, if she gets away early. Probably with such a small party she will."

"Oh, I shouldn't count on that," said he. "We are having some tableaux, and they always take longer than you think. Dear me, I shouldn't have said that, as they were to be impromptu, but I really believe my head is going. You know how thorough Lucia is; she is taking a great deal of trouble about them."

"I hadn't heard about that," said Mrs Quantock.

She thought a moment.

"Well; I don't want to spoil Lucia's evening," she said, "for I'm sure nothing could be so ridiculous as three people doing tableaux for two others. And on the other hand, I don't want her to spoil mine, for what's to prevent her going on with the tableaux till church-time next morning if she wishes to keep Miss Bracely away from my house? I'm sure after the way she behaved about my Guru——— Well, never mind that. How would it be if we had the tableaux first at Lucia's, and then came on here? If Lucia cares to suggest that to me, and my guests consent, I don't mind doing that."

By six o'clock on Tuesday evening therefore all the telephone bells of Riseholme were merrily ringing again. Mrs Quantock stipulated that Lucia's party should end at 10.45 precisely, if it didn't end before, and that everyone should then be free to flock across to her house. She proposed a romp that should even outshine Olga's, and was deep in the study of a manual of "Round Games," which included "Hunt the Slipper."…

Georgie and Peppino took turns at the telephone, ringing up all Mrs Quantock's guests, and informing them of the double pleasure which awaited them on Saturday. Since Georgie had let out the secret of the impromptu tableaux to Mrs Quantock there was no reason why the rest of Riseholme should not learn of this firsthand from The Hurst, instead of second-hand (with promises not to repeat it) from Mrs Quantock. It appeared that she had a better nature than Lucia credited her with, but to expect her not to tell everybody about the tableaux would be putting virtue to an unfair test.

"So that's all settled," said Georgie, as he returned with the last acceptance, "and how fortunately it has happened after all. But what a day it has been. Nothing but telephoning from morning till night. If we go on like this the company will pay a dividend this year, and return us some of our own pennies."

Lucia had got a quantity of pearl beads and was stringing them for the tableau of Mary Queen of Scots.

"Now that everyone knows," she said, "we might allow ourselves a little more elaboration in our preparations. There is an Elizabethan axe at the Ambermere Arms which I might borrow for Peppino. Then about the Brunnhilde tableau. It is dawn, is it not? We might have the stage quite dark when the curtain goes up, and turn up a lamp very slowly behind the scene, so that it shines on my face. A lamp being turned up very slowly is wonderfully effective. It produces a perfect illusion. Could you manage that with one hand and play the music of the awakening with the other, Georgino?"

"I'm quite sure I couldn't," said he.

"Well then Peppino must do it before he comes on. We will have movement in this tableau; I think that will be quite a new idea. Peppino shall come in—just two steps—when he has turned the lamp up, and he will take off my shield and armour——"

"But the music will never last out," cried Georgie. "I shall have to start earlier."

"Yes, perhaps that would be better," said Lucia calmly. "That real piece of chain-armour too, I am glad I remembered Peppino had that. Marshall is cleaning it now, and it will give a far finer effect than the tawdry stuff they use in opera. Then I sit up very slowly, and wave first my right arm and then my left, and then both. I should like to practise that now on the sofa!"

Lucia had just lain down, when the telephone sounded again and Georgie got up.

"That's to announce a dividend," he said, and tripped into the hall.

"Is that Mrs Lucas'?" said a voice he knew.

"Yes, Miss Olga," he said, "and this is me."

"Oh, Mr Georgie, how fortunate," she said. "You can give my message now to Mrs Lucas, can't you? I'm a perfect fool, you know, and horribly forgetful."

"What's the matter?" asked Georgie faintly.

"It's about Saturday. I've just remembered that Georgie and I—not you, you know—are going away for the weekend. Will you tell Mrs Lucas how sorry I am?"

Georgie went back to the music room, where Lucia had just got both her arms waving. But at the sight of his face she dropped them and took a firm hold of herself.

"Well, what is it?" she said.

Georgie gave the message, and she got off the sofa, rising to her feet, while her mind rose to the occasion.

"I am sorry that Miss Bracely will not see our tableaux," she said. "But as she was not acting in them I do not know that it makes much difference."

A deadly flatness, although Olga's absence made no difference, descended on the three. Lucia did not resume her arm-work, for after all these years her acting might be supposed to be good enough for Riseholme without further practice, and nothing more was heard of the borrowing of the axe from the Ambermere Arms. But having begun to thread her pearl-beads, she finished them; Georgie, however, cared no longer whether the gold border of King Cophetua's mantle went quite round the back or not, and having tacked on the piece he was working at, rolled it up. It was just going to be an ordinary party, after all. His cup was empty.

But Lucia's was not yet quite full, for at this moment Miss Lyall's pony hip-bath stopped at the gate, and a small stableboy presented a note, which required an answer. In spite of all Lucia's self-control, the immediate answer it got was a flush of heightened colour.

"Mere impertinence," she said. "I will read it aloud."

"Dear Mrs Lucas,

"I was in Riseholme this morning, and learn from Mrs Weston that Miss Bracely will be at your house on Saturday night. So I shall be enchanted to come to dinner after all. You must know that I make a rule of not going out in the evening, except for some special reason, but it would be a great pleasure to hear her sing again. I wonder if you would have dinner at 7:30 instead of 8, as I do not like being out very late."

There was a short pause.

"Caro," said Lucia, trembling violently, "perhaps you would kindly tell Miss Lyall that I do not expect Miss Bracely on Saturday, and that I do not expect Lady Ambermere either."

"My dear—" he began.

"I will do it myself then," she said.

It was as Georgie walked home after the delivery of this message that he wanted to fly away and be at rest with Foljambe and Dicky. He had been frantically excited ever since Sunday at the idea of doing tableaux before Olga, and today in especial had been a mere feverish hash of telephoning and sewing which all ended in nothing at all, for neither tableaux nor romps seemed to hold the least attraction for him now that Olga was not going to be there. And then all at once it dawned on him that he must be in love with Olga, for why else should her presence or absence make such an astounding difference to him? He stopped dead opposite Mrs Quantock's mulberry tree.

"More misery! More unhappiness!" he said to himself. Really if life at Riseholme was to become a series of agitated days ending in devastating discoveries, the sooner he went away with Foljambe and Dicky the better. He did not quite know what it was like to be in love, for the nearest he had previously ever got to it was when he saw Olga awake on the mountain-top and felt that he had missed his vocation in not being Siegfried, but from that he guessed. This time, too, it was about Olga, not about her as framed in the romance of legend and song, but of her as she appeared at Riseholme, taking as she did now, an ecstatic interest in the affairs of the place. So short a time ago, when she contemplated coming here first, she had spoken of it as a lazy backwater. Now she knew better than that, for she could listen to Mrs Weston far longer than anybody else, and ask for more histories when even she had run dry. And yet Lucia seemed hardly to interest her at all. Georgie wondered why that was.

He raised his eyes as he muttered these desolated syllables and there was Olga just letting herself out of the front garden of the Old Place. Georgie's first impulse was to affect not to see her, and turn into his bachelor house, but she had certainly seen him, and made so shrill and piercing a whistle on her fingers that, pretend as he would not to have seen her, it was ludicrous to appear not to have heard her. She beckoned to him.

"Georgie, the most awful thing has happened," she said, as they came within speaking distance. "Oh, I called you Georgie by mistake then. When one once does that, one must go on doing it on purpose. Guess!" she said in the best Riseholme manner.

"You can come to Lucia's party after all," said he.

"No, I can't. Well, you'll never guess because you move in such high circles, so I'll tell you. Mrs Weston's Elizabeth is going to be married to Colonel Boucher's Atkinson. I don't know his Christian name, nor her surname, but they're the ones!"

"You don't say so!" said Georgie, stung for a moment out of his own troubles. "But will they both leave? What will either of the others do? Mrs Weston can't have a manservant, and how on earth is she to get on without Elizabeth? Besides——"

A faint flush mounted to his cheek.

"I know. You mean babies," said Olga ruthlessly. "Didn't you?"

"Yes," said Georgie.

"Then why not say so? You and I were babies once, though no one is old enough to remember that, and we shouldn't have liked our parents and friends to have blushed when they mentioned us. Georgie, you are a prude."

"No, I'm not," said Georgie, remembering he was probably in love with a married woman.

"It doesn't matter whether you are or not. Now there's only one thing that can happen to Mrs Weston and the Colonel. They must marry each other too. Then Atkinson can continue to be Colonel Boucher's man and Elizabeth the parlour-maid, unless she is busy with what made you blush. Then they can get help in; you will lend them Foljambe, for instance. It's time you began to be of some good in your wicked selfish life. So that's settled. It only remains for us to make them marry each other."

"Aren't you getting on rather fast?" asked Georgie.

"I'm not getting on at all at present I'm only talking. Come into my house instantly, and we'll drink vermouth. Vermouth always makes me brilliant unless it makes me idiotic, but we'll hope for the best."

Presently they were seated in Olga's music-room, with a bottle of vermouth between them.

"Now drink fair, Georgie," she said, "and as you drink tell me all about the young people's emotional history."

"Atkinson and Elizabeth?" asked Georgie.

93

"No, my dear, Colonel Boucher and Mrs Weston. They have an emotional history. I am sure you all thought they were going to marry each other once. And they constantly dine together tete-a-tete. Now that's a very good start. Are you quite sure he hasn't got a wife and family in Egypt, or she a husband and family somewhere else? I don't want to rake up family skeletons."

"I've never heard of them," said Georgie.

"Then we'll take them as non-existent. You certainly would have heard of them if there were any, and very likely if there weren't. And they both like eating, drinking and the latest intelligence. Don't they?"

"Yes. But——"

"But what? What more do you or they want? Isn't that a better start for married life than many people get?"

"But aren't they rather old?" asked Georgie.

"Not much older than you and me, and if it wasn't that I've got my own
Georgie, I would soon have somebody else's. Do you know who I mean?"
"No!" said Georgie firmly. Though all this came at the end of a most harrowing day, it or the vermouth exhilarated him.

"Then I'll tell you just what Mrs Weston told me. 'He's always been devoted to Lucia,' said Mrs Weston, 'and he has never looked at anybody else. There was Piggy Antrobus——' Now do you know who I mean?"

Georgie suddenly giggled.

"Yes," he said.

"Then don't talk about yourself so much, my dear, and let us get to the point. Now this afternoon I dropped in to see Mrs Weston and as she was telling me about the tragedy, she said by accident (just as I called you Georgie just now by accident) 'And I don't know what Jacob will do without Atkinson.' Now is or is not Colonel Boucher's name Jacob? There you are then! That's one side of the question. She called him Jacob by accident and so she'll call him Jacob on purpose before very long."

Olga nodded her head up and down in precise reproduction of Mrs Weston.

"I'd hardly got out of the house," she said in exact imitation of Mrs Weston's voice, "before I met Colonel Boucher. It would have been about three o'clock—no it couldn't have been three, because I had got back home and was standing in the hall when it struck three, and my clock's a shade fast if anything. Well, Colonel Boucher said to me, 'Haw, hum, quite a domestic crisis, by Jove.' And so I pretended I didn't know, and he told me all about it. So I said 'Well, it is a domestic crisis, and you'll lose Atkinson.' 'Haw, hum,' said he, 'and poor Jane, I should say, Mrs Weston, will lose Elizabeth.' There!"

She got up and lit a cigarette.

"Oh, Georgie, do you grasp the inwardness of that?" she said. "Their dear old hearts were laid bare by the trouble that had come upon them, and each of them spoke of the other, as each felt for the other. Probably neither of them had said Jacob or Jane in the whole course of their lives. But the Angel of the Lord descended and troubled the waters. If you think that's profane, have some more vermouth. It's making me brilliant, though you wouldn't have thought it. Now listen!"

She sat down again close to him, her face brimming with a humorous enthusiasm. Humour in Riseholme was apt to be a little unkind; if you mentioned the absurdities of your friends, there was just a speck of malice in your wit. But with her there was none of that, she gave an imitation of Mrs Weston with the most ruthless fidelity, and yet it was kindly to the bottom. She liked her for talking in that emphatic voice and being so particular as to what time it was. "Now first of all you are coming to dine with me tonight," said Olga.

"Oh, I'm afraid that tonight——" began Georgie, shrinking from any further complications. He really must have a quiet evening, and go to bed very early.

"What are you afraid of tonight?" she asked. "You're only going to wash your hair. You can do that tomorrow. So you and I, that's two, and Mrs Weston and Colonel Jacob, that's four, which is enough, and I don't believe there's anything to eat in the house. But there's something to drink, which is my point. Not for you and me, mind; we've got to keep our heads and be clever. Don't have any more vermouth. But Jane and Jacob are going to have quantities of champagne. Not tipsy, you understand, but at their best, and unguardedly appreciative of each other and us. And when they go away, they will exchange a chaste kiss at Mrs Weston's door, and she will ask him in. No! I think she'll ask him in first. And when they wake up tomorrow morning, they will both wonder how they could possibly, and jointly ask themselves what everybody else will say. And then they'll thank God and Olga and Georgie that they did, and live happily for an extraordinary number of years. My dear, how infinitely happier they will be together than they are being now. Funny old dears! Each at its own fireside, saying that it's too old, bless them! And you and I will sing 'Voice that breathed o'er Eden' and in the middle our angel-voices will crack, and we will sob into our handkerchief, and Eden will be left breathing deeply all by itself like the Guru. Why did you never tell me about the Guru? Mrs Weston's a better friend to me than you are, and I must ring for my cook—no I'll telephone first to Jacob and Jane—and see what there is to eat afterwards. You will sit here quietly, and when I have finished I will tell you what your part is."

During dinner, according to Olga's plan of campaign, the conversation was to be general, because she hated to have two conversations going on when only four people were present, since she found that she always wanted to join in the other one. This was the main principle she inculcated on Georgie, stamping it on his memory by a simile of peculiar vividness. "Imagine there is an Elizabethan spittoon in the middle of the table," she said, "and keep on firmly spitting into it. I want you when there's any pause to spit about two things, one, how dreadfully unhappy both Jacob and Jane will be without their paragons, the other, how pleasant is conversation and companionship. I shall be chaffing you, mind, all the time and saying you must get married. After dinner I shall probably stroll in the garden with Jacob. Don't come. Keep him after dinner for some little time, for then's my opportunity of talking to Jane, and give him at least three glasses of port. Gracious it's time to dress, and the Lord prosper us."

Georgie found himself the last to arrive, when he got back to Olga's and all three of them shook hands rather as people shake hands before a funeral. They went into dinner at once and Olga instantly began, "How many years did you say your admirable Atkinson had been with you?" she asked Colonel Boucher.

"Twenty; getting on for twenty-one," said he. "Great nuisance; 'pon my word it's worse than a nuisance."

Georgie had a bright idea.

"But what's a nuisance, Colonel?" he asked.

"Eh, haven't you heard? I thought it would have been all over the place by now. Atkinson's going to be married."

"No!" said Georgie. "Whom to?"

Mrs Weston could not bear not to announce this herself. "To my Elizabeth," she said. "Elizabeth came to me this morning. 'May I speak to you a minute, ma'am?' she asked, and I thought nothing more than that perhaps she had broken a tea-cup. 'Yes,' said I quite cheerfully, 'and what have you come to tell me?'"

It was getting almost too tragic and Olga broke in.

"Let's try to forget all about it, for an hour or two," she said. "It was nice of you all to take pity on me and come and have dinner, otherwise I should have been quite alone. If there's one thing I cannot bear it's being alone in the evening. And to think that anybody chooses to be alone when he needn't! Look at that wretch there," and she pointed to Georgie, "who lives all by himself instead of marrying. Liking to be alone is the worst habit I know; much worse than drink."

"Now do leave me alone," said Georgie.

"I won't, my dear, and when dinner is over Mrs Weston and I are going to put our heads together, and when you come out we shall announce to you the name of your bride. I should put a tax of twenty shillings on the pound on all bachelors; they should all marry or starve."

Suddenly she turned to Colonel Boucher.

"Oh, Colonel," she said. "What have I been saying? How dreadfully stupid of me not to remember that you were a bachelor too. But I wouldn't have you starve for anything. Have some more fish instantly to shew you forgive me. Georgie change the subject you're always talking about yourself."

Georgie turned with admirable docility to Mrs Weston.

"It's too miserable for you," he said. "How will you get on without Elizabeth? How long has she been with you?"
Mrs Weston went straight back to where she had left off.

"So I said, 'What have you come to tell me?' quite cheerfully, thinking it was a tea-cup. And she said, 'I'm going to be married, ma'am,' and she blushed so prettily that you'd have thought she was a girl of twenty, though she was seventeen when she came to me,—no, she was just eighteen, and that's fifteen years ago, and that makes her thirty-three. 'Well, Elizabeth,' I said, 'you haven't told me yet who it is, but whether it's the Archbishop of Canterbury or the Prince

96

of Wales—for I felt I had to make a little joke like that—I hope you'll make him as happy as you've made me all these years.'"

"You old darling," said Olga. "I should have gone into hysterics, and forbade the banns."

"No, Miss Bracely, you wouldn't," said Mrs Weston, "you'd have been just as thankful as me, that she'd got a good husband to take care of and to be taken care of by, because then she said, 'Lor ma'am, it's none of they—not them great folks. It's the Colonel's Atkinson.' You ask the Colonel for Atkinson's character, Miss Bracely, and then you'd be just as thankful as I was."

"The Colonel's Atkinson is a slow coach, just like Georgie," said Olga. "He and Elizabeth have been living side by side all these years, and why couldn't the man make up his mind before? The only redeeming circumstance is that he has done it now. Our poor Georgie now—"

"Now you're going to be rude to Colonel Boucher again," said Georgie.
"Colonel, we've been asked here to be insulted."
Colonel Boucher had nothing stronger than a mild tolerance for Georgie and rather enjoyed snubbing him.

"Well, if you call a glass of wine and a dinner like this an insult," he said, "'pon my word I don't know what you'd call a compliment."

"I know what I call a compliment," said Olga, "and that's your all coming to dine with me at such short notice. About Georgie's approaching nuptials now—"

"You're too tarsome" said he. "If you go on like that, I shan't ask you to the wedding. Let's talk about Elizabeth's. When are they going to get married, Mrs Weston?"

"That's what I said to Elizabeth. 'Get an almanack, Elizabeth,' said I, 'so that you won't choose a Sunday. Don't say the 20th of next month without looking it out. But if the 20th isn't a Sunday or a Friday mind, for though I don't believe in such things, still you never know—' There was Mrs Antrobus now," said Mrs Weston suddenly, putting in a footnote to her speech to Elizabeth, "it was on a Friday she married, and within a year she got as deaf as you see her now. Then Mr Weston's uncle, his uncle by marriage I should say, he was another Friday marriage and they missed their train when going off on their honeymoon, and had to stay all night where they were without a sponge or a tooth brush between them, for all their luggage was in the train being whirled away to Torquay. 'So make it the 20th, Elizabeth,' I said, 'if it isn't a Friday or a Sunday, and I shall have time to look round me, and so will the Colonel, though I don't expect that either of us will find your equals! And don't cry, Elizabeth,' I said, for she was getting quite watery, 'for if you cry about a marriage, what'll be left for a funeral?'"

"Ha! Upon my word, I call that splendid of you," said the Colonel. "I told Atkinson I wished I had never set eyes on him, before I wished him joy."

Olga got up.

"Look after Colonel Boucher, Georgie," she said, "and ring for anything you want. Look at the moon! Isn't it heavenly. How Atkinson and Elizabeth must be enjoying it."

The two men spent a half-hour of only moderately enjoyable conversation, for Georgie kept the grindstone of the misery of his lot without Atkinson, and the pleasure of companionship firmly to the Colonel's nose. It was no use for him to attempt to change the subject to the approaching tableaux, to a vague rumour that Piggy had fallen face downwards in the ducking-pond, that Mrs Quantock and her husband had turned a table this afternoon with remarkable results, for it had tapped out that his name was Robert and hers Daisy. Whichever way he turned, Georgie herded him back on to the stony path that he had been bidden to take, with the result that when Georgie finally permitted him to go into the music-room, he was athirst for the more genial companionship of the ladies. Olga got up as they entered.

"Georgie's so lazy," she said, "that it's no use asking him. But do let you and me have a turn up and down my garden, Colonel. There's a divine moon and it's quite warm."

They stepped out into the windless night.

"Fancy it's being October," she said. "I don't believe there is any winter in Riseholme, nor autumn either, for that matter. You are all so young, so deliciously young. Look at Georgie in there: he's like a boy still, and as for Mrs Weston, she's twenty-five: not a day older."

"Yes, wonderful woman," said he. "Always agreeable and lively. Handsome, too: I consider Mrs Weston a very handsome woman. Hasn't altered an atom since I knew her."

"That's the wonderful thing about you all!" said she. "You are all just as brisk and young as you were ten years ago. It's ridiculous. As for you, I'm not sure that you're not the most ridiculous of the lot. I feel as if I had been having dinner with three delightful cousins a little younger—not much, but just a little—than myself. Gracious! How you all made me romp the other night here. What a pace you go, Colonel! What's your walking like if you call this a stroll?"

Colonel Boucher moderated his pace. He thought Olga had been walking so quickly.

"I'm very sorry," he said. "Certainly Riseholme is a healthy bracing place. Perhaps we do keep our youth pretty well. God bless me, but the days go by without one's noticing them. To think that I came here with Atkinson close on ten years ago."

This did very well for Olga: she swiftly switched off onto it.

"It's quite horrid for you losing your servant," she said. "Servants do become friends, don't they, especially to anyone living alone. Georgie and Foljambe, now! But I shouldn't be a bit surprised if Foljambe had a mistress before very long."

"No, really? I thought you were just chaffing him at dinner. Georgie marrying, is he? His wife'll take some of his needlework off his hands. May I—ah—may I enquire the lady's name?"

Olga decided to play a great card. She had just found it, so to speak, in her hand, and it was most tempting. She stopped.

"But can't you guess?" she said. "Surely I'm not absolutely on the wrong track?"

"Ah, Miss Antrobus," said he. "The one I think they call Piggy. No, I should say there was nothing in that."

98

"Oh, that had never occurred to me," said she. "I daresay I'm quite wrong. I only judged from what I thought I noticed in poor Georgie. I daresay it's only what he should have done ten years ago, but I fancy there's a spark alive still. Let us talk about something else, though we won't go in quite yet, shall we?" She felt quite safe in her apparent reluctance to tell him; the Riseholme gluttony for news made it imperative for him to ask more.

"Really, I must be very dull," he said. "I daresay an eye new to the place sees more. Who is it, Miss Bracely?"

She laughed.

"Ah, how bad a man is at observing a man!" she said. "Didn't you see
Georgie at dinner? He hardly took his eyes off her."
She had a great and glorious reward. Colonel Boucher's face grew absolutely blank in the moonlight with sheer astonishment.

"Well, you surprise me," he said. "Surely a fine woman, though lame, wouldn't look at a needle-woman—well, leave it at that."

He stamped his feet and put his hands in his pockets.

"It's growing a bit chilly," he said. "You'll be catching cold, Miss Bracely, and what will your husband say if he finds out I've been strolling about with you out of doors after dinner?"

"Yes, we'll go in," she said. "It is chilly. How thoughtful you are for me."

Georgie little knowing the catspaw that had been made of him, found himself being detached from Mrs Weston by the Colonel, and this suited him very well, for presently Olga said she would sing, unless anybody minded, and called on him to accompany her. She stood just behind him, leaning over him sometimes with a hand on his shoulder, and sang three ruthless simple English songs, appropriate to the matter in hand. She sang, "I Attempt from Love's Sickness to Fly," and "Sally in Our Alley," and "Come Live with Me," and sometimes beneath the rustle of leaves turned over she whispered to him, "Georgie, I'm cleverer than anybody ever was, and I shall die in the night," she said once. Again more enigmatically she said, "I've been a cad, but I'll tell you about it when they've gone. Stop behind." And then some whiskey came in, and she insisted on the "young people" having some of that; finally she saw them off at the door, and came running back to Georgie. "I've been a cad," she said, "because I hinted that you were in love with Mrs Weston. My dear, it was simply perfect! I believe it to have been the last straw, and if you don't forgive me you needn't. Wasn't it clever? He simply couldn't stand that, for it came on the top of your being so young."

"Well, really—" said Georgie.

"I know. And I must be a cad again. I'm going up to my bedroom, you may come, too, if you like, because it commands a view of Church Road. I shouldn't sleep a wink unless I knew that he had gone in with her. It'll be precisely like Faust and Marguerite going into the house, and you and I are Mephistopheles and Martha. Come quick!"

From the dark of the window they watched Mrs Weston's bath-chair being pushed up the lit road.

"It's the Colonel pushing it," whispered Olga, squeezing him into a corner of the window. "Look! There's Tommy Luton on the path. Now they've stopped at her gate ... I can't bear the suspense.... Oh, Georgie, they've gone in! And Atkinson will stop, and so will Elizabeth, and you've promised to lend them Foljambe. Which house will they live at, do you think? Aren't you happy?"

Chapter TWELVE

The miserable Lucia started a run of extreme bad luck about this time, of which the adventure or misadventure of the Guru seemed to be the prelude, or perhaps the news of her want of recognition of the August moon, which Georgie had so carefully saluted, may have arrived at that satellite by October. For she had simply "cut" the August moon....

There was the fiasco about Olga coming to the tableaux, which was the cause of her sending that very tart reply, via Miss Lyall, to Lady Ambermere's impertinence, and the very next morning, Lady Ambermere, coming again into Riseholme, perhaps for that very purpose, had behaved to Lucia as Lucia had behaved to the moon, and cut her. That was irritating, but the counter-irritant to it had been that Lady Ambermere had then gone to Olga's, and been told that she was not at home, though she was very audibly practising in her music-room at the time. Upon which Lady Ambermere had said "Home" to her people, and got in with such unconcern of the material world that she sat down on Pug.

Mrs Quantock had heard both "Home" and Pug, and told the cut Lucia, who was a hundred yards away about it. She also told her about the engagement of Atkinson and Elizabeth, which was all she knew about events in those houses. On which Lucia with a kind smile had said, "Dear Daisy, what slaves some people are to their servants. I am sure Mrs Weston and Colonel Boucher will be quite miserable, poor things. Now I must run home. How I wish I could stop and chat on the green!" And she gave her silvery laugh, for she felt much better now that she knew Olga had said she was out to Lady Ambermere, when she was so audibly in.

Then came a second piece of bad luck. Lucia had not gone more than a hundred yards past Georgie's house, when he came out in a tremendous hurry. He rapidly measured the distance between himself and Lucia, and himself and Mrs Quantock, and made a bee-line for Mrs Quantock, since she was the nearest. Olga had just telephoned to him....

"Good morning," he said breathlessly, determined to cap anything she said. "Any news?"

"Yes, indeed," she said. "Haven't you heard?"

Georgie had one moment of heart-sink.

"What?" he said.

"Atkinson and Eliz——" she began.

"Oh, that," said he scornfully. "And talking of them, of course you've heard the rest. Haven't you? Why, Mrs Weston and Colonel Boucher are going to follow their example, unless they set it themselves, and get married first."

"No!" said Mrs Quantock in the loudest possible Riseholme voice of surprise.

"Oh, yes. I really knew it last night. I was dining at Old Place and they were there. Olga and I both settled there would be something to talk in the morning. Shall we stroll on the green a few minutes?"

Georgie had a lovely time. He hurried from person to person, leaving Mrs Quantock to pick up a few further gleanings. Everyone was there except Lucia, and she, but for the accident of her being further off than Mrs Quantock, would have been the first to know.

When this tour was finished Georgie sat to enjoy the warm comforting glow of envy that surrounded him. Nowadays the meeting place at the Green had insensibly transferred itself to just opposite Old Place, and it was extremely interesting to hear Olga practising as she always did in the morning. Interesting though it was, Riseholme had at first been a little disappointed about it, for everyone had thought that she would sing Brunnhilde's part or Salome's part through every day, or some trifle of that kind. Instead she would perform an upwards scale in gradual crescendo, and on the highest most magnificent note would enunciate at the top of her voice, "Yawning York!" Then starting soft again she would descend in crescendo to a superb low note and enunciate "Love's Lilies Lonely." Then after a dozen repetitions of this, she would start off with full voice, and get softer and softer until she just whispered that York was yawning, and do the same with Love's Lilies. But you never could tell what she might not sing, and some mornings there would be long trills and leapings onto high notes: long notes and leaping onto trills, and occasionally she sang a real song. That was worth waiting for, and Georgie did not hesitate to let drop that she had sung four last night to his accompaniment. And hardly had he repeated that the third time, when she appeared at her window, and before all Riseholme called out "Georgie!" with a trill at the end, like a bird shaking its wings. Before all Riseholme!

So in he went. Had Lucia known that, it would quite have wiped the gilt off Lady Ambermere's being refused admittance. In point of fact it did wipe the gilt off when, about an hour afterwards, Georgie went to lunch because he told her. And if there had been any gilt left about anywhere, that would have vanished, too, when in answer to some rather damaging remark she made about poor Daisy's interests in the love-affairs of other people's servants, she learned that it was of the love-affairs of their superiors that all Riseholme had been talking for at least an hour by now.

Again there was ill-luck about the tableaux on Saturday, for in the Brunnhilde scene, Peppino in his agitation, turned the lamp that was to be a sunrise, completely out, and Brunnhilde had to hail the midnight, or at any rate a very obscure twilight. Georgie, it is true, with wonderful presence of mind, turned on an electric light when he had finished playing, but it was more like a flash of lightning than a slow, wonderful dawn. The tableaux were over well before 10.45, and though Lucia in answer to the usual pressings, said she would "see about" doing them again, she felt that Mrs Weston and Colonel Boucher, who made their first public appearance as the happy pair, attracted more than their proper share of attention. The only consolation was that the romps that followed at poor Daisy's were a complete fiasco. It was in vain, too, at supper, that she went from table to table, and helped people to lobster salad and champagne, and had not enough chairs, and generally imitated all that had apparently made Olga's party so supreme a success. But on this occasion the recipe for the dish and not the dish itself was served up, and the hunting of the slipper produced no exhilaration in the chase....

But far more untoward events followed. Olga came back on the next Monday, and immediately after Lucia received a card for an evening "At Home," with "Music" in the bottom left-hand corner. It happened to be wet that afternoon, and seeing Olga's shut motor

101

coming from the station with four men inside, she leaped to the conclusion that these were four musicians for the music. A second motor followed with luggage, and she quite distinctly saw the unmistakable shape of a 'cello against the window. After that no more guessing was necessary, for it was clear that poor Olga had hired the awful string-quartet from Brinton, that played in the lounge at the Royal Hotel after dinner. The Brinton string-quartet! She had heard them once at a distance and that was quite enough. Lucia shuddered as she thought of those doleful fiddlers. It was indeed strange that Olga with all the opportunities she had had for hearing good music, should hire the Brinton string-quartet, but, after all, that was entirely of a piece with her views about the gramophone. Perhaps the gramophone would have its share in this musical evening. But she had said she would go: it would be very unkind to Olga to stop away now, for Olga must know by this time her passion for music, so she went. She sincerely hoped that she would not be conducted to the seat of honour, and be obliged to say a few encouraging words to the string-quartet afterwards.

Once again she came rather late, for the music had begun. It had only just begun, for she recognised—who should recognise if not she?—the early bars of a Beethoven quartet. She laid her hand on Peppino's arm.

"Brinton: Beethoven," she said limply.

She slipped into a chair next Daisy Quantock, and sat in her well-known position when listening to music, with her head forward, her chin resting on her hand, and the far-away look in her eyes. Nothing of course could wholly take away the splendour of that glorious composition, and she was pleased that there was no applause between the movements, for she had rather expected that Olga would clap, and interrupt the unity of it all. Occasionally, too, she was agreeably surprised by the Brinton string-quartet: they seemed to have some inklings, though not many. Once she winced very much when a string broke.

Olga (she was rather a restless hostess) came up to her when it was over.

"So glad you could come," she said. "Aren't they divine?"

Lucia gave her most indulgent smile.

"Perfect music! Glorious!" she said. "And they really played it very creditably. But I am a little spoiled, you know, for the last time I heard that it was performed by the Spanish Quartet. I know one ought never to compare, but have you ever heard the Spanish Quartet, Miss Bracely?"

Olga looked at her in surprise.

"But they are the Spanish Quartet!" she said pointing to the players.

Lucia had raised her voice rather as she spoke, for when she spoke on music she spoke for everybody to hear. And a great many people undoubtedly did hear, among whom, of course, was Daisy Quantock. She gave one shrill squeal of laughter, like a slate-pencil, and from that moment granted plenary absolution to poor dear Lucia for all her greed and grabbing with regard to the Guru.

But instantly all Olga's good-nature awoke: unwittingly (for her remark that this was the Spanish Quartet had been a mere surprised exclamation), she had made a guest of hers uncomfortable, and must at once do all she could to remedy that.

"It's a shocking room for echoes, this," she said. "Do all of you come up a little nearer, and you will be able to hear the playing so much better. You lose all shade, all fineness here. I came here on purpose to ask you to move up, Mrs Lucas: there are half a dozen chairs unoccupied near the platform."

It was a kindly intention that prompted the speech, but for all real Riseholme practical purposes, quite barren, for many people had heard Lucia's remarks, and Peppino also had already been wincing at the Brinton quartet. In that fell moment the Bolshevists laid bony fingers on the sceptre of her musical autocracy.... But who would have guessed that Olga would get the Spanish Quartet from London to come down to Riseholme?

Staggering from these blows, she had to undergo an even shrewder stroke yet. Already, in the intelligence department, she had been sadly behind-hand in news, her tableaux-party had been anything but a success, this one little remark of Olga's had shaken her musically, but at any rate up till this moment she had shewn herself mistress of the Italian tongue, while to strengthen that she was being very diligent with her dictionary, grammar and Dante's Paradiso. Then as by a bolt out of a clear sky that temple, too, was completely demolished, in the most tragic fashion.

A few days after the disaster of the Spanish-Brinton Quartet, Olga received a letter from Signor Cortese, the eminent Italian composer, to herald the completion of his opera, "Lucretia." Might he come down to Riseholme for a couple of nights, and, figuratively, lay it at her feet, in the hope that she would raise it up, and usher it into the world? All the time he had been writing it, as she knew, he had thought of her in the name part and he would come down today, tomorrow, at a moment's notice by day or night to submit it to her. Olga was delighted and sent an effusive telegram of many sheets, full of congratulation and welcome, for she wanted above all things to "create" the part. So would Signor Cortese come down that very day?

She ran upstairs with the news to her husband.

"My dear, 'Lucretia' is finished," she said, "and that angel practically offers it me. Now what are we to do about dinner tonight? Jacob and Jane are coming, and neither you nor they, I suppose, speak one word of Italian, and you know what mine is, firm and intelligible and operatic but not conversational. What are we to do? He hates talking English.... Oh, I know, if I can only get Mrs Lucas. They always talk Italian, I believe, at home. I wonder if she can come. She's musical, too, and I shall ask her husband, I think: that'll be a man over, but it will be another Italiano———"

Olga wrote at once to Lucia, mentioning that Cortese was staying with them, but, quite naturally, saying nothing about the usefulness of Peppino and her being able to engage the musician in his own tongue, for that she took for granted. An eager affirmative (such a great pleasure) came back to her, and for the rest of the day, Lucia and Peppino made up neat little sentences to let off to the dazzled Cortese, at the moment when they said "good-night," to shew that they could have talked Italian all the time, had there been any occasion for doing so.

Mrs Weston and Colonel Boucher had already arrived when Lucia and her husband entered, and Lucia had quite a shock to see on what intimate terms they were with their hostess. They actually called each other Olga and Jacob and Jane, which was most surprising and almost painful. Lucia (perhaps because she had not known about it soon enough) had been a little satirical about the engagement, rather as if it was a slight on her that Jacob had not been content with celibacy and Jane with her friendship, but she was sure she wished them both "nothing but well." Indeed the moment she got over the shock of seeing them so intimate with Olga, she could not have been surpassed in cordiality.

"We see but little of our old friends now," she said to Olga and Jane jointly, "but we must excuse their desire for solitude in their first glow of their happiness. Peppino and I remember that sweet time, oh, ever so long ago."

This might have been tact, or it might have been cat. That Peppino and she sympathised as they remembered their beautiful time was tact, that it was so long ago was cat. Altogether it might be described as a cat chewing tact. But there was a slight air of patronage about it, and if there was one thing Mrs Weston would not, and could not and did not even intend to stand, it was that. Besides it had reached her ears that Mrs Lucas had said something about there being no difficulty in finding bridesmaids younger than the bride.

"Fancy! How clever of you to remember so long ago," she said. "But, then, you have the most marvellous memory, dear, and keep it wonderfully!"

Olga intervened.

"How kind of you and Mr Lucas to come at such short notice," she said. "Cortese hates talking English, so I shall put him between you and me, and you'll talk to him all the time, won't you? And you won't laugh at me, will you, when I join in with my atrocious attempts? And I shall buttress myself on the other side with your husband, who will firmly talk across me to him."

Lucia had to say something. A further exposure was at hand, quite inevitably. It was no use for her and Peppino to recollect a previous engagement.

"Oh, my Italian is terribly rusty," she said, knowing that Mrs Weston's eye was on her.... Why had she not sent Mrs Weston a handsome wedding-present that morning?

"Rusty? We will ask Cortese about that when you've had a good talk to him. Ah, here he is!"

Cortese came into the room, florid and loquacious, pouring out a stream of apology for his lateness to Olga, none of which was the least intelligible to Lucia. She guessed what he was saying, and next moment Olga, who apparently understood him perfectly, and told him with an enviable fluency that he was not late at all, was introducing him to her, and explaining that "la Signora" (Lucia understood this) and her husband talked Italian. She did not need to reply to some torrent of amiable words from him, addressed to her, for he was taken on and introduced to Mrs Weston, and the Colonel. But he instantly whirled round to her again, and asked her something. Not knowing the least what he meant, she replied:

"Si: tante grazie."

He looked puzzled for a moment and then repeated his question in English.
"In what deestrict of Italy 'ave you voyaged most?"

Lucia understood that: so did Mrs Weston, and Lucia pulled herself together.

"In Rome," she said. "Che bella citta! Adoro Roma, e il mio marito. Non e vere, Peppino?"

Peppino cordially assented: the familiar ring of this fine intelligible Italian restored his confidence, and he asked Cortese whether he was not very fond of music....

Dinner seemed interminable to Lucia. She kept a watchful eye on Cortese, and if she saw he was about to speak to her, she turned hastily to Colonel Boucher, who sat on her other side, and asked him something about his cari cani, which she translated to him. While he answered she made up another sentence in Italian about the blue sky or Venice, or very meanly said her husband had been there, hoping to direct the torrent of Italian eloquence to him. But she knew that, as an Italian conversationalist, neither she nor Peppino had a rag of reputation left them, and she dismally regretted that they had not chosen French, of which they both knew about as much, instead of Italian, for the vehicle of their linguistic distinction.

Olga meantime continued to understand all that Cortese said, and to reply to it with odious fluency, and at the last, Cortese having said something to her which made her laugh, he turned to Lucia.

"I've said to Meesis Shottlewort" ... and he proceeded to explain his joke in English.

"Molto bene," said Lucia with a dying flicker. "Molto divertente. Non e vero, Peppino."

"Si, si," said Peppino miserably.

And then the final disgrace came, and it was something of a relief to have it over. Cortese, in excellent spirits with his dinner and his wine and the prospect of Olga taking the part of Lucretia, turned beamingly to Lucia again.

"Now we will all spick English," he said. "This is one very pleasant evening. I enjoy me very much. Ecco!"

Just once more Lucia shot up into flame.

"Parlate Inglese molto bene," she said, and except when Cortese spoke to Olga, there was no more Italian that night.

Even the unique excitement of hearing Olga "try over" the great scene in the last act could not quite absorb Lucia's attention after this awful fiasco, and though she sat leaning forward with her chin in her hand, and the far-away look in her eyes, her mind was furiously busy as to how to make anything whatever out of so bad a job. Everyone present knew that her Italian, as a medium for conversation, had suffered a complete break-down, and it was no longer any real use, when Olga did not quite catch the rhythm of a passage, to murmur "Uno, due, tre" unconsciously to herself; she might just as well have said "one, two, three" for any effect it had on Mrs Weston. The story would be all over Riseholme next day, and she felt sure that Mrs Weston, that excellent observer and superb reporter, had not failed to take it all in, and would not fail to do justice to it. Blow after blow had been rained upon her palace door, it was little wonder that the whole building was a-quiver. She had thought of starting a Dante-class this winter, for printed Italian, if you had a dictionary and a translation in order to prepare for the class, could be easily interpreted: it was the spoken word which you had to understand without any preparation at all, and not in the least knowing what was coming, that had presented such insurmountable difficulties. And yet who, when the story of this evening was known, would seek instruction from a teacher of that sort? Would Mrs Weston come to her Dante-class? Would she? Would she? No, she would not.

Lucia lay long awake that night, tossing and turning in her bed in that delightful apartment in "Midsummer Night's Dream," and reviewing the fell array of these unlucky affairs. As she eyed them, black shapes against the glow of her firelight, it struck her that the same malevolent influence inspired them all. For what had caused the failure and flatness of her tableaux (omitting the unfortunate incident about the lamp) but the absence of Olga? Who was it who had occasioned her unfortunate remark about the Spanish Quartet but Olga, whose clear duty it had been, when she sent the invitation for the musical party, to state (so that there could be no mistake about it) that those eminent performers were to entrance them? Who could have guessed that she would have gone to the staggering expense of having them down from London? The Brinton quartet was the utmost that any sane imagination could have pictured, and Lucia's extremely sane imagination had pictured just that, with such extreme vividness that it had never occurred to her that it could be anybody else. Certainly Olga should have put "Spanish Quartet" in the bottom left-hand corner instead of "Music" and then Lucia would have known all about it, and have been speechless with emotion when they had finished the Beethoven, and wiped her eyes, and pulled herself together again. It really looked as if Olga had laid a trap for her....

Even more like a trap were the horrid events of this evening. Trap was not at all too strong a word for them. To ask her to the house, and then suddenly spring upon her the fact that she was expected to talk Italian.... Was that an open, an honourable proceeding? What if Lucia had actually told Olga (and she seemed to recollect it) that she and Peppino often talked Italian at home? That was no reason why she should be expected, off-hand like that, to talk Italian anywhere else. She should have been told what was expected of her, so as to give her the chance of having a previous engagement. Lucia hated underhand ways, and they were particularly odious in one whom she had been willing to educate and refine up to the highest standards of Riseholme. Indeed it looked as if Olga's nature was actually incapable of receiving cultivation. She went on her own rough independent lines, giving a romp one night, and not coming to the tableaux on another, and getting the Spanish Quartet without consultation on a third, and springing this dreadful Pentecostal party on them on a fourth. Olga clearly meant mischief: she wanted to set herself up as leader of Art and Culture in Riseholme. Her conduct admitted of no other explanation.

Lucia's benevolent scheme of educating and refining vanished like morning mists, and through her drooping eyelids, the firelight seemed strangely red.... She had been too kind, too encouraging: now she must collect her forces round her and be stern. As she dozed off to sleep, she reminded herself to ask Georgie to lunch next day. He and Peppino and she must have a serious talk. She had seen Georgie comparatively little just lately, and she drowsily and uneasily wondered how that was.

Georgie by this time had quite got over the desolation of the moment when standing in the road opposite Mrs Quantock's mulberry-tree he had given vent to that bitter cry of "More misery: more unhappiness!" His nerves on that occasion had been worn to fiddlestrings with all the fuss and fiasco of planning the tableaux, and thus fancying himself in love had been just the last straw. But the fact that he had been Olga's chosen confidant in her wonderful scheme of causing Mrs Weston and the Colonel to get engaged, and the distinction of being singled out by Olga to this friendly intimacy, had proved a great tonic. It was quite clear that the existence of Mr Shuttleworth constituted a hopeless bar to the fruition of his passion, and, if he was completely honest with himself, he was aware that he did not really hate Mr Shuttleworth for standing in his path. Georgie was gentle in all his ways, and his manner of falling in love was very gentle, too. He admired Olga immensely, he found her stimulating and amusing, and since it was out of the question really to be her lover, he would have enjoyed next best to that, being her brother, and such little pangs of jealousy as he might experience from time to time, were rather in the nature of small electric shocks voluntarily received. He was devoted to her with a warmth that his supposed devotion to Lucia had never kindled in him; he even went so far as to dream about her in an agitated though respectful manner. Without being conscious of any unreality about his sentiments, he really wanted to dress up as a lover rather than to be one, for he could form no notion at present of what it felt to be absorbed in anyone else. Life was so full as it was: there really was no room for anything else, especially if that something else must be of the quality which rendered everything else colourless.

This state of mind, this quality of emotion was wholly pleasurable and quite exciting, and instead of crying out "More misery! more unhappiness!" he could now, as he passed the mulberry, say to himself "More pleasures! more happiness!"

Yet as he ran down the road to lunch with Lucia he was conscious that she was likely to stand, an angel perhaps, but certainly one with a flaming sword, between him and all the interests of the new life which was undoubtedly beginning to bubble in Riseholme, and to which Georgie found it so pleasant to take his little mug, and have it filled with exhilarating liquid. And if Lucia proved to be standing in his path, forbidding his approach, he, too, was armed for combat, with a revolutionary weapon, consisting of a rolled-up copy of some of Debussy's music for the piano—Olga had lent it him a few days,—and he had been very busy over "Poissons d'or." He was further armed by the complete knowledge of the Italian debacle of last night, which, from his knowledge of Lucia, he judged must constitute a crisis. Something would have to happen.... Several times lately Olga had, so to speak, run full-tilt into Lucia, and had passed on leaving a staggering form behind her. And in each case, so Georgie clearly perceived, Olga had not intended to butt into or stagger anybody. Each time, she had knocked Lucia down purely by accident, but if these accidents occurred with such awful frequency, it was to be expected that Lucia would find another name for them: they would have to be christened. With all his Riseholme appetite for complications and events Georgie guessed that he was not likely to go empty away from this lunch. In addition there were other topics of extraordinary interest, for really there had been very odd experiences at Mrs Quantock's last night, when the Italian debacle was going on, a little way up the road. But he was not going to bring that out at once.

Lucia hailed him with her most cordial manner, and with a superb effrontery began to talk Italian just as usual, though she must have guessed that Georgie knew all about last night.

"Bon arrivato, amico mio," she said. "Why, it must be three days since we met. Che la falto il signorino? And what have you got there?"

Georgie, having escaped being caught over Italian, had made up his mind not to talk any more ever.

"Oh, they are some little things by Debussy," he said. "I want to play one of them to you afterwards. I've just been glancing through it."

"Bene, molto bene!" said she. "Come in to lunch. But I can't promise to like it, Georgino. Isn't Debussy the man who always makes me want to howl like a dog at the sound of the gong? Where did you get these from?"

"Olga lent me them," said Georgie negligently. He really did call her
Olga to her face now, by request.

Lucia's bugles began to sound.

"Yes, I should think Miss Bracely would admire that sort of music," she said. "I suppose I am too old-fashioned, though I will not condemn your little pieces of Debussy before I have heard them. Old-fashioned! Yes! I was certainly too old-fashioned for the music she gave us last night. Dio mi!"

"Oh, didn't you enjoy it?" asked he.

Lucia sat down, without waiting for Peppino.

"Poor Miss Bracely!" she said. "It was very kind of her in intention to ask me, but she would have been kinder to have asked Mrs Antrobus instead, and have told her not to bring her ear-trumpet. To hear that lovely voice, for I do her justice, and there are lovely notes in her voice, lovely, to hear that voice shrieking and screaming away, in what she called the great scene, was simply pitiful. There was no melody, and above all there was no form. A musical composition is like an architectural building; it must be built up and constructed. How often have I said that! You must have colour, and you must have line, otherwise I cannot concede you the right to say you have music."

Lucia finished her egg in a hurry, and put her elbows on the table.

"I hope I am not hide-bound and limited," she said, "and I think you will acknowledge, Georgie, that I am not. Even in the divinest music of all, I am not blind to defects, if there are defects. The Moonlight Sonata, for instance. You have often heard me say that the two last movements do not approach the first in perfection of form. And if I am permitted to criticise Beethoven, I hope I may be allowed to suggest that Mr Cortese has not produced an opera which will render Fidelio ridiculous. But really I am chiefly sorry for Miss Bracely. I should have thought it worth her while to render herself not unworthy to interpret Fidelio, whatever time and trouble that cost her, rather than to seek notoriety by helping to foist on to the world a fresh combination of engine-whistles and grunts. Non e vero, Peppino? How late you are."

Lucia had not determined on this declaration of war without anxious consideration. But it was quite obvious to her that the enemy was daily gaining strength, and therefore the sooner she came to open hostilities the better, for it was equally obvious to her mind that Olga was a pretender to the throne she had occupied for so long. It was time to mobilise, and she had first to state her views and her plan of campaign to the chief of her staff.

"No, we did not quite like our evening, Peppino and I, did we, caro?" she went on. "And Mr Cortese! His appearance! He is like a huge hairdresser. His touch on the piano. If you can imagine a wild bull butting at the keys, you will have some idea of it. And above all, his Italian! I gathered that he was a Neapolitan, and we all know what Neapolitan dialect is like. Tuscans and Romans, who between them I believe—Lingua Toscano in Bocca Romana, you remember—know how to speak their own tongue, find Neapolitans totally unintelligible. For myself, and I speak for mio sposo as well, I do not want to understand what Romans do not understand. La bella lingua is sufficient for me."

"I hear that Olga could understand him quite well," said Georgie betraying his complete knowledge of all that had happened.

"That may be so," said Lucia. "I hope she understood his English too, and his music. He had not an 'h' when he spoke English, and I have not the slightest doubt in my own mind that his Italian was equally illiterate. It does not matter; I do not see that Mr Cortese's linguistic accomplishments concern us. But his music does, if poor Miss Bracely, with her lovely notes, is going to study it, and appear as Lucretia. I am sorry if that is so. Any news?"

Really it was rather magnificent, and it was war as well; of that there could not be the slightest doubt. All Riseholme, by this time, knew that Lucia and Peppino had not been able to understand a word of what Cortese had said, and here was the answer to the back-biting suggestion, vividly put forward by Mrs Weston on the green that morning, that the explanation was that Lucia and Peppino did not know Italian. They could not reasonably be expected to know Neapolitan dialect; the language of Dante satisfied their humble needs. They found it difficult to understand Cortese when he spoke English, but that did not imply that they did not know English. Dante's tongue and Shakespeare's tongue sufficed them....

"And what were the words of the libretto like?" asked Georgie.

Lucia fixed him with her beady eyes, ready and eager to show how delighted she was to bestow approbation wherever it was deserved.

"Wonderful!" she said. "I felt, and so did Peppino, that the words were as utterly wasted on that formless music as was poor Miss Bracely's voice. How did it go, Peppino? Let me think!"

Lucia raised her head again with the far-away look.

"Amore misterio!" she said. "Amore profondo! Amore profondo del vasto mar." "Ah, there was our poor bella lingua again. I wonder who wrote the libretto."

"Mr Cortese wrote the libretto," said Georgie.

Lucia did not hesitate for a moment, but gave her silvery laugh.

"Oh, dear me, no," she said. "If you had heard him talk you would know he could not have. Well, have we not had enough of Mr Cortese and his works? Any news? What did you do last night, when Peppino and I were in our purgatorio?"

Georgie was almost equally glad to get off the subject of Italian. The less said in or of Italian the better.

"I was dining with Mrs Quantock," he said. "She had a very interesting Russian woman staying with her, Princess Popoffski."
Lucia laughed again.

"Dear Daisy!" she said. "Tell me about the Russian princess. Was she a Guru? Dear me, how easily some people are taken in! The Guru! Well, we were all in the same boat there. We took the Guru on poor Daisy's valuation, and I still believe he had very remarkable gifts, curry-cook or not. But Princess Popoffski now——"

"We had a seance," said Georgie.

"Indeed! And Princess Popoffski was the medium?"

Georgie grew a little dignified.

"It is no use adopting that tone, cara," he said, relapsing into
Italian. "You were not there; you were having your purgatory at Olga's.
It was very remarkable. We touched hands all round the table; there was
no possibility of fraud."
Lucia's views on psychic phenomena were clearly known to Riseholme; those who produced
them were fraudulent, those who were taken in by them were dupes. Consequently there was
irony in the baby-talk of her reply.

"Me dood!" she said. "Me very dood, and listen carefully. Tell Lucia!"

Georgie recounted the experiences. The table had rocked and tapped out names. The table
had whirled round, though it was a very heavy table. Georgie had been told that he had two
sisters, one of whom in Latin was a bear.

"How did the table know that?" he asked. "Ursa, a bear, you know. And then, while we were
sitting there, the Princess went off into a trance. She said there was a beautiful spirit present,
who blessed us all. She called Mrs Quantock Margarita, which, as you may know, is the Italian
for Daisy."

Lucia smiled.

"Thank you for explaining, Georgino," she said.

There was no mistaking the irony of that, and Georgie thought he would be ironical too.

"I didn't know if you knew," he said. "I thought it might be Neapolitan dialect."

"Pray, go on!" said Lucia, breathing through her nose.

"And she said I was Georgie," said Georgie, "but that there was another
Georgie not far off. That was odd, because Olga's house, with Mr
Shuttleworth, were so close. And then the Princess went into very deep
trance, and the spirit that was there took possession of her."
"And who was that?" asked Lucia.

"His name was Amadeo. She spoke in Amadeo's voice, indeed it was Amadeo who was
speaking. He was a Florentine and knew Dante quite well. He materialised; I saw him."

A bright glorious vision flashed upon Lucia. The Dante-class might not, even though it was
clearly understood that Cortese spoke unintelligible Neapolitan, be a complete success, if the
only attraction was that she herself taught Dante, but it would be quite a different proposition
if Princess Popoffski, controlled by Amadeo, Dante's friend, was present. They might read a
Canto first, and then hold a seance of which Amadeo—via Princess Popoffski—would take
charge. While this was simmering in her mind, it was important to drop all irony and be
extremely sympathetic.

"Georgino! How wonderful!" she said. "As you know, I am sceptical by nature, and want all
evidence carefully sifted. I daresay I am too critical, and that is a fault. But fancy getting in

touch with a friend of Dante's! What would one not give? Tell me: what is this Princess like? Is she the sort of person one could ask to dinner?"

Georgie was still sore over the irony to which he had been treated. He had, moreover, the solid fact behind him that Daisy Quantock (Margarita) had declared that in no circumstances would she permit Lucia to annex her Princess. She had forgiven Lucia for annexing the Guru (and considering that she had only annexed a curry-cook, it was not so difficult) but she was quite determined to run her Princess herself.

"Yes, you might ask her," he said. If irony was going about, there was no reason why he should not have a share.

Lucia bounced from her seat, as if it had been a spring cushion.

"We will have a little party," she said. "We three, and dear Daisy and her husband and the Princess. I think that will be enough; psychics hate a crowd, because it disturbs the influences. Mind! I do not say I believe in her power yet, but I am quite open-minded; I should like to be convinced. Let me see! We are doing nothing tomorrow. Let us have our little dinner tomorrow. I will send a line to dear Daisy at once, and say how enormously your account of the seance has interested me. I should like dear Daisy to have something to console her for that terrible fiasco about her Guru. And then, Georgino mio, I will listen to your Debussy. Do not expect anything; if it seems to me formless, I shall say so. But if it seems to me promising, I shall be equally frank. Perhaps it is great; I cannot tell you about that till I have heard it. Let me write my note first."

That was soon done, and Lucia, having sent it by hand, came into the music-room, and drew down the blinds over the window through which the autumn sun was streaming. Very little art, as she had once said, would "stand" daylight; only Shakespeare or Dante or Beethoven and perhaps Bach, could compete with the sun.

Georgie, for his part, would have liked rather more light, but after all Debussy wrote such very odd chords and sequences that it was not necessary to wear his spectacles.

Lucia sat in a high chair near the piano, with her chin in her hand, tremendously erect.

Georgie took off his rings and laid them on the candle-bracket, and ran his hands nimbly over the piano.

"Poissons d'or," he said. "Goldfish!"

"Yes; Pesci d'oro," said Lucia, explaining it to Peppino.

Lucia's face changed as the elusive music proceeded. The far-away look died away, and became puzzled; her chin came out of her hand, and the hand it came out of covered her eyes.

Before Georgie had got to the end the answer to her note came, and she sat with it in her hand, which, released from covering her eyes, tried to beat time. On the last note she got up with a regretful sigh.

"Is it finished?" she asked. "And yet I feel inclined to say 'When is it going to begin?' I haven't been fed; I haven't drank in anything. Yes, I warned you I should be quite candid. And there's my verdict. I am sorry. Me vewy sowwy! But you played it, I am sure, beautifully, Georgino; you were a buono avvocato; you said all that could be said for your client. Shall I open this note before we discuss it more fully? Give Georgino a cigarette, Peppino! I am sure he deserves one, after all those accidentals."

She pulled up the blind again in order to read her note and as she read her face clouded.

"Ah! I am sorry for that," she said. "Peppino, the Princess does not go out in the evening; they always have a seance there. I daresay Daisy means to ask us some evening soon. We will keep an evening or two open. It is a long time since I have seen dear Daisy; I will pop round this afternoon."

Chapter THIRTEEN
Spiritualism, and all things pertaining to it, swept over Riseholme like the amazing growth of some tropical forest, germinating and shooting out its surprising vegetation, and rearing into huge fantastic shapes. In the centre of this wonderful jungle was a temple, so to speak, and that temple was the house of Mrs Quantock....

A strange Providence was the origin of it all. Mrs Quantock, a week before, had the toothache, and being no longer in the fold of Christian Science, found that it was no good at all to tell herself that it was a false claim. False claim it might be, but it was so plausible at once that it quite deceived her, and she went up to London to have its falsity demonstrated by a dentist. Since the collapse of Yoga and the flight of the curry-cook, she had embarked on no mystical adventure, and she starved for some new fad. Then when her first visit to the dentist was over (the tooth required three treatments) and she went to a vegetarian restaurant to see if there was anything enlightening to be got out of that, she was delighted to find herself sitting at a very small table with a very communicative lady who ate cabbages in perfectly incredible quantities. She had a round pale face like the moon behind the clouds, enormous eyebrows that almost met over her nose, and a strange low voice, of husky tone, and a pronunciation quite as foreign as Signor Cortese's. She wore some very curious rings with large engraved amethysts and turquoises in them, and since in the first moments of their conversation she had volunteered the information that vegetarianism was the only possible diet for any who were cultivating their psychical powers, Mrs Quantock asked her if these weird finger-ornaments had any mystical signification. They had; one was Gnostic, one was Rosicrucian, and the other was Cabalistic.... It is easy to picture Mrs Quantock's delight; adventure had met her with smiling mouth and mysterious eyes. In the course of an animated conversation of half an hour, the lady explained that if Mrs Quantock was, like her, a searcher after psychical truths, and cared to come to her flat at half-past four that afternoon, she would try to help her. She added with some little diffidence that the fee for a seance was a guinea, and, as she left, took a card out of a case, encrusted with glowing rubies, and gave it her. That was the Princess Popoffski.

Now here was a curious thing. For the last few evenings at Riseholme, Mrs Quantock had been experimenting with a table, and found that it creaked and tilted and tapped in the most encouraging way when she and Robert laid their hands on it. Then something—whatever it was that moved the table—had indicated by raps that her name was Daisy and his Robert, as well as giving them other information, which could not so easily be verified. Robert had grown quite excited about it, and was vexed that the seances were interrupted by his wife's expedition to London. But now how providential that was. She had walked straight from the dentist into the arms of Princess Popoffski.

It was barely half-past four when Mrs Quantock arrived at the Princess's flat, in a pleasant quiet side street off Charing Cross Road. A small dapper little gentleman received her, who explained that he was the Princess's secretary, and conducted her through several small rooms into the presence of the Sybil. These rooms, so Mrs Quantock thrillingly noticed, were dimly lit by oil lamps that stood in front of shrines containing images of the great spiritual guides from Moses down to Madame Blavatski, a smell of incense hung about, there were vases of flowers on the tables, and strange caskets set with winking stones. In the last of these rooms the Princess was seated, and for the moment Mrs Quantock hardly recognised her, for she wore a blue robe, which left her massive arms bare, and up them writhed serpent-shaped bracelets of many coils. She fixed her eyes on Mrs Quantock, as if she had never seen her before, and made no sign of recognition.

"The Princess has been meditating," said the secretary in a whisper.
"She'll come to herself presently."
For a moment meditation unpleasantly reminded Mrs Quantock of the Guru, but nothing could have been less like that ill-starred curry-cook than this majestic creature. Eventually she gave a great sigh and came out of her meditation.

"Ah, it is my friend," she said. "Do you know that you have a purple halo?"

This was very gratifying, especially when it was explained that only the most elect had purple halos, and soon other elect souls assembled for the seance. In the centre of the table was placed a musical box and a violin, and hardly had the circle been made, and the lights turned down, when the most extraordinary things began to happen. A perfect storm of rappings issued from the table, which began to rock violently, and presently there came peals of laughter in a high voice, and those who had been here before said that it was Pocky. He was a dear naughty boy, so Mrs Quantock's neighbour explained to her, so full of fun, and when on earth had been a Hungarian violinist. Still invisible, Pocky wished them all much laughter and joy, and then suddenly said "'Ullo, 'ullo, 'ere's a new friend. I like her," and Mrs Quantock's neighbour, with a touch of envy in her voice, told her that Pocky clearly meant her. Then Pocky said that they had been having heavenly music on the other side that day, and that if the new friend would say "Please" he would play them some of it.

So Mrs Quantock, trembling with emotion, said "Please, Pocky," and instantly he began to play on the violin the spirit tune which he had just been playing on the other side. After that, the violin clattered back onto the middle of the table again, and Pocky, blowing showers of kisses to them all, went away amid peals of happy laughter.

Silence fell, and then a deep bass voice said, "I am coming, Amadeo!" and out of the middle of the table appeared a faint luminousness. It grew upwards and began to take form. Swathes of white muslin shaped themselves in the darkness, and there appeared a white face, in among the topmost folds of the muslin, with a Roman nose and a melancholy expression. He was not gay like Pocky, but he was intensely impressive, and spoke some lines in Italian, when asked to repeat a piece of Dante. Mrs Quantock knew they were Italian, because she recognised "notte" and "uno" and "caro," familiar words on Lucia's lips.

The seance came to an end, and Mrs Quantock having placed a guinea with the utmost alacrity in a sort of offertory plate which the Princess's secretary negligently but prominently put down on a table in one of the other rooms, waited to arrange for another seance. But most unfortunately the Princess was leaving town next day on a much needed holiday, for she had been giving three seances a day for the last two months and required rest.

"Yes, we're off tomorrow, the Princess and I," said he, "for a week at the Royal Hotel at Brinton. Pleasant bracing air, always sets her up. But after that she'll be back in town. Do you know that part of the country?"

Daisy could hardly believe her ears.

"Brinton?" she said. "I live close to Brinton."

Her whole scheme flashed completely upon her, even as Athene sprang full-grown from the brain of Zeus.

"Do you think that she might be induced to spend a few days with me at Riseholme?" she said. "My husband and I are so much interested in psychical things. You would be our guest, too, I hope. If she rested for a few days at Brinton first? If she came on to me afterwards? And then if she was thoroughly rested, perhaps she would give us a seance or two. I don't know—"

Mrs Quantock felt a great diffidence in speaking of guineas in the same sentence with Princesses, and had to make another start.

"If she were thoroughly rested," she said, "and if a little circle perhaps of four, at the usual price would be worth her while. Just after dinner, you know, and nothing else to do all day but rest. There are pretty drives and beautiful air. All very quiet, and I think I may say more comfortable than the hotel. It would be such a pleasure."

Mrs Quantock heard the clinking of bracelets from the room where the Princess was still reposing, and there she stood in the door, looking unspeakably majestic, but very gracious. So Mrs Quantock put her proposition before her, the secretary coming to the rescue on the subject of the usual fees, and when two days afterwards Mrs Quantock returned to Riseholme, it was to get ready the spare room and Robert's room next to it for these thrilling visitors, whose first seance Georgie and Piggy had attended, on the evening of the Italian debacle....

The Quantocks had taken a high and magnificent line about the "usual fees" for the seances, an expensive line, but then Roumanian oils had been extremely prosperous lately. No mention whatever of these fees was made to their guests, no offertory-plate was put in a prominent position in the hall, there was no fumbling for change or the discreet pressure of coins into the secretary's hand; the entire cost was borne by Roumanian oils. The Princess and Mrs Quantock, apparently, were old friends; they spoke to each other at dinner as "dear friend," and the Princess declared in the most gratifying way that they had been most intimate in a previous incarnation, without any allusion to the fact that in this incarnation they had met for the first time last week at a vegetarian restaurant. She was kind enough, it was left to be understood, to give a little seance after dinner at the house of her "dear friend," and so, publicly, the question of money never came up.

Now the Princess was to stay three nights, and therefore, as soon as Mrs Quantock had made sure of that, she proceeded to fill up each of the seances without asking Lucia to any of them. It was not that she had not fully forgiven her for her odious grabbing of the Guru, for she had done that on the night of the Spanish quartette; it was rather that she meant to make sure that there would by no possibility be anything to forgive concerning her conduct with regard to the Princess. Lucia could not grab her and so call Daisy's powers of forgiveness into play again, if she never came near her, and Daisy meant to take proper precautions that she should not come near her. Accordingly Georgie and Piggy were asked to the first seance (if it did not go very well, it would not particularly matter with them), Olga and Mr Shuttleworth were bidden to the second, and Lady Ambermere with Georgie again to the third. This—quite apart from the immense interest of psychic phenomena—was deadly work, for it would be bitter indeed to Lucia to know, as she most undoubtedly would, that Lady Ambermere, who had cut her so firmly, was dining twice and coming to a seance. Daisy, it must again be repeated, had quite forgiven Lucia about the Guru, but Lucia must take the consequences of what she had done.

It was after the first seance that the frenzy for spiritualism seized Riseholme. The Princess with great good-nature, gave some further exhibitions of her psychical power in addition to the seances, and even as Georgie the next afternoon was receiving Lucia's cruel verdict about Debussy, the Sybil was looking at the hands of Colonel Boucher and Mrs Weston, and unerringly probing into their past, and lifting the corner of the veil, giving them both glimpses into the future. She knew that the two were engaged for that she had learned from Mrs Quantock in her morning's drive, and did not attempt to conceal the fact, but how could it be accounted for that looking impressively from the one to the other, she said that a woman no longer young but tall, and with fair hair had crossed their lives and had been connected with one of them for years past? It was impossible to describe Elizabeth more accurately than that, and Mrs Weston in high excitement confessed that her maid who had been with her for fifteen years entirely corresponded with what the Princess had seen in her hand. After that it took only a moment's further scrutiny for the Princess to discover that Elizabeth was going to be happy too. Then she found that there was a man connected with Elizabeth, and Colonel Boucher's hand, to which she transferred her gaze, trembled with delightful anticipation. She seemed to see a man there; she was not quite sure, but was there a man who perhaps had been known to him for a long time? There was. And then by degrees the affairs of Elizabeth and Atkinson were unerringly unravelled. It was little wonder that the Colonel pushed Mrs Weston's bath-chair with record speed to "Ye signe of ye daffodil," and by the greatest good luck obtained a copy of the "Palmist's Manual."

At another of these informal seances attended by Goosie and Mrs Antrobus, even stranger things had happened, for the Princess's hands, as they held a little preliminary conversation, began to tremble and twitch even more strongly than Colonel Boucher's, and Mrs Quantock hastily supplied her with a pencil and a quantity of sheets of foolscap paper, for this trembling and twitching implied that Reschia, an ancient Egyptian priestess, was longing to use the Princess's hand for automatic writing. After a few wild scrawls and plunges with the pencil, the Princess, though she still continued to talk to them, covered sheet after sheet in large flowing handwriting. This, when it was finished and the Princess sunk back in her chair, proved to be the most wonderful spiritual discourse, describing the happiness and harmony which pervaded the whole universe, and was only temporarily obscured by the mists of materiality. These mists were wholly withdrawn from the vision of those who had passed over. They lived in the midst of song and flowers and light and love…. Towards the end there was a less intelligible passage about fire from the clouds. It was rendered completely intelligible the very next day when there was a thunderstorm, surely an unusual occurrence in November. If that had not happened Mrs Quantock's interpretation of it, as referring to Zeppelins, would have been found equally satisfactory. It was no wonder after that, that Mrs Antrobus, Piggy and Goosie spent long evenings with pencils and paper, for the Princess said that everybody had the gift of automatic writing, if they would only take pains and patience to develop it. Everybody had his own particular guide, and it was the very next day that Piggy obtained a script clearly signed Annabel Nicostratus and Jamifleg followed very soon after for her mother and sister, and so there was no jealousy.

But the crown and apex of these manifestations was undoubtedly the three regular seances which took place to the three select circles after dinner. Musical boxes resounded, violins gave forth ravishing airs, the sitters were touched by unseen fingers when everybody's hands were touching all around the table, and from the middle of it materialisations swathed in muslin were built up. Pocky came, visible to the eye, and played spirit music. Amadeo, melancholy and impressive, recited Dante, and Cardinal Newman, not visible to the eye but audible to the ear, joined in the singing "Lead, Kindly Light," which the secretary requested them to encourage him with, and blessed them profusely at the conclusion. Lady Ambermere was so much impressed, and so nervous of driving home alone, that she insisted on Georgie's going back to the Hall with her, and consigning her person to Pug and Miss Lyall, and for the three days of the Princess's visit, there was practically no subject discussed at the parliaments on the Green, except the latest manifestations. Olga went to town for a crystal, and Georgie for a planchette, and Riseholme temporarily became a spiritualistic republic, with the Princess as priestess and Mrs Quantock as President.

Lucia, all this time, was almost insane with pique and jealousy, for she sat in vain waiting for an invitation to come to a seance, and would, long before the three days were over, have welcomed with enthusiasm a place at one of the inferior and informal exhibitions. Since she could not procure the Princess for dinner, she asked Daisy to bring her to lunch or tea or at any hour day or night which was convenient. She made Peppino hang about opposite Daisy's house, with orders to drop his stick, or let his hat blow off, if he saw even the secretary coming out of the gate, so as possibly to enter into conversation with him, while she positively forced herself one morning into Daisy's hall, and cried "Margarita" in silvery tones. On this occasion Margarita came out of the drawing-room with a most determined expression on her face, and shut the door carefully behind her.

"Dearest Lucia," she said, "how nice to see you! What is it?"

"I just popped in for a chat," said she. "I haven't set eyes on you since the evening of the Spanish quartette."

"No! So long ago as that is it? Well, you must come in again sometime very soon, won't you? The day after tomorrow I shall be much less busy. Promise to look in then."

"You have a visitor with you, have you not?" asked Lucia desperately.

"Yes! Two, indeed, dear friends of mine. But I am afraid you would not like them. I know your opinion about anything connected with spiritualism, and—isn't it silly of us?—we've been dabbling in that."

"Oh, but how interesting," said Lucia. "I—I am always ready to learn, and alter my opinions if I am wrong."

Mrs Quantock did not move from in front of the drawing-room door.

"Yes?" she said. "Then we will have a great talk about it, when you come to see me the day after tomorrow. But I know I shall find you hard to convince."

She kissed the tips of her fingers in a manner so hopelessly final that there was nothing to do but go away.

Then with poor generalship, Lucia altered her tactics, and went up to the Village Green where Piggy was telling Georgie about the script signed Annabel. This was repeated again for Lucia's benefit.

"Wasn't it too lovely?" said Piggy. "So Annabel's my guide, and she writes a hand quite unlike mine."

Lucia gave a little scream, and put her fingers to her ears.

"Gracious me!" she said. "What has come over Riseholme? Wherever I go I hear nothing but talk of seances, and spirits, and automatic writing. Such a pack of nonsense, my dear Piggy. I wonder at a sensible girl like you."

Mrs Weston, propelled by the Colonel, whirled up in her bath-chair.

"'The Palmist's Manual' is too wonderful," she said, "and Jacob and I sat up over it till I don't know what hour. There's a break in his line of life, just at the right place, when he was so ill in Egypt, which is most remarkable, and when Tommy Luton brought round my bath-chair this morning—I had it at the garden-door, because the gravel's just laid at my front-door, and the wheels sink so far into it—'Tommy,' I said, 'let me look at your hand a moment,' and there on his line of fate, was the little cross that means bereavement. It came just right didn't it, Jacob? when he was thirteen, for he's fourteen this year, and Mrs Luton died just a year ago. Of course I didn't tell Tommy that, for I only told him to wash his hands, but it was most curious. And has your planchette come yet, Mr Georgie? I shall be most anxious to know what it writes, so if you've got an evening free any night soon just come round for a bit of dinner, and we'll make an evening of it, with table turning and planchette and palmistry. Now tell me all about the seance the first night. I wish I could have been present at a real seance, but of course Mrs Quantock can't find room for everybody, and I'm sure it was most kind of her to let the Colonel and me come in yesterday afternoon. We were thrilled with it, and who knows but that the Princess didn't write the Palmist's Manual for on the title page it says it's by P. and that might be Popoffski as easily as not, or perhaps Princess."

This allusion to there not being room for everybody was agony to Lucia.
She laughed in her most silvery manner.
"Or, perhaps Peppino," she said. "I must ask mio caro if he wrote it. Or does it stand for Pillson? Georgino, are you the author of the Palmist's Manual? Ecco! I believe it was you."

This was not quite wise, for no one detested irony more than Mrs Weston, or was sharper to detect it. Lucia should never have been ironical just then, nor indeed have dropped into Italian.

"No" she said. "I'm sure it was neither Il Signer Peppino nor Il Signer Pillson who wrote it. I believe it was the Principessa. So, ecco! And did we not have a delicious evening at Miss Bracely's the other night? Such lovely singing, and so interesting to learn that Signor Cortese made it all up. And those lovely words, for though I didn't understand much of them, they sounded so exquisite. And fancy Miss Bracely talking Italian so beautifully when we none of us knew she talked it at all."

Mrs Weston's amiable face was crimson with suppressed emotion, of which these few words were only the most insignificant leakage, and a very awkward pause succeeded which was luckily broken by everybody beginning to talk again very fast and brightly. Then Mrs Weston's chair scudded away; Piggy skipped away to the stocks where Goosie was sitting with a large sheet of foolscap, in case her hand twitched for automatic script, and Lucia turned to Georgie, who alone was left.

"Poor Daisy!" she said. "I dropped in just now, and really I found her very odd and strange. What with her crazes for Christian Science, and Uric Acid and Gurus and Mediums, one wonders if she is quite sane. So sad! I should be dreadfully sorry if she had some mental collapse; that sort of thing is always so painful. But I know of a first-rate place for rest-cures; I think it would be wise if I just casually dropped the name of it to Mr Robert, in case. And this last craze seems so terribly infectious. Fancy Mrs Weston dabbling in palmistry! It is too comical, but I hope I did not hurt her feelings by suggesting that Peppino or you wrote the Manual. It is dangerous to make little jokes to poor Mrs Weston."

Georgie quite agreed with that, but did not think it necessary to say in what sense he agreed with it. Every day now Lucia was pouring floods of light on a quite new side of her character, which had been undeveloped, like the print from some photographic plate lying in the dark so long as she was undisputed mistress of Riseholme. But, so it struck him now, since the advent of Olga, she had taken up a critical ironical standpoint, which previously she had reserved for Londoners. At every turn she had to criticise and condemn where once she would only have praised. So few months ago, there had been that marvellous Hightum garden party, when Olga had sung long after Lady Ambermere had gone away. That was her garden party; the splendour and success of it had been hers, and no one had been allowed to forget that until Olga came back again. But the moment that happened, and Olga began to sing on her own account (which after all, so Georgie thought, she had a perfect right to do), the whole aspect of affairs was changed. She romped, and Riseholme did not like romps; she sang in church, and that was theatrical; she gave a party with the Spanish quartette, and Brinton was publicly credited with the performance. Then had come Mrs Quantock and her Princess, and, lo, it would be kind to remember the name of an establishment for rest-cures, in the hope of saving poor Daisy's sanity. Again Colonel Boucher and Mrs Weston were intending to get married, and consulted a Palmist's Manual, so they too helped to develop as with acid the print that had lain so long in the dark.

"Poor thing!" said Lucia, "it is dreadful to have no sense of humour, and I'm sure I hope that Colonel Boucher will thoroughly understand that she has none before he speaks the fatal words. But then he has none either, and I have often noticed that two people without any sense of humour find each other most witty and amusing. A sense of humour, I expect, is not a very common gift; Miss Bracely has none at all, for I do not call romping humour. As for poor Daisy, what can rival her solemnity in sitting night after night round a table with someone who may or may not be a Russian princess—Russia of course is a very large place, and one does not know how many princesses there may be there—and thrilling over a pot of luminous paint and a false nose and calling it Amadeo the friend of Dante."

This was too much for Georgie.

"But you asked Mrs Quantock and the Princess to dine with you," he said, "and hoped there would be a seance afterwards. You wouldn't have done that, if you thought it was only a false nose and a pot of luminous paint."

"I may have been impulsive," said Lucia speaking very rapidly. "I daresay I'm impulsive, and if my impulses lie in the direction of extending such poor hospitality as I can offer to my friends, and their friends, I am not ashamed of them. Far otherwise. But when I see and observe the awful effect of this so-called spiritualism on people whom I should have thought sensible and well-balanced—I do not include poor dear Daisy among them—then I am only

118

thankful that my impulses did not happen to lead me into countenancing such piffle, as your sister so truly observed about POOR Daisy's Guru."

They had come opposite Georgie's house, and suddenly his drawing-room window was thrown up. Olga's head looked out.

"Don't have a fit, Georgie, to find me here" she said. "Good morning, Mrs Lucas; you were behind the mulberry, and I didn't see you. But something's happened to my kitchen range, and I can't have lunch at home. Do give me some. I've brought my crystal, and we'll gaze and gaze. I can see nothing at present except my own nose and the window. Are you psychical, Mrs Lucas?"

This was the last straw; all Lucia's grievances had been flocking together like swallows for their flight, and to crown all came this open annexation of Georgie. There was Olga, sitting in his window, all unasked, and demanding lunch, with her silly ridiculous crystal in her hand, wondering if Lucia was psychical.

Her silvery laugh was a little shrill. It started a full tone above its normal pitch.

"No, dear Miss Bracely," she said. "I am afraid I am much too commonplace and matter-of-fact to care about such things. It is a great loss I know, and deprives me of the pleasant society of Russian princesses. But we are all made differently; that is very lucky. I must get home, Georgie."

It certainly seemed very lucky that everyone was not precisely like Lucia at that moment, or there would have been quarrelling.
She walked quickly off, and Georgie entered his house. Lucia had really been remarkably rude, and, if allusion was made to it, he was ready to confess that she seemed a little worried. Friendship would allow that, and candour demanded it. But no allusion of any sort was made. There was a certain flush on Olga's face, and she explained that she had been sitting over the fire.

The Princess's visit came to an end next day, and all the world knew that she was going back to London by the 11.00 a.m. express. Lady Ambermere was quite aware of it, and drove in with Pug and Miss Lyall, meaning to give her a lift to the station, leaving Mrs Quantock, if she wanted to see her guest off, to follow with the Princess's luggage in the fly which, no doubt, had been ordered. But Daisy had no intention of permitting this sort of thing, and drove calmly away with her dear friend in Georgie's motor, leaving the baffled Lady Ambermere to follow or not as she liked. She did like, though not much, and found herself on the platform among a perfect crowd of Riseholmites who had strolled down to the station on this lovely morning to see if parcels had come. Lady Ambermere took very little notice of them, but managed that Pug should give his paw to the Princess as she took her seat, and waved her hand to Mrs Quantock's dear friend, as the train slid out of the station.

"The late lord had some Russian relations," she said majestically. "How did you get to know her?"

"I met her at Potsdam" was on the tip of Mrs Quantock's tongue, but she was afraid that Lady Ambermere might not understand, and ask her when she had been to Potsdam. It was grievous work making jokes for Lady Ambermere.

The train sped on to London, and the Princess opened the envelope which her hostess had discreetly put in her hand, and found that that was all right. Her hostess had also provided her with an admirable lunch, which her secretary took out of a Gladstone bag. When that was finished, she wanted her cigarettes, and as she looked for these, and even after she had found them, she continued to search for something else. There was the musical box there, and some curious pieces of elastic, and the violin was in its case, and there was a white mask. But she still continued to search....

About the same time as she gave up the search, Mrs Quantock wandered upstairs to the Princess's room. A less highly vitalised nature than hers would have been in a stupor of content, but she was more in a frenzy of content than in a stupor. How fine that frenzy was may be judged from the fact that perhaps the smallest ingredient in it was her utter defeat of Lucia. She cared comparatively little for that glorious achievement, and she was not sure that when the Princess came back again, as she had arranged to do on her next holiday, she would not ask Lucia to come to a seance. Indeed she had little but pity for the vanquished, so great were the spoils. Never had Riseholme risen to such a pitch of enthusiasm, and with good cause had it done so now, for of all the wonderful and exciting things that had ever happened there, these seances were the most delirious. And better even than the excitement of Riseholme was the cause of its excitement, for spiritualism and the truth of inexplicable psychic phenomena had flashed upon them all. Tableaux, romps, Yoga, the Moonlight Sonata, Shakespeare, Christian Science, Olga herself, Uric Acid, Elizabethan furniture, the engagement of Colonel Boucher and Mrs Weston, all these tremendous topics had paled like fire in the sunlight before the revelation that had now dawned. By practice and patience, by zealous concentration on crystals and palms, by the waiting for automatic script to develop, you attained to the highest mysteries, and could evoke Cardinal Newman, or Pocky....

There was the bed in which the Sybil had slept; there was the fresh vase of flowers, difficult to procure in November, but still obtainable, which she loved to have standing near her. There was the chest of drawers in which she had put her clothes, and Mrs Quantock pulled them open one by one, finding fresh emanations and vibrations everywhere. The lowest one stuck a little, and she had to use force to it....

The smile was struck from her face, as it flew open. Inside it were billows and billows of the finest possible muslin. Fold after fold of it she drew out, and with it there came a pair of false eyebrows. She recognised them at once as being Amadeo's. The muslin belonged to Pocky as well.

She needed but a moment's concentrated thought, and in swift succession rejected two courses of action that suggested themselves. The first was to use the muslin herself; it would make summer garments for years. The chief reason against that was that she was a little old for muslin. The second course was to send the whole paraphernalia back to her dear friend, with or without a comment. But that would be tantamount to a direct accusation of fraud. Never any more, if she did that, could she dispense her dear friend to Riseholme like an expensive drug. She would not so utterly burn her boats. There remained only one other judicious course of action, and she got to work.

It had been a cold morning, clear and frosty, and she had caused a good fire to be lit in the Princess's bedroom, for her to dress by. It still prospered in the grate, and Mrs Quantock, having shut the door and locked it, put on to it the false eyebrows, which, as they turned to ash, flew up the chimney. Then she fed it with muslin; yards and yards of muslin she poured on to it; never had there been so much muslin nor that so exquisitely fine. It went to her heart to burn it, but there was no time for minor considerations; every atom of that evidence must be purged by fire. The Princess would certainly not write and say that she had left some eyebrows and a hundred yards of muslin behind her, for, knowing what she did, it would be to her interests as well as Mrs Quantock's that those properties should vanish, as if they never had been.

Up the chimney in sheets of flame went this delightful fabric; sometimes it roared there, as if it had set the chimney on fire, and she had to pause, shielding her scorched face, until the hollow rumbling had died down. But at last the holocaust was over, and she unlocked the door again. No one knew but she, and no one should ever know. The Guru had turned out to be a curry-cook, but no intruding Hermy had been here this time. As long as crystals fascinated and automatic writing flourished, the secret of the muslin and the eyebrows should repose in one bosom alone. Riseholme had been electrified by spiritualism, and, even now, the seances had been cheap at the price, and in spite of this discovery, she felt by no means sure that she would not ask the Princess to come again and minister to their spiritual needs.

She had hardly got downstairs when Robert came in from the Green, where he had been recounting the experiences of the last seance.

"Looked as if there was a chimney on fire," he said. "I wish it was the kitchen chimney. Then perhaps the beef mightn't be so raw as it was yesterday."

Thus is comedy intertwined with tragedy!

Chapter FOURTEEN

Georgie was very busily engaged during the first weeks of December on a water-colour sketch of Olga sitting at her piano and singing. The difficulty of it was such that at times he almost despaired of accomplishing it, for the problem of how to draw her face and her mouth wide open and yet retain the likeness seemed almost insoluble. Often he sat in front of his own looking-glass with his mouth open, and diligently drew his own face, in order to arrive at the principles of the changes of line which took place. Certainly the shape of a person's face, when his mouth was wide open altered so completely that you would have thought him quite unrecognisable, however skilfully the artist reproduced his elongated countenance, and yet Georgie could easily recognise that face in the glass as his. Forehead, eyes and cheek-bones alone retained their wonted aspect; even the nose seemed to lengthen if you opened your mouth very wide…. Then how again was he to indicate that she was singing and not yawning, or preparing for a sneeze? His most successful sketch at present looked precisely as if she was yawning, and made Georgie's jaws long to yawn too. Perhaps the shape of the mouth in the two positions was really the same, and it was only the sound that led you to suppose that an open-mouthed person was singing. But perhaps the piano would supply the necessary suggestion; Olga would not sit down at the piano merely to yawn or sneeze, for she could do that anywhere.

Then a brilliant idea struck him: he would introduce a shaded lamp standing on the piano, and then her face would be in red shadow. Naturally this entailed fresh problems with regard to light, but light seemed to present less difficulty than likeness. Besides he could make her dress, and the keys of the piano very like indeed. But when he came to painting again he despaired. There must be red shadow on her face and yellow light on her hands, and on her green dress, and presently the whole thing looked not so much like Olga singing by lamp-light, as a lobster-salad spread out in the sunlight. The more he painted, the more vividly did the lettuce leaves and the dressing and the lobster emerge from the paper. So he took away the lamp, and shut Olga's mouth, and there she would be at her piano just going to sing.

These artistic agonies had rewards which more than compensated for them, for regularly now he took his drawing-board and his paint-box across to her house, and sat with her while she practised. There were none of love's lilies low or yawning York now, for she was very busy learning her part in Lucretia, spending a solid two hours at it every morning, and Georgie began to perceive what sort of work it implied to produce the spontaneous ease with which Brunnhilde hailed the sun. More astounding even was the fact that this mere learning of notes was but the preliminary to what she called "real work." And when she had got through the mere mechanical part of it, she would have to study. Then when her practice was over, she would indulgently sit with her head in profile against a dark background, and Georgie would suck one end of his brush and bite the other, and wonder whether he would ever produce anything which he could dare to offer her. By daily poring on her face, he grew not to admire only but to adore its youth and beauty, by daily contact with her he began to see how fresh and how lovely was the mind that illuminated it.

"Georgie, I'm going to scold you," she said one day, as she took up her place against the black panel. "You're a selfish little brute. You think of nothing but your own amusement. Did that ever strike you?"

Georgie gasped with surprise. Here was he spending the whole of every morning trying to do something which would be a worthy Christmas present for her (to say nothing of the hours he had spent with his mouth open in front of his glass, and the cost of the beautiful frame which he had ordered) and yet he was supposed to be only thinking about himself. Of course Olga did not know that the picture was to be hers....

"How tarsome you are!" he said. "You're always finding fault with me.
Explain."
"Well, you're neglecting your old friends for your new one," she said. "My dear, you should never drop an old friend. For instance, when did you last play duets with Mrs Lucas?"

"Oh, not so very long ago," said Georgie.

"Quite long enough, I am sure. But I don't actually mean sitting down and thumping the piano with her. When did you last think about her and make plans for her and talk baby-language?"

"Who told you I ever did?" asked Georgie.

"Gracious! How can I possibly remember that sort of thing? I should say at a guess that everybody told me. Now poor Mrs Lucas is feeling out of it, and neglected and dethroned. It's all on my mind rather, and I'm talking to you about it, because it's largely your fault. Now we're talking quite frankly, so don't fence, and say it's mine. I know exactly what you mean, but you are perfectly wrong. Primarily, it's Mrs Lucas's fault, because she's quite the stupidest woman I ever saw, but it's partly your fault too."

She turned round.

"Come, Georgie, let's have it out," she said. "I'm perfectly powerless to do anything, because she detests me, and you've got to help her and help me, and drop your selfishness. Before I came here, she used to run you all, and give you treats like going to her tableaux and listening to her stupid old Moonlight Sonata, and talking seven words of Italian. And then I came along with no earthly intention except to enjoy my holidays, and she got it into her head that I was trying to run the place instead of her. Isn't that so? Just say 'yes.'"

"Yes," said Georgie.

"Well, that puts me in an odious position and a helpless position. I did my best to be nice to her; I went to her house until she ceased to ask me, and asked her here for everything that I thought would amuse her, until she ceased to come. I took no notice of her rudeness which was remarkable, or of her absurd patronising airs, which didn't hurt me in the smallest degree. But Georgie, she would continue to make such a dreadful ass of herself, and think it was my fault. Was it my fault that she didn't know the Spanish quartette when she heard it, or that she didn't know a word of Italian, when she pretended she did, or that the other day (it was the last time I saw her, when you played your Debussy to us at Aunt Jane's) she talked to me about inverted fifths?"

Olga suddenly burst out laughing, and Georgie assumed the Riseholme face of intense curiosity.

"You must tell me all about that," he said, "and I'll tell you the rest which you don't know."

Olga succumbed too, and began to talk in Aunt Jane's voice, for she had adopted her as an aunt.

"Well, it was last Monday week" she said "or was it Sunday? No it couldn't have been Sunday because I don't have anybody to tea that day, as Elizabeth goes over to Jacob's and spends the afternoon with Atkinson, or the other way about, which doesn't signify, as the point is that Elizabeth should be free. So it was Monday, and Aunt Jane—it's me talking again—had the tea-party at which you played Poisson d'Or. And when it was finished, Mrs Lucas gave a great sigh, and said 'Poor Georgino! Wasting his time over that rubbish,' though she knew quite well that I had given it to you. And so I said, 'Would you call it rubbish, do you think?' and she said 'Quite. Every rule of music is violated. Don't those inverted fifths make you wince, Miss Bracely?'"

Olga laughed again, and spoke in her own voice.

"Oh, Georgie, she is an ass," she said. "What she meant I suppose was consecutive fifths; you can't invert a fifth. So I said (I really meant it as a joke), 'Of course there is that, but you must forgive Debussy that for the sake of that wonderful passage of submerged tenths!' And she took it quite gravely and shook her head, and said she was afraid she was a purist. What happened next? That's all I know."

"Directly afterwards," said Georgie, "she brought the music to me, and asked me to show her where the passage of tenths came. I didn't know, but I found some tenths, and she brightened up and said 'Yes, it is true; those submerged tenths are very impressive.' Then I suggested that the submerged tenth was not a musical expression, but referred to a section of the population. On which she said no more, but when she went away she asked me to send her some book on 'Harmony.' I daresay she is looking for the submerged tenth still."

Olga lit a cigarette and became grave again.

"Well, it can't go on," she said. "We can't have the poor thing feeling angry and out of it. Then there was Mrs Quantock absolutely refusing to let her see the Princess."

"That was her own fault," said Georgie. "It was because she was so greedy about the Guru."

"That makes it all the bitterer. And I can't do anything, because she blames me for it all. I would ask her and her Peppino here every night, and listen to her dreary tunes every evening, and let her have it all her own way, if it would do any good. But things have gone too far; she wouldn't come. It has all happened without my noticing it. I never added it all up as it went along, and I hate it."

Georgie thought of the spiritualistic truths.

"If you're an incarnation," he said in a sudden glow of admiration, "you're the incarnation of an angel. How you can forgive her odious manners to you——"

"My dear, shut up," said Olga. "We've got to do something. Now how would it be if you gave a nice party on Christmas night, and asked her at once? Ask her to help you in getting it up; make it clear she's going to run it."

"All right. You'll come, won't you?"

"Certainly I will not. Perhaps I will come in after dinner with Goosie or some one of that sort. Don't you see it would spoil it all if I were at dinner? You must rather pointedly leave me out. Give her a nice expensive refined Christmas present too. You might give her that picture you're doing of me—No, I suppose she wouldn't like that. But just comfort her and make her feel you can't get on without her. You've been her right hand all these years. Make her give her tableaux again. And then I think you must ask me in afterwards. I long to see her and Peppino as Brunnhilde and Siegfried. Just attend to her, Georgie, and buck her up. Promise me you will. And do it as if your heart was in it, otherwise it's no good."

Georgie began packing up his paint-box. This was not the plan he had hoped for on Christmas Day, but if Olga wished this, it had got to be done.

"Well, I'll do my best," he said.

"Thanks ever so much. You're a darling. And how is your planchette getting on? I've been lazy about my crystal, but I get so tired of my own nose."

"Planchette would write nothing but a few names," said Georgie, omitting the fact that Olga's was the most frequent. "I think I shall drop it."

This was but reasonable, for since Riseholme had some new and absorbing excitement every few weeks, to say nothing of the current excitement of daily life, it followed that even the most thrilling pursuits could not hold the stage for very long. Still, the interest in spiritualism had died down with the rapidity of the seed on stony ground.

"Even Mrs Quantock seems to have cooled," said Olga. "She and her husband were here last night, and they looked rather bored when I suggested table-turning. I wonder if anything has happened to put her off it?"

"What do you think could have?" asked Georgie with Riseholme alacrity.

"Georgie, do you really believe in the Princess and Pocky?" she asked.

Georgie looked round to see that there was no one within hearing.

"I did at the time," he said, "at least I think I did. But it seems less likely now. Who was the Princess anyway? Why didn't we ever hear of her before? I believe Mrs Quantock met her in the train or something."

"So do I," said Olga. "But not a word. It makes Aunt Jane and Uncle Jacob completely happy to believe in it all. Their lines of life are enormous, and they won't die till they're over a hundred. Now go and see Mrs Lucas, and if she doesn't ask you to lunch you can come back here."

Georgie put down his picture and painting-apparatus at his house, and went on to Lucia's, definitely conscious that though he did not want to have her to dinner on Christmas Day, or go back to his duets and his A. D. C. duties, there was a spice and savour in so doing that came entirely from the fact that Olga wished him to, that by this service he was pleasing her. In itself it was distasteful, in itself it tended to cut him off from her, if he had to devote his time to Lucia, but he still delighted in doing it.

"I believe I am falling in love with her this time," said Georgie to himself.... "She's wonderful; she's big; she's——"

At that moment his thoughts were violently diverted, for Robert Quantock came out of his house in a tremendous hurry, merely scowling at Georgie, and positively trotted across the Green in the direction of the news-agent's. Instantly Georgie recollected that he had seen him there already this morning before his visit to Olga, buying a new twopenny paper in a yellow cover called "Todd's News." They had had a few words of genial conversation, and what could have happened in the last two hours that made Robert merely gnash his teeth at Georgie now, and make a second visit to the paper-shop?

It was impossible not to linger a moment and see what Robert did when he got to the paper-shop, and with the aid of his spectacles Georgie perceived that he presently loaded himself with a whole packet of papers in yellow covers, presumably "Todd's News." Flesh and blood could not resist the cravings of curiosity, and making a detour, so as to avoid being gnashed at again by Robert, who was coming rapidly back in his direction, he strolled round to the paper-shop and asked for a copy of "Todd's News." Instantly the bright December morning grew dark with mystery, for the proprietor told him that Mr Quantock has bought every copy he possessed of it. No further information could be obtained, except that he had bought a copy of every other daily paper as well.

Georgie could make nothing of it whatever, and having observed Robert hurry into his house again, went on his errand to Lucia. Had he seen what Robert did when he got home, it is doubtful if he could have avoided breaking into the house and snatching a copy of "Todd's News" from him....

Robert went to his study, and locked the door. He drew out from under his blotting-pad the first copy of "Todd's News" that he bought earlier in the morning, and put it with the rest. Then with a furrowed brow he turned to the police-reports in the "Times" and after looking at them laid the paper down. He did the same to the "Daily Telegraph," the "Daily Mail," the "Morning Post," the "Daily Chronicle." Finally (this was the last of the daily papers) he perused "The Daily Mirror," tore it in shreds, and said "Damn."

He sat for a while in thought, trying to recollect if anybody in Riseholme except Colonel Boucher took in the "Daily Mirror." But he felt morally certain that no one did, and letting himself out of his study, and again locking the door after him, he went into the street, and saw at a glance that the Colonel was employed in whirling Mrs Weston round the Green. Instead of joining them he hurried to the Colonel's house and, for there was no time for half-measures, fixed Atkinson with his eye, and said he would like to write a note to Colonel Boucher. He was shown into his sitting-room, and saw the "Daily Mirror" lying open on the table. As soon as he was left alone, he stuffed it into his pocket, told Atkinson he would speak to the Colonel instead, and intercepted the path of the bath-chair. He was nearly run over, but stood his ground, and in a perfectly firm voice asked the Colonel if there was any news in the morning papers. With the Colonel's decided negative ringing joyfully in his ears, he went home again, and locked himself for the second time into his study.

There is a luxury, when some fell danger has been averted by promptness and presence of mind, in living through the moments of that danger again, and Robert opened "Todd's News," for that gave the fuller account, and read over the paragraph in the police news headed "Bogus Russian Princess." But now he gloated over the lines which had made him shudder before when he read how Marie Lowenstein, of 15, Gerald Street, Charing Cross Road, calling herself Princess Popoffski, had been brought up at the Bow Street Police Court for fraudulently professing to tell fortunes and produce materialised spirits at a seance in her flat. Sordid details followed: a detective who had been there seized an apparition by the throat, and turned on the electric light. It was the woman Popoffski's throat that he held, and her secretary, Hezekiah Schwarz, was discovered under the table detaching an electric hammer. A fine was inflicted….

A moment's mental debate was sufficient to determine Robert not to tell his wife. It was true that she had produced Popoffski, but then he had praised and applauded her for that; he, no less than she, had been convinced of Popoffski's integrity, high rank and marvellous psychic powers, and together they had soared to a pinnacle of unexampled greatness in the Riseholme world. Besides poor Daisy would be simply flattened out if she knew that Popoffski was no better than the Guru. He glanced at the pile of papers, and at the fire place….

It had been a cold morning, clear and frosty, and a good blaze prospered in the grate. Out of each copy, of "Todd's News" he tore the page on which were printed the police reports, and fed the fire with them. Page after page he put upon it; never had so much paper been devoted to one grate. Up the chimney they flew in sheets of flame; sometimes he was afraid he had set it on fire, and he had to pause, shielding his scorched face, until the hollow rumbling had died down. With the page from two copies of the "Daily Mirror" the holocaust was over, and he unlocked the door again. No one in Riseholme knew but he, and no one should ever know. Riseholme had been electrified by spiritualism, and even now the seances had been cheap at the price.

The debris of all these papers he caused to be removed by the housemaid, and this was hardly done when his wife came in from the Green.

"I thought there was a chimney on fire, Robert," she said. "You would have liked it to be the kitchen-chimney as you said the other day."

"Stuff and nonsense, my dear," said he. "Lunch-time, isn't it?"

"Yes. Ah, there's the post. None for me, and two for you."

She looked at him narrowly as he took his letters. Perhaps their subconscious minds (according to her dear friend's theory) held communication, but only the faintest unintelligible ripple of that appeared on the surface.

"I haven't heard from my Princess since she went away," she remarked.

Robert gave a slight start; he was a little off his guard from the reaction after his anxiety.

"Indeed!" he said. "Have you written to her?"

She appeared to try to remember.

"Well, I really don't believe I have," she said. "That is remiss of me.
I must send her a long budget one of these days."
This time he looked narrowly at her. Had she a secret, he wondered, as well as he? What could it be?…

Georgie found his mission none too easy, and it was only the thought that it was a labour of love, or something very like it, that enabled him to persevere. Even then for the first few minutes he thought it might prove love's labour's lost, so bright and unreal was Lucia.

He had half crossed Shakespeare's garden, and had clearly seen her standing at the window of the music-room, when she stole away, and next moment the strains of some slow movement, played very loud, drowned the bell on the mermaid's tail so completely that he wondered whether it had rung at all. As a matter of fact, Lucia and Peppino were in the midst of a most serious conversation when Georgie came through the gate, which was concerned with deciding what was to be done. A party at The Hurst sometime during Christmas week was as regular as the festival itself, but this year everything was so unusual. Who were to be asked in the first place? Certainly not Mrs Weston, for she had talked Italian to Lucia in a manner impossible to misinterpret, and probably, so said Lucia with great acidity, she would be playing children's games with her promesso. It was equally impossible to ask Miss Bracely and her husband, for relations were already severed on account of the Spanish quartette and Signer Cortese, and as for the Quantocks, did Peppino expect Lucia to ask Mrs Quantock again ever? Then there was Georgie, who had become so different and strange, and … Well here was Georgie. Hastily she sat down at the piano, and Peppino closed his eyes for the slow movement.

The opening of the door was lost on Lucia, and Peppino's eyes were closed. Consequently Georgie sat down on the nearest chair, and waited. At the end Peppino sighed, and he sighed too.

"Who is that?" said Lucia sharply. "Why is it you, Georgie? What a stranger. Aren't you? Any news?"

This was all delivered in the coldest of tones, and Lucia snatched a morsel of wax off Eb.

"I've heard none," said Georgie in great discomfort. "I just dropped in."

Lucia fixed Peppino with a glance. If she had shouted at the top of her voice she could not have conveyed more unmistakably that she was going to manage this situation.

"Ah, that is very pleasant," she said. "Peppino and I have been so busy lately that we have seen nobody. We are quite country-cousins, and so the town-mouse must spare us a little cheese. How is dear Miss Bracely now?"

"Very well," said Georgie. "I saw her this morning."

Lucia gave a sigh of relief.

"That is good," she said. "Peppino, do you hear? Miss Bracely is quite well. Not overtired with practising that new opera? Lucy Grecian, was it? Oh, how silly I am! Lucretia; that was it, by that extraordinary Neapolitan. Yes. And what next? Our good Mrs Weston, now! Still thinking about her nice young man? Making orange-flower wreaths, and choosing bridesmaids? How naughty I am! Yes. And then dear Daisy? How is she? Still entertaining princesses? I look in the Court Circular every morning to see if Princess Pop—Pop—Popoff isn't it? if Princess Popoff has popped off to see her cousin the Czar again. Dear me!"

The amount of malice, envy and all uncharitableness which Lucia managed to put into this quite unrehearsed speech was positively amazing. She had not thought it over beforehand for a moment; it came out with the august spontaneity of lightning leaping from a cloud. Not till that moment had Georgie guessed at a tithe of all that Olga had felt so certain about, and a double emotion took hold of him. He was immensely sorry for Lucia, never having conjectured how she must have suffered before she attained to so superb a sourness, and he adored the intuition that had guessed it and wanted to sweeten it.

The outburst was not quite over yet, though Lucia felt distinctly better.

"And you, Georgie," she said, "though I'm sure we are such strangers that I ought to call you Mr Pillson, what have you been doing? Playing Miss Bracely's accompaniments, and sewing wedding-dresses all day, and raising spooks all night? Yes."

Lucia had caught this "Yes" from Lady Ambermere, having found it peculiarly obnoxious. You laid down a proposition, or asked a question, and then confirmed it yourself.

"And Mr Cortese," she said, "is he still roaring out his marvellous English and Italian? Yes. What a full life you lead, Georgie. I suppose you have no time for your painting now."

This was not a bow drawn at a venture, for she had seen Georgie come out of Old Place with his paint-box and drawing-board, but this direct attack on him did not lessen the power of the "sweet charity" which had sent him here. He blew the bugle to rally all the good-nature for which he was capable.

"No, I have been painting lately," he said, "at least I have been trying to. I'm doing a little sketch of Miss Bracely at her piano, which I want to give her on Christmas Day. But it's so difficult. I wish I had brought it round to ask your advice, but you would only have screamed with laughter at it. It's a dreadful failure: much worse than those I gave you for your birthdays. Fancy your keeping them still in your lovely music-room. Send them to the pantry, and I'll do something better for you next."

Lucia, try as she might, could not help being rather touched by that.
There they all were: "Golden Autumn Woodland," "Bleak December,"
"Yellow Daffodils," and "Roses of Summer."...
"Or have them blacked over by the boot-boy," she said. "Take them down,

Georgie, and let me send them to be blacked."

This was much better: there was playfulness behind the sarcasm now, which peeped out from it. He made the most of that.

"We'll do that presently," he said. "Just now I want to engage you and Peppino to dine with me on Christmas Day. Now don't be tarsome and say you're engaged. But one can never tell with you."

"A party?" asked Lucia suspiciously.

"Well, I thought we would have just one of our old evenings together again," said Georgie, feeling himself remarkably clever. "We'll have the Quantocks, shan't we, and Colonel and Mrs Colonel, and you and Peppino, and me, and Mrs Rumbold? That'll make eight, which is more than Foljambe likes, but she must lump it. Mr Rumbold is always singing carols all Christmas evening with the choir, and she will be alone."

"Ah, those carols" said Lucia, wincing.

"I know: I will provide you with little wads of cotton-wool. Do come and we'll have just a party of eight. I've asked no one yet and perhaps nobody will come. I want you and Peppino, and the rest may come or stop away. Do say you approve."

Lucia could not yield at once. She had to press her fingers to her forehead.

"So kind of you, Georgie," she said, "but I must think. Are we doing anything on Christmas night, carrissimo? Where's your engagement-book? Go and consult it."

This was a grand manoeuvre, for hardly had Peppino left the room when she started up with a little scream and ran after him.

"Me so stupid," she cried. "Me put it in smoking-room, and poor caro will look for it ever so long. Back in minute, Georgino."

Naturally this was perfectly clear to Georgie. She wanted to have a short private consultation with Peppino, and he waited rather hopefully for their return, for Peppino, he felt sure, was bored with this Achilles-attitude of sitting sulking in the tent. They came back wreathed in smiles, and instantly embarked on the question of what to do after dinner. No romps: certainly not, but why not the tableaux again? The question was still under debate when they went in to lunch. It was settled affirmatively during the macaroni, and Lucia said that they all wanted to work her to death, and so get rid of her. They had thought—she and Peppino— of having a little holiday on the Riviera, but anyhow they would put if off till after Christmas. Georgie's mouth was full of crashing toast at the moment, and he could only shake his head. But as soon as the toast could be swallowed, he made the usual reply with great fervour.

Georgie was hardly at all complacent when he walked home afterwards, and thought how extremely good-natured he had been, for he could not but feel that this marvellous forbearance was a sort of mistletoe growth on him, quite foreign really to his nature. Never before had Lucia showed so shrewish and venomous a temper; he had not thought her capable of it. For the gracious queen, there was substituted a snarling fish-wife, but then as Georgie calmly pursued the pacific mission of comfort to which Olga had ordained him, how the fish-wife's wrinkles had been smoothed out, and the asps withered from her tongue. Had his imagination ever pictured Lucia saying such things to him, it would have supplied him with no sequel but a complete severance of relations between them. Instead of that he had consulted her and truckled to her: truckled: yes, he had truckled, and he was astonished at himself. Why had he truckled? And the beautiful mouth and kindly eyes of Olga supplied the answer. Certainly he must drop in at once, and tell her the result of the mission. Perhaps she would reward him by calling him a darling again. Really he deserved that she should say something nice to him.

It was a day of surprises for Georgie. He found Olga at home, and recounted, without loving any of the substance, the sarcasms of Lucia, and his own amazing tact and forbearance. He did not comment, he just narrated the facts in the vivid Riseholme manner, and waited for his reward.

Olga looked at him a moment in silence: then she deliberately wiped her eyes.

"Oh, poor Mrs Lucas" she said. "She must have been miserable to have behaved like that! I am so sorry. Now what else can you do, Georgie, to make her feel better?"

"I think I've done everything that could have been required of me," said Georgie. "It was all I could do to keep my temper at all. I will give my party at Christmas, because I promised you I would."

"Oh, but it's ten days to Christmas yet," said Olga. "Can't you paint her portrait, and give it her for a present. Oh, I think you could, playing the Moonlight-Sonata."

Georgie felt terribly inclined to be offended and tell Olga that she was tired of him: or to be dignified and say he was unusually busy. Never had he shown such forbearance towards downright rudeness as he had shown to Lucia, and though he had shown that for Olga's sake, she seemed to be without a single spark of gratitude, but continued to urge her request.

"Do paint a little picture of her," she repeated. "She would love it, and make it young and interesting. Think over it, anyhow: perhaps you'll think of something better than that. And now won't you go and secure all your guests for Christmas at once?"

Georgie turned to leave the room, but just as he got to the door she spoke again:

"I think you're a brick," she said.

Somehow this undemonstrative expression of approval began to glow in Georgie's heart as he walked home. Apparently she took it for granted that he was going to behave with all the perfect tact and good-temper that he had shown. It did not surprise her in the least, she had almost forgotten to indicate that she had noticed it at all. And that, as he thought about it, seemed a far deeper compliment than if she had told him how wonderful he was. She took it for granted, no more nor less, that he would be kind and pleasant, whatever Lucia said. He had not fallen short of her standard....

Chapter FIFTEEN

Georgie's Christmas party had just taken its seats at his round rosewood table without a cloth, and he hoped that Foljambe would be quick with the champagne, because there had been rather a long wait before dinner, owing to Lucia and Peppino being late, and conversation had been a little jerky. Lucia, as usual, had sailed into the room, without a word of apology, for she was accustomed to come last when she went out to dinner, and on her arrival dinner was always announced immediately. The few seconds that intervened were employed by her in saying just one kind word to everybody. Tonight, however, these gratifying utterances had not been received with the gratified responses to which she was accustomed: there was a different atmosphere abroad, and it was as if she were no more than one-eighth of the entire party.... But it would never do to hurry Foljambe, who was a little upset already by the fact of there being eight to dinner, which was two more than she approved of.

Lucia was on Georgie's right, Mrs Colonel as she had decided to call herself, on his left. Next her was Peppino, then Mrs Quantock, then the Colonel, then Mrs Rumbold (who resembled a grey hungry mouse), and Mr Quantock completed the circle round to Lucia again. Everyone had a small bunch of violets in the napkin, but Lucia had the largest. She had also a footstool.

"Capital good soup," remarked Mr Quantock. "Can't get soup like this at home."

There was dead silence. Why was there never a silence when Olga was there, wondered Georgie. It wasn't because she talked, she somehow caused other people to talk.

"Tommy Luton hasn't got measles," said Mrs Weston. "I always said he hadn't, though there are measles about. He came to work as usual this morning, and is going to sing in the carols tonight."

She suddenly stopped.

Georgie gave an imploring glance at Foljambe, and looked at the champagne glasses. She took no notice. Lucia turned to Georgie, with an elbow on the table between her and Mr Quantock.

"And what news, Georgie?" she said. "Peppino and I have been so busy that we haven't seen a soul all day. What have you been doing? Any planchette?"

She looked brightly at Mrs Quantock.

"Yes, dear Daisy, I needn't ask you what you've been doing. Table-turning, I expect. I know how interested you are in psychical matters. I should be, too, if only I could be certain that I was not dealing with fraudulent people."

Georgie felt inclined to give a hollow groan and sink under the table when this awful polemical rhetoric began. To his unbounded surprise Mrs Quantock answered most cordially.

"You are quite right, dear Lucia," she said. "Would it not be terrible to find that a medium, some dear friend perhaps, whom one implicitly trusted, was exposed as fraudulent? One sees such exposures in the paper sometimes. I should be miserable if I thought I had ever sat with a medium who was not honest. They fine the wretches well, though, if they are caught, and they deserve it."

Georgie observed, and couldn't the least understand, a sudden blank expression cross Robert's face. For the moment he looked as if he were dead but had been beautifully stuffed. But Georgie gave but a cursory thought to that, for the amazing supposition dawned on him that Lucia had not been polemical at all, but was burying instead of chopping with the hatchet. It was instantly confirmed, for Lucia took her elbow off the table, and turned to Robert.

"You and dear Daisy have been very lucky in your spiritualistic experiences," she said. "I hear on all sides what a charming medium you had. Georgie quite lost his heart to her."

"'Pon my word; she was delightful," said Robert.

"Of course she was a dear friend of Daisy's, but one has to be very careful when one hears of the dreadful exposures, as my wife said, that occur sometimes. Fancy finding that a medium whom you believed to be perfectly honest had yards and yards of muslin and a false nose or two concealed about her. It would sicken me of the whole business."

A loud pop announced that Foljambe had allowed them all some champagne at last, but Georgie hardly heard it, for glancing up at Daisy Quantock, he observed that the same dead and stuffed look had come over her face which he had just now noticed on her husband's countenance. Then they both looked up at each other with a glance that to him bristled with significance. An agonised questioning, an imploring petition for silence seemed to inspire it; it was as if each had made unwittingly some hopeless faux pas. Then they instantly looked away from each other again; their necks seemed to crack with the rapidity with which they turned them right and left, and they burst into torrents of speech to the grey hungry mouse and the Colonel respectively.

Georgie was utterly mystified: his Riseholme instinct told him that there was something below all this, but his Riseholme instinct could not supply the faintest clue as to what it was. Both of the Quantocks, it seemed clear, knew something perilous about the Princess, but surely if Daisy had read in the paper that the Princess had been exposed and fined, she would not have touched on so dangerous a subject. Then the curious incident about "Todd's News" inevitably occurred to him, but that would not fit the case, since it was Robert and not Daisy who had bought that inexplicable number of the yellow print. And then Robert had hinted at the discovery of yards and yards of muslin and a false nose. Why had he done that unless he had discovered them, or unless … Georgie's eyes grew round with the excitement of the chase … unless Robert had some other reason to suspect the integrity of the dear friend, and had said this at hap-hazard. In that case what was Robert's reason for suspicion? Had he, not Daisy, read in the paper of some damaging disclosures, and had Daisy (also having reason to suspect the Princess) alluded to the damaging exposures in the paper by pure hap-hazard? Anyhow they had both looked dead and stuffed when the other alluded to mediumistic frauds, and both had said how lucky their own experiences had been. "Oh!"—Georgie almost said it aloud—What if Robert had seen a damaging exposure in "Todd's News," and therefore bought up every copy that was to be had? Then, indeed, he would look dead and stuffed, when Daisy alluded to damaging exposures in the paper. Had a stray copy escaped him, and did Daisy know? What did Robert know? Had they exquisite secrets from each other?

Lucia was being talked to across him by Mrs Weston, who had also pinned down the attention of Peppino on the other side of her. At that precise moment the flood of Mrs Quantock's spate of conversation to the Colonel dried up, and Robert could find nothing more to say to the hungry mouse. Georgie in this backwater of his own thoughts was whirled into the current again. But before he sank he caught Mrs Quantock's eye and put a question that arose from his exciting backwater.

"Have you heard from the Princess lately?" he asked.

Robert's head went round with the same alacrity as he had turned it away.

"Oh, yes," said she. "Two days ago was it, Robert?"

"I heard yesterday," said Robert firmly.

Mrs Quantock looked at her husband with an eager encouraging earnestness.

"So you did!" she said. "I'm getting jealous. Interesting, dear?"

"Yes, dear, haw, haw," said Robert, and again their eyes met.

This time Georgie had no doubts at all. They were playing the same game now: they smiled and smirked at each other. They had not been playing the same game before. Now they recognised that there was a conspiracy between them.... But he was host, his business for the moment was to make his guests comfortable, and not pry into their inmost bosoms. So before Mrs Weston realised that she had the whole table attending to her, he said:

"I shall get it out of Robert after dinner. And I'll tell you, Mrs Quantock."
"Before Atkinson came to the Colonel," said Mrs Weston, going on precisely where she had left off, "and that was five years before Elizabeth came to me—let me see—was it five or was it four and a half?—four and a half we'll say, he had another servant whose name was Ahab Crowe."

"No!" said Georgie.

"Yes!" said Mrs Weston, hastily finishing her champagne, for she saw Foljambe coming near—"Yes, Ahab Crowe. He married, too, just like Atkinson is going to, and that's an odd coincidence in itself. I tell the Colonel that if Ahab Crowe hadn't married, he would be with him still, and who can say that he'd have fancied Elizabeth? And if he hadn't, I don't believe that the Colonel and I would ever have—well, I'll leave that alone, and spare my blushes. But that's not what I was saying. Whom do you think Ahab Crowe married? You can have ten guesses each, and you would never come right, for it can't be a common name. It was Miss Jackdaw. Crowe: Jackdaw. I never heard anything like that, and if you ask the Colonel about it, he'll confirm every word I've said. Boucher, Weston, why that's quite commonplace in comparison, and I'm sure that's an event enough for me."

Lucia gave her silvery laugh.

"Dear Mrs Weston," she said, "you must really tell me at once when the happy day will be. Peppino and I are thinking of going to the Riviera——"

Georgie broke in.

"You shan't do anything of the kind," he said. "What's to happen to us? 'Oo very selfish, Lucia."
The conversation broke up again into duets and trios, and Lucia could have a private conversation with her host. But half-an-hour ago, so Georgie reflected, they had all been walking round each other like dogs going on tiptoe with their tails very tightly curled, and growling gently to themselves, aware that a hasty snap, or the breach of the smallest observance of etiquette, might lead to a general quarrel. But now they all had the reward of their icy politenesses: there was no more ice, except on their plates, and the politeness was not a matter of etiquette. At present, they might be considered a republic, but no one knew what was going to happen after dinner. Not a word had been said about the tableaux.

Lucia dropped her voice as she spoke to him, and put in a good deal of

Italian for fear she might be overheard.

"Non cognosce anybody?" she asked. "I tablieri, I mean. And are we all to sit in the aula, while the salone is being got ready?"

"Si," said Georgie. "There's a fire. When you go out, keep them there. I domestichi are making salone ready."

"Molto bene. Then Peppino and you and I just steal away. La lampa is acting beautifully. We tried it over several times."

"Everybody's tummin'," said Georgie, varying the cipher.

"Me so nervosa!" said Lucia. "Fancy me doing Brunnhilde before singing Brunnhilde. Me can't bear it."

Georgie knew that Lucia had been thrilled and delighted to know that Olga so much wanted to come in after dinner and see the tableaux, so he found it quite easy to induce Lucia to nerve herself up to an ordeal so passionately desired. Indeed he himself was hardly less excited at the thought of being King Cophetua.

At that moment, even as the crackers were being handed round, the sound of the carol-singers was heard from outside, and Lucia had to wince, as "Good King Wenceslas" looked out. When the Page and the King sang their speeches, the other voices grew piano, so that the effect was of a solo voice accompanied. When the Page sang, Lucia shuddered.

"That's the small red-haired boy who nearly deafens me in church," she whispered to Georgie. "Don't you hope his voice will crack soon?"

She said this very discreetly, so as not to hurt Mrs Rumbold's feelings, for she trained the choir. Everyone knew that the king was Mr Rumbold, and said "Charming" to each other, after he had sung.

"I liked that boy's voice, too," said Mrs Weston. "Tommy Luton used to have a lovely voice, but this one's struck me as better-trained even than Tommy Luton's. Great credit to you, Mrs Rumbold."

The grey hungry mouse suddenly gave a shrill cackle of a laugh, quite inexplicable. Then Georgie guessed.

He got up.

"Now nobody must move," he said, "because we haven't drunk 'absent friends' yet. I'm just going out to see that they have a bit of supper in the kitchen before they go on."

His trembling legs would scarcely carry him to the door, and he ran out. There were half a dozen little choir boys, four men and one tall cloaked woman....

"Divine!" he said to Olga. "Aunt Jane thought your voice very well trained. Come in soon, won't you?"

"Yes: all flourishing?"

"Swimming," said Georgie. "Lucia hoped your voice would crack soon. But it's all being lovely."

He explained about food in the kitchen and hurried back to his guests.
There was the riddle of the Quantocks to solve: there were the tableaux vivants imminent: there was the little red-haired boy coming in soon.
What a Christmas night!
Soon after Georgie's hall began to fill up with guests, and yet not a word was said about tableaux. It grew so full that nobody could have said for certain whether Lucia and Peppino were there or not. Olga certainly was: there was no mistaking that fact. And then Foljambe opened the drawing-room door and sounded a gong.

The lamp behaved perfectly and an hour later one Brunnhilde was being extremely kind to the other, as they sat together. "If you really want to know my view, dear Miss Bracely," said Lucia, "it's just that. You must be Brunnhilde for the time being. Singing, of course, as you say, helps it out: you can express so much by singing. You are so lucky there. I am bound to say I had qualms when Peppino—or was it Georgie—suggested we should do Brunnhilde-Siegfried. I said it would be so terribly difficult. Slow: it has to be slow, and to keep gestures slow when you cannot make them mere illustrations of what you are singing—well, I am sure, it is very kind of you to be so flattering about it—but it is difficult to do that."

"And you thought them all out for yourself?" said Olga. "Marvellous!"

"Ah, if I had ever seen you do it," said Lucia, "I am sure I should have picked up some hints! And King Cophetua! Won't you give me a little word for our dear King Cophetua? I was so glad after the strain of Brunnhilde to have my back to the audience. Even then there is the difficulty of keeping quite still, but I am sure you know that quite as well as I do, from having played Brunnhilde yourself. Georgie was very much impressed by your performance of it. And Mary Queen of Scots now! The shrinking of the flesh, and the resignation of the spirit! That is what I tried to express. You must come and help me next time I attempt this sort of thing again. That will not be quite soon, I am afraid, for Peppino and I am thinking of going to the Riviera for a little holiday."

"Oh, but how selfish!" said Olga. "You mustn't do that."

Lucia gave the silvery laugh.

"You are all very tiresome about my going to the Riviera," she said. "But I don't promise that I shall give it up yet. We shall see! Gracious! How late it is. We must have sat very late over dinner. Why were you not asked to dinner, I wonder! I shall scold Georgie for not asking you. Ah, there is dear Mrs Weston going away. I must say good-night to her. She would think it very strange if I did not. Colonel Boucher, too! Oh, they are coming this way to save us the trouble of moving."

A general move was certainly taking place, not in the direction of the door, but to where Olga and Lucia were sitting.

"It's snowing," said Piggy excitedly to Olga. "Will you mark my footsteps well, my page?"

"Piggy, you—you Goosie," said Olga hurriedly. "Goosie, weren't the tableaux lovely?"

"And the carols," said Goosie. "I adored the carols. I guessed. Did you guess, Mrs Lucas?"

Olga resorted to the mean trick of treading on Goosie's foot and apologising. That was cowardly because it was sure to come out sometime. And Goosie again trod on dangerous ground by saying that if the Page had trod like that, there was no need for any footsteps to be marked for him.

It was snowing fast, and Mrs Weston's wheels left a deep track, but in spite of that, Daisy and Robert had not gone fifty yards from the door when they came to a full stop.

"Now, what is it?" said Daisy. "Out with it. Why did you talk about the discovery of muslin?"

"I only said that we were fortunate in a medium whom after all you picked up at a vegetarian restaurant," said he. "I suppose I may indulge in general conversation. If it comes to that, why did you talk about exposure in the papers?"

"General conversation," said Mrs Quantock all in one word. "So that's all, is it?"

"Yes," said Robert, "you may know something, and—"

"Now don't put it all on me," said Daisy. "If you want to know what I think, it is that you've got some secret."

"And if you want to know what I think," he retorted, "it is that I know you have."

Daisy hesitated a moment, the snow was white on her shoulder and she shook her cloak.

"I hate concealment," she said. "I found yards and yards of muslin and a pair of Amadeo's eyebrows in that woman's bedroom the very day she went away."

"And she was fined last Thursday for holding a seance at which a detective was present," said Robert. "15 Gerard Street. He seized Amadeo or Cardinal Newman by the throat, and it was that woman."

She looked hastily round.

"When you thought that the chimney was on fire, I was burning muslin," she said.

"When you thought the chimney was on fire, I was burning every copy of 'Todd's News,'" said he. "Also a copy of the 'Daily Mirror,' which contained the case. It belonged to the Colonel. I stole it."

She put her hand through his arm.

"Let's get home," she said. "We must talk it over. No one knows one word except you and me?"

"Not one, my dear," said Robert cordially. "But there are suspicions.
Georgie suspects, for instance. He saw me buy all the copies of 'Todd's
News,' at least he was hanging about. Tonight he was clearly on the
track of something, though he gave us a very tolerable dinner."
They went into Robert's study: it was cold, but neither felt it, for they glowed with excitement and enterprise.

136

"That was a wonderful stroke of yours, Robert," said she. "It was masterly: it saved the situation. The 'Daily Mirror,' too: how right you were to steal it. A horrid paper I always thought. Yes, Georgie suspects something, but luckily he doesn't know what he suspects."

"That's why we both said we had just heard from that woman," said Robert.
"Of course. You haven't got a copy of 'Todd's News,' have you?"

"No: at least I burned every page of the police reports," said he. "It was safer."

"Quite so. I cannot show you Amadeo's eyebrows for the same reason. Nor the muslin. Lovely muslin, my dear: yards of it. Now what we must do is this: we must continue to be interested in psychical things; we mustn't drop them, or seem to be put off them. I wish now I had taken you into my confidence at the beginning and told you about Amadeo's eyebrows."

"My dear, you acted for the best," said he. "So did I when I didn't tell you about 'Todd's News.' Secrecy even from each other was more prudent, until it became impossible. And I think we should be wise to let it be understood that we hear from the Princess now and then. Perhaps in a few months she might even visit us again. It—it would be humorous to be behind the scenes, so to speak, and observe the credulity of the others."

Daisy broke into a broad grin.

"I will certainly ask dear Lucia to a seance, if we do," she said. "Dear me! How late it is: there was such a long wait between the tableaux. But we must keep our eyes on Georgie, and be careful how we answer his impertinent questions. He is sure to ask some. About getting that woman down again, Robert. It might be fool-hardy, for we've had an escape, and shouldn't put our heads into the same noose again. On the other hand, it would disarm suspicion for ever, if, after a few months, I asked her to spend a few days of holiday here. You said it was a fine only, not imprisonment?"

The week was a busy one: Georgie in particular never had a moment to himself. The Hurst, so lately a desert, suddenly began to rejoice with joy and singing and broke out into all manner of edifying gaieties. Lucia, capricious queen, quite forgot all the vitriolic things she had said to him, and gave him to understand that he was just as high in favour as ever before, and he was as busy with his duties as ever he had been. Whether he would have fallen into his old place so readily if he had been a free agent, was a question that did not arise, for though it was Lucia who employed him, it was Olga who drove him there. But he had his consolation, for Lucia's noble forgiveness of all the disloyalties against her, included Olga's as well, and out of all the dinners and music parties, and recitations from Peppino's new book of prose poems which was already in proof, and was read to select audiences from end to end, there was none to which Olga was not bidden, and none at which she failed to appear. Lucia even overlooked the fact that she had sung in the carols on Christmas night, though she had herself declared that it was the voice of the red-haired boy which was so peculiarly painful to her. Georgie's picture of her (she never knew that Olga had really commissioned it) hung at the side of the piano in the music room, where the print of Beethoven had hung before, and it gave her the acutest gratification. It represented her sitting, with eyes cast down at her piano, and was indeed much on the same scheme as the yet unfinished one of Olga, which had been postponed in its favour, but there was no time for Georgie to think out another position, and his hand was in with regard to the perspective of pianos. So there it hung with its title, "The Moonlight Sonata," painted in gilt letters on its frame, and Lucia, though she continued to say that he had made her far, far too young, could not but consider that he had caught her expression exactly....

So Riseholme flocked back to The Hurst like sheep that have been astray, for it was certain to find Olga there, even as it had turned there, deeply breathing, to the classes of the Guru. It had to sit through the prose-poems of Peppino, it had to listen to the old, old tunes and sigh at the end, but Olga mingled her sighs with theirs, and often after a suitable pause Lucia would say winningly to Olga:

"One little song, Miss Bracely. Just a stanza? Or am I trespassing too much on your good-nature? Where is your accompanist? I declare I am jealous of him: I shall pop into his place some day! Georgino, Miss Bracely is going to sing us something. Is not that a treat? Sh-sh, please, ladies and gentlemen."

And she rustled to her place, and sat with the farthest-away expression ever seen on mortal face, while she trespassed on Miss Bracely's good-nature.

Then Georgie had the other picture to finish, which he hoped to get ready in time to be a New Year's present, since Olga had insisted on Lucia's being done first. He had certainly secured an admirable likeness of her, and there was in it just all that his stippled, fussy representation of Lucia lacked. "Bleak December" and "Yellow Daffodils" and the rest of the series lacked it, too: for once he had done something in the doing of which he had forgotten himself. It was by no means a work of genius, for Georgie was not possessed of one grain of that, and the talent it displayed was by no means of a high order, but it had something of the naturalness of a flower that grew from the earth which nourished it.

On the last day of the year he was putting a few final touches to it, little high reflected lights on the black keys, little blacknesses of shadow in the moulding of the panel behind his hand. He had finished with her altogether, and now she sat in the window-seat, looking out, and playing with the blind-tassel. He had been so much absorbed in his work that he had scarcely noticed that she had been rather unusually silent.

"I've got a piece of news for you," she said at length.

Georgie held his breath, as he drew a very thin line of body-colour along the edge of Ab.

"No! What is it?" he said. "Is it about the Princess?"

Olga seemed to hail this as a diversion.

"Ah, let's talk about that for a minute," she said. "What you ought to have done was to order another copy of 'Todd's News' at once."

"I know I ought, but I couldn't get one when I thought of it afterwards. That was tarsome. But I feel sure there was something about her in it."

"And you can't get anything out of the Quantocks?"

"No, though I've laid plenty of traps for them. There's an understanding between them now. They both know something. When I lay a trap, it isn't any use: they look at the trap, and then they look at each other afterwards."

"What sort of traps?"

"Oh, anything. I say suddenly, 'What a bore it is that there are so many frauds among mediums, especially paid ones.' You see, I don't believe for a moment that these seances were held for nothing, though we didn't pay for going to them. And then Robert says that he would never trust a paid medium, and she looks at him approvingly, and says 'Dear Princess'! The other day—it was a very good trap—I said, 'Is it true that the Princess is coming to stay with Lady Ambermere?' It wasn't a lie: I only asked."

"And then?" said Olga.

"Robert gave an awful twitch, not a jump exactly, but a twitch. But she was on the spot and said, 'Ah, that would be nice. I wonder if it's true. The Princess didn't mention it in her last letter.' And then he looked at her approvingly. There is something there, no one shall convince me otherwise."

Olga suddenly burst out laughing.

"What's the matter?" asked Georgie.

"Oh, it's all so delicious!" she said. "I never knew before how terribly interesting little things were. It's all wildly exciting, and there are fifty things going on just as exciting. Is it all of you who take such a tremendous interest in them that makes them so absorbing, or is it that they are absorbing in themselves, and ordinary dull people, not Riseholmites, don't see how exciting they are? Tommy Luton's measles: the Quantocks' secret: Elizabeth's lover! And to think that I believed I was coming to a backwater."

Georgie held up his picture and half closed his eyes. "I believe it's finished," he said. "I shall have it framed, and put it in my drawing-room."

This was a trap, and Olga fell into it.

"Yes, it will look nice there," she said. "Really, Georgie, it is very clever of you."

He began washing his brushes.

"And what was your news?" he said.

She got up from her seat.

"I forgot all about it, with talking of the Quantocks' secret," she said. "That just shows you: I completely forgot, Georgie. I've just accepted an offer to sing in America, a four months' engagement, at fifty thousand million pounds a night. A penny less, and I wouldn't have gone. But I really can't refuse. It's all been very sudden, but they want to produce Lucretia there before it appears in England. Then I come back, and sing in London all the summer. Oh, me!"

There was dead silence, while Georgie dried his brushes.

"When do you go?" he asked.

"In about a fortnight."

"Oh," said he.

She moved down the room to the piano and shut it without speaking, while he folded the paper round his finished picture.

"Why don't you come, too?" she said at length. "It would do you no end of good, for you would get out of this darling two-penny place which will all go inside a nut-shell. There are big things in the world, Georgie: seas, continents, people, movements, emotions. I told my Georgie I was going to ask you, and he thoroughly approves. We both like you, you know. It would be lovely if you would come. Come for a couple of months, anyhow: of course you'll be our guest, please."

The world, at that moment, had grown absolutely black to him, and it was by that that he knew who, for him, was the light of it. He shook his head.

"Why can't you come?" she said.

He looked at her straight in the face.

"Because I adore you," he said.

Note from the Editor

Odin's Library Classics strives to bring you unedited and unabridged works of classical literature. As such, this is the complete and unabridged version of the original English text unless noted. In some instances, obvious typographical errors have been corrected. This is done to preserve the original text as much as possible. The English language has evolved since the writing and some of the words appear in their original form, or at least the most commonly used form at the time. This is done to protect the original intent of the author. If at any time you are unsure of the meaning of a word, please do your research on the etymology of that word. It is important to preserve the history of the English language.

Taylor Anderson

Made in the USA
Coppell, TX
11 November 2024